USDIN ★ HAYES ★ NALTY

THE AVANT-GUARDS ™

VOLUME ONE

Published by
BOOM! BOX ™

BOOM! BOX™

THE AVANT-GUARDS Volume One, December 2020.
Published by BOOM! Box, a division of Boom Entertainment, Inc.
The Avant-Guards is ™ & © 2020 Scheme Machine Studios,
LLC. Originally published in single magazine form as THE AVANT-
GUARDS No. 1-4. ™ & © 2019 Scheme Machine Studios, LLC.
All rights reserved. BOOM! Box™ and the BOOM! Box logo are
trademarks of Boom Entertainment, Inc., registered in various
countries and categories. All characters, events, and institutions
depicted herein are fictional. Any similarity between any of the
names, characters, persons, events, and/or institutions in this
publication to actual names, characters, and persons, whether
living or dead, events, and/or institutions is unintended and purely
coincidental. BOOM! Box does not read or accept unsolicited
submissions of ideas, stories, or artwork.

BOOM! Studios, 5670 Wilshire Boulevard, Suite 400, Los Angeles,
CA 90036-5679. Printed in China. Second Printing.

ISBN: 978-1-68415-367-1, eISBN: 978-1-64144-350-0

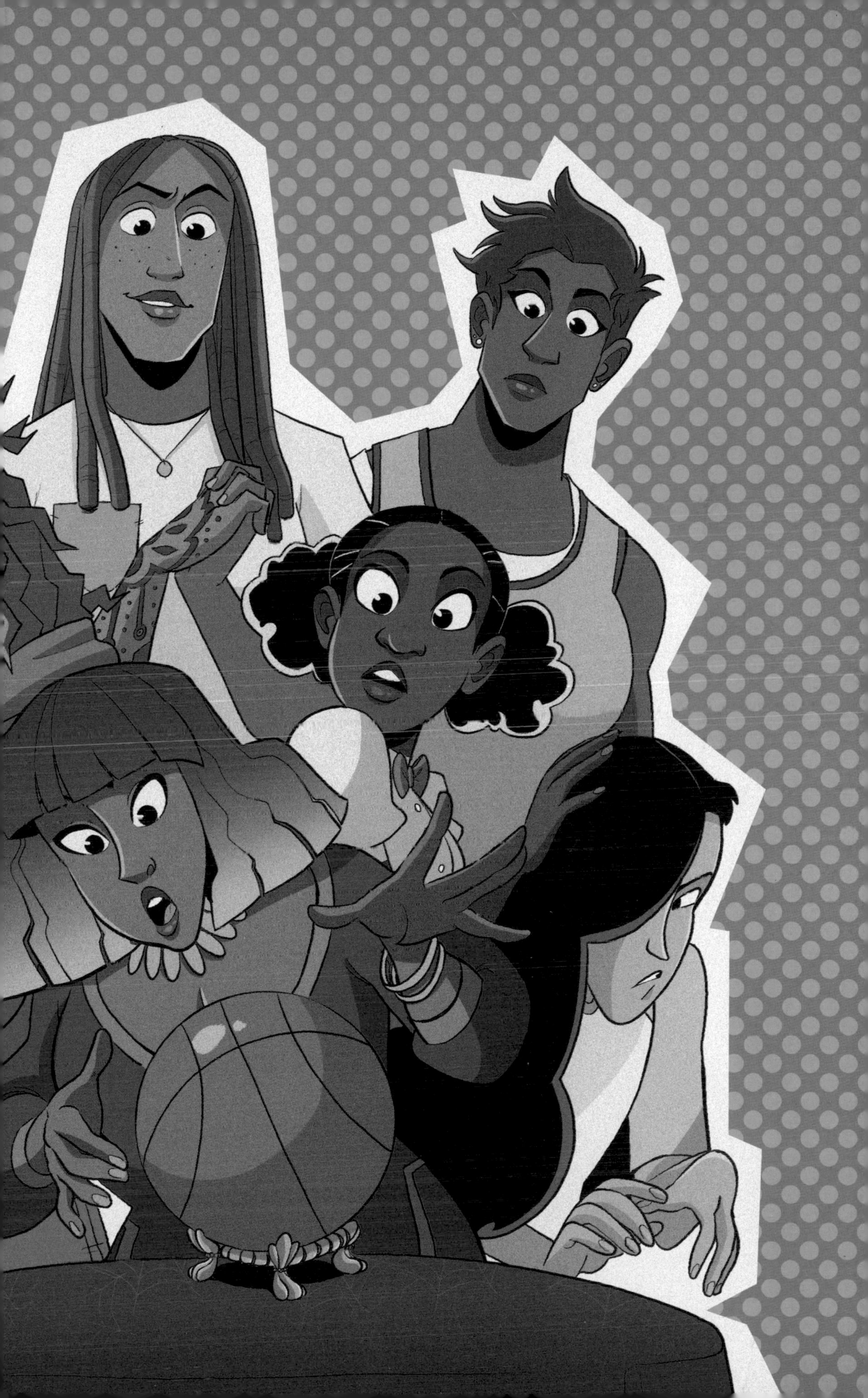

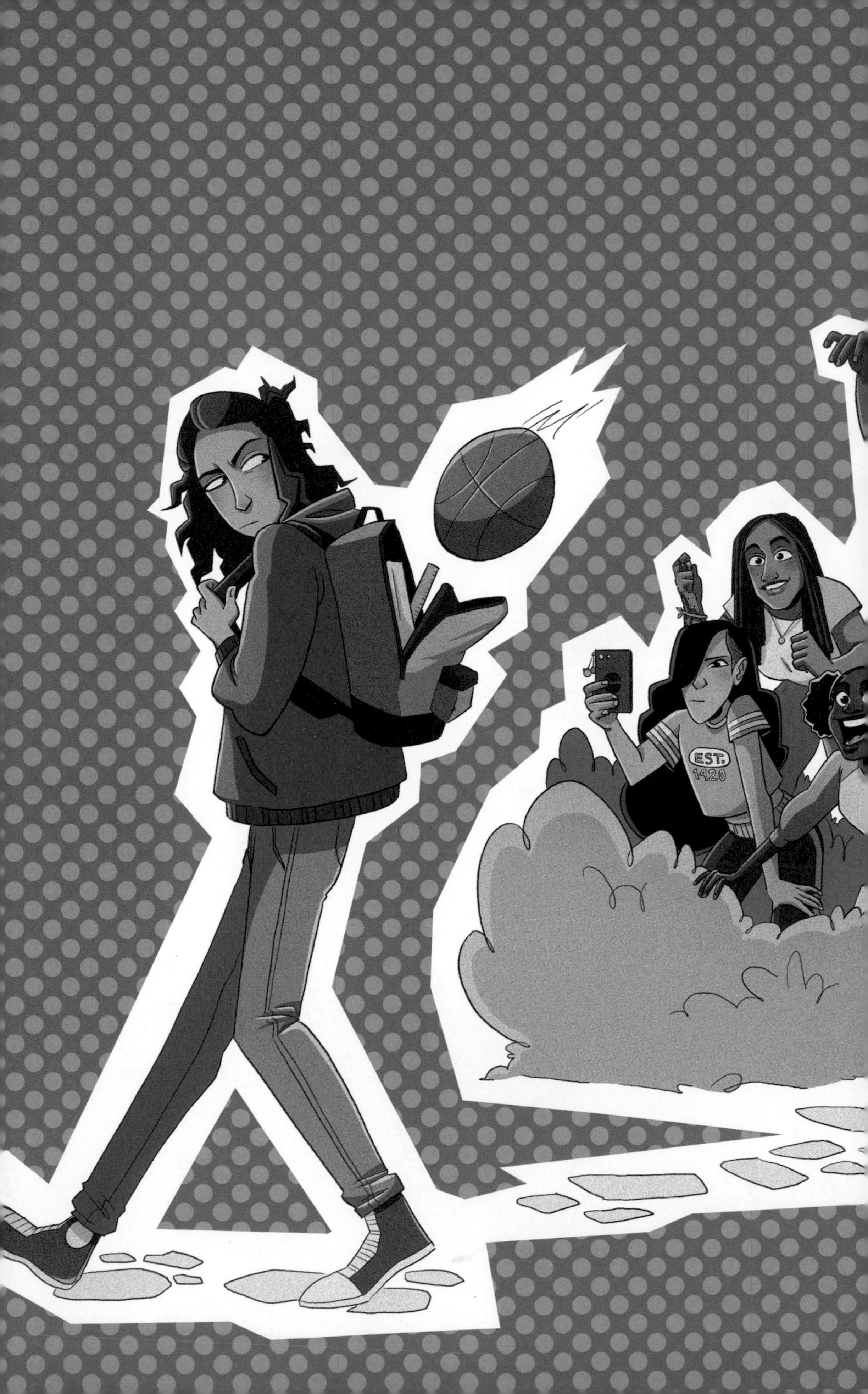
EST.
1420

CREATED & WRITTEN BY
CARLY USDIN

ILLUSTRATED BY
NOAH HAYES

COLORED BY
REBECCA NALTY

LETTERED BY
ED DUKESHIRE

COVER BY
NOAH HAYES
WITH COLORS BY **REBECCA NALTY**

SERIES DESIGNER
GRACE PARK

COLLECTION DESIGNER
JILLIAN CRAB

EDITOR
SOPHIE PHILIPS-ROBERTS

SENIOR EDITOR
SHANNON WATTERS

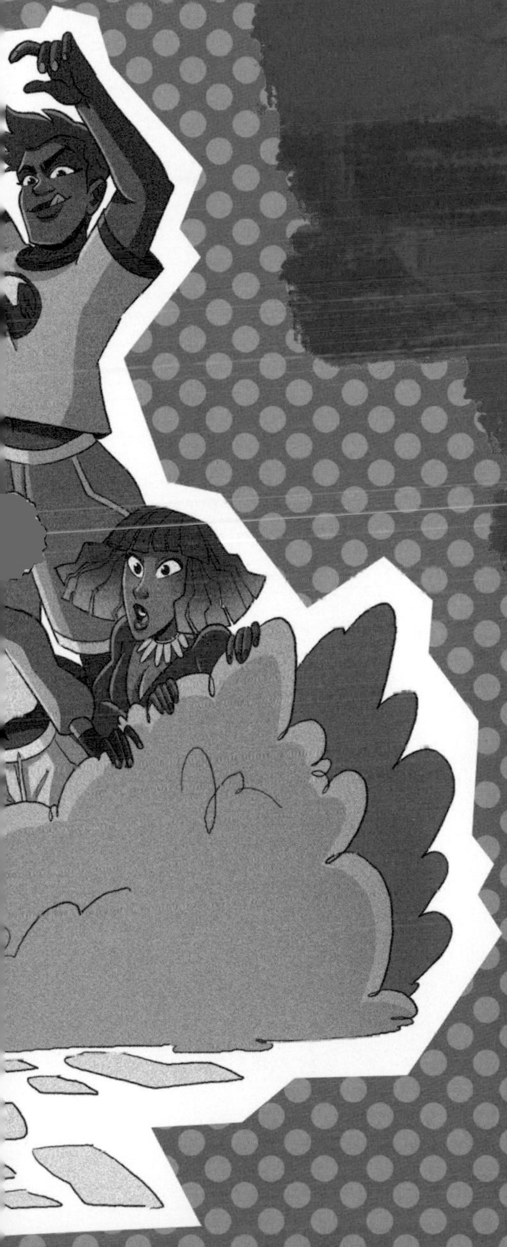

CHAPTER ONE

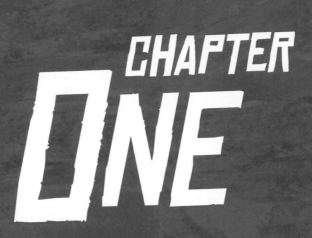

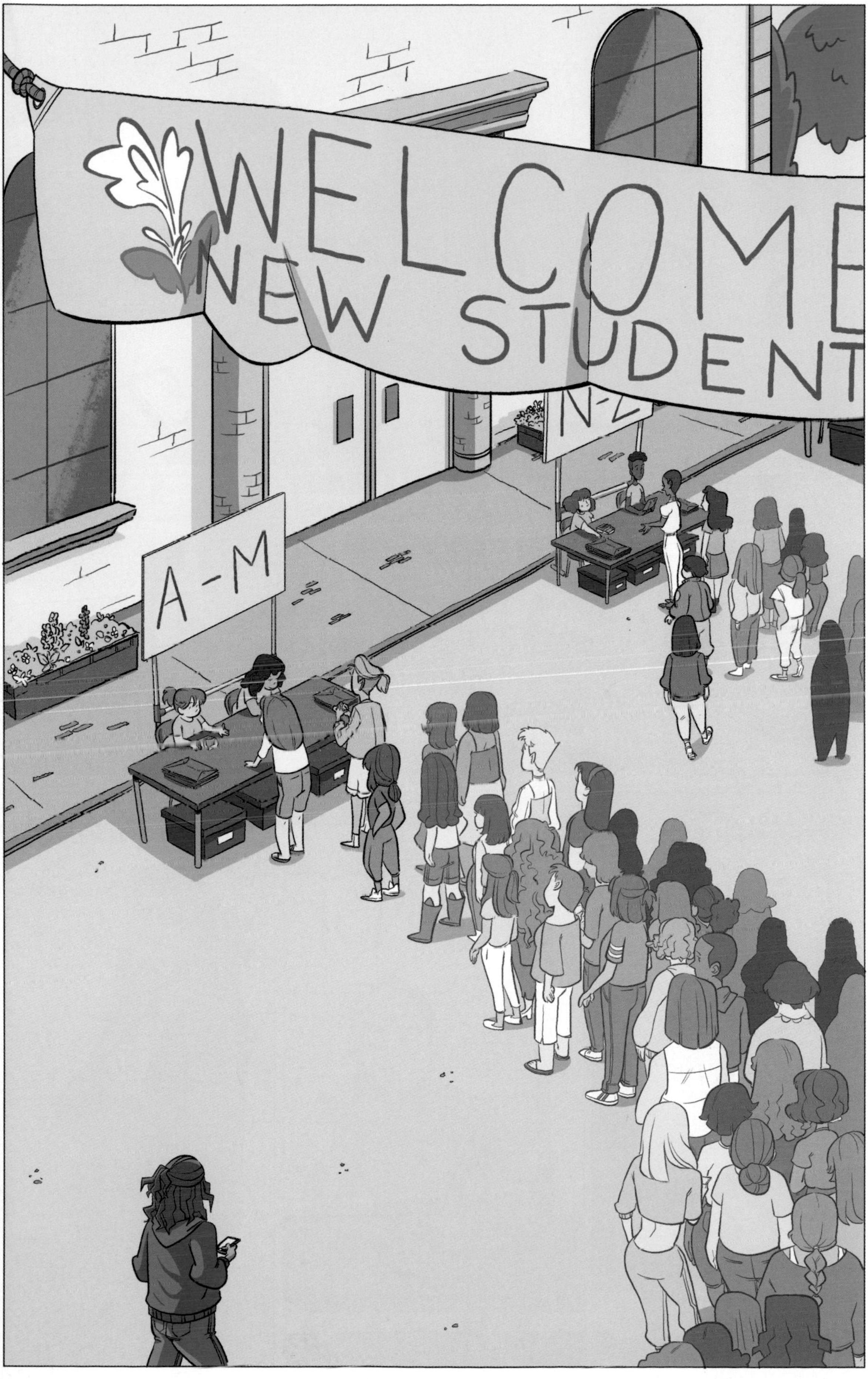
WELCOME
NEW STUDENT
A-M
N-Z

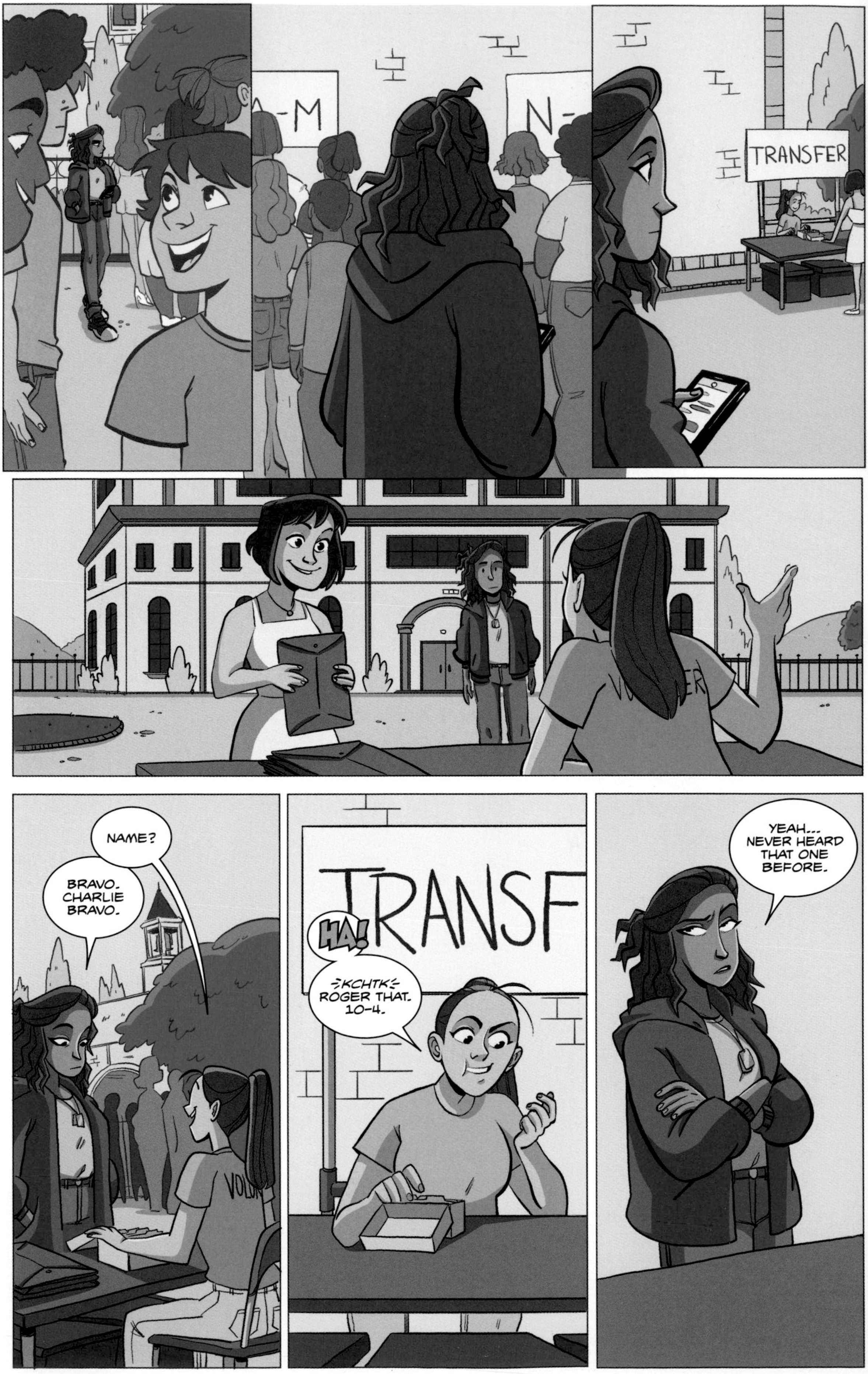
A-M
N-
TRANSFER
NAME?
BRAVO. CHARLIE BRAVO.
TRANSF
HA!
KCHTK ROGER THAT. 10-4.
YEAH... NEVER HEARD THAT ONE BEFORE.

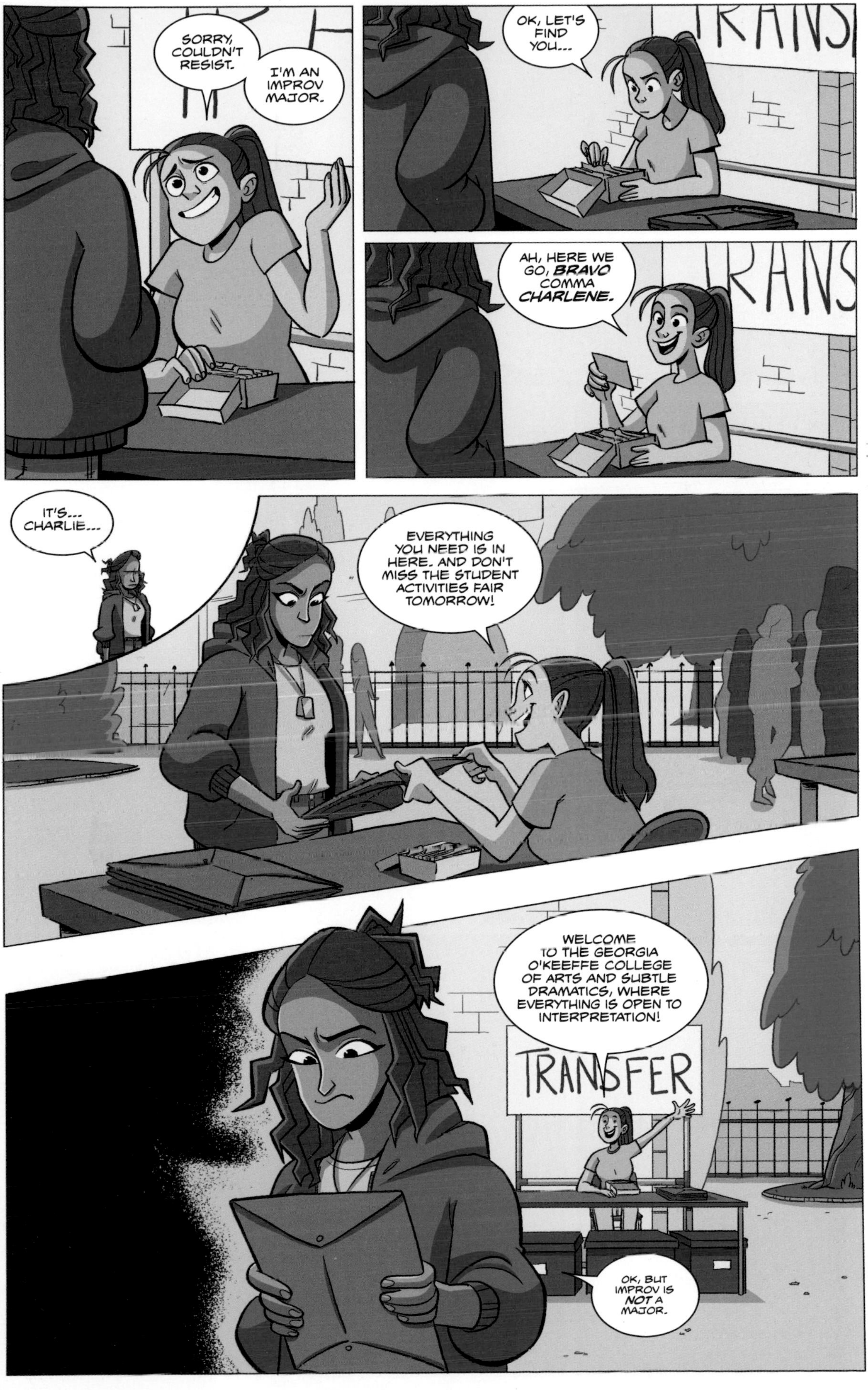
SORRY, COULDN'T RESIST.
I'M AN IMPROV MAJOR.
OK, LET'S FIND YOU...
AH, HERE WE GO, BRAVO COMMA CHARLENE.
IT'S... CHARLIE...
EVERYTHING YOU NEED IS IN HERE. AND DON'T MISS THE STUDENT ACTIVITIES FAIR TOMORROW!
WELCOME TO THE GEORGIA O'KEEFFE COLLEGE OF ARTS AND SUBTLE DRAMATICS, WHERE EVERYTHING IS OPEN TO INTERPRETATION!
TRANSFER
OK, BUT IMPROV IS NOT A MAJOR.

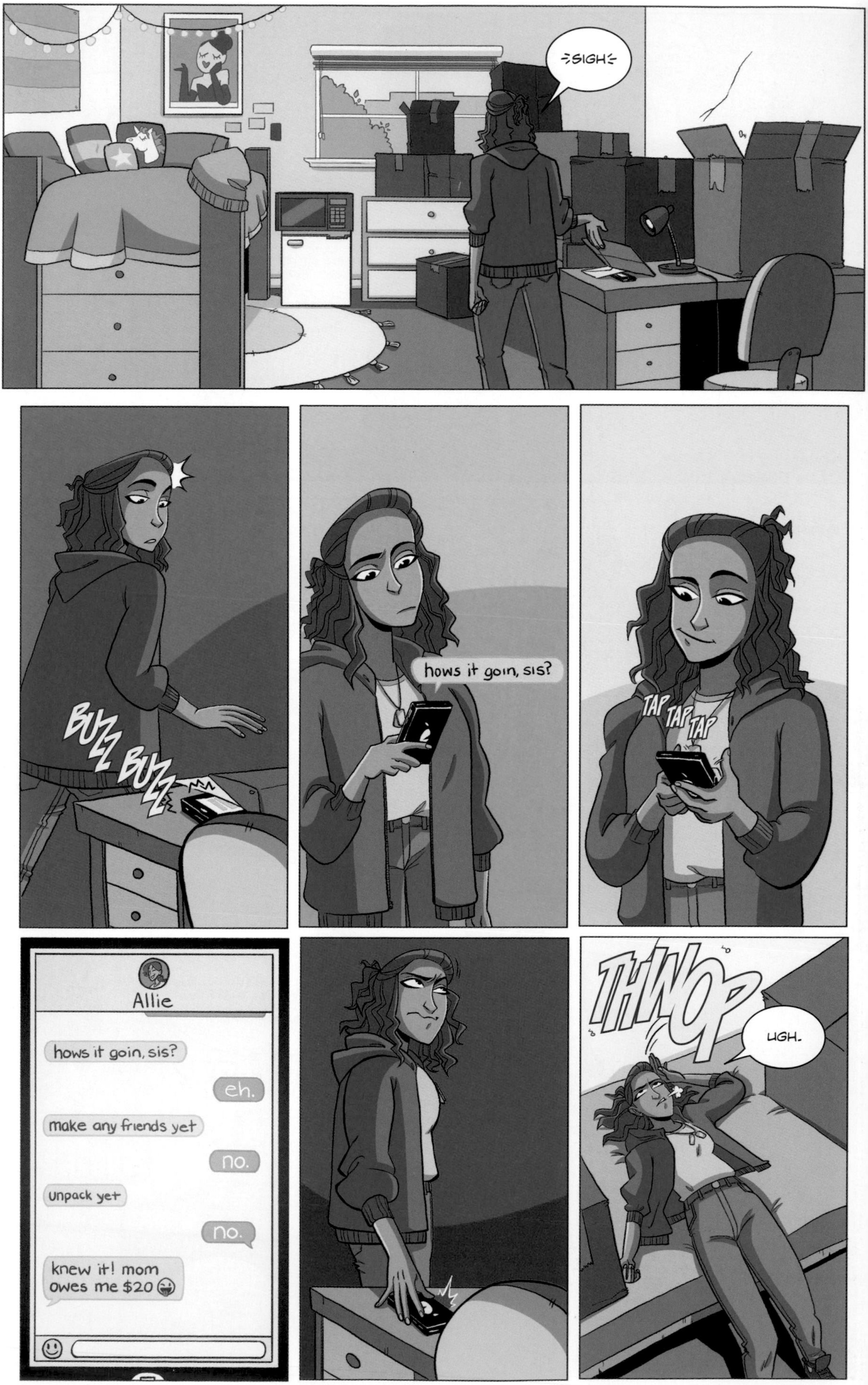
SIGH
BUZZ BUZZ
hows it goin, sis?
TAP TAP TAP
Allie
hows it goin, sis?
eh.
make any friends yet
no.
unpack yet
no.
knew it! mom owes me $20
THWOP
UGH.

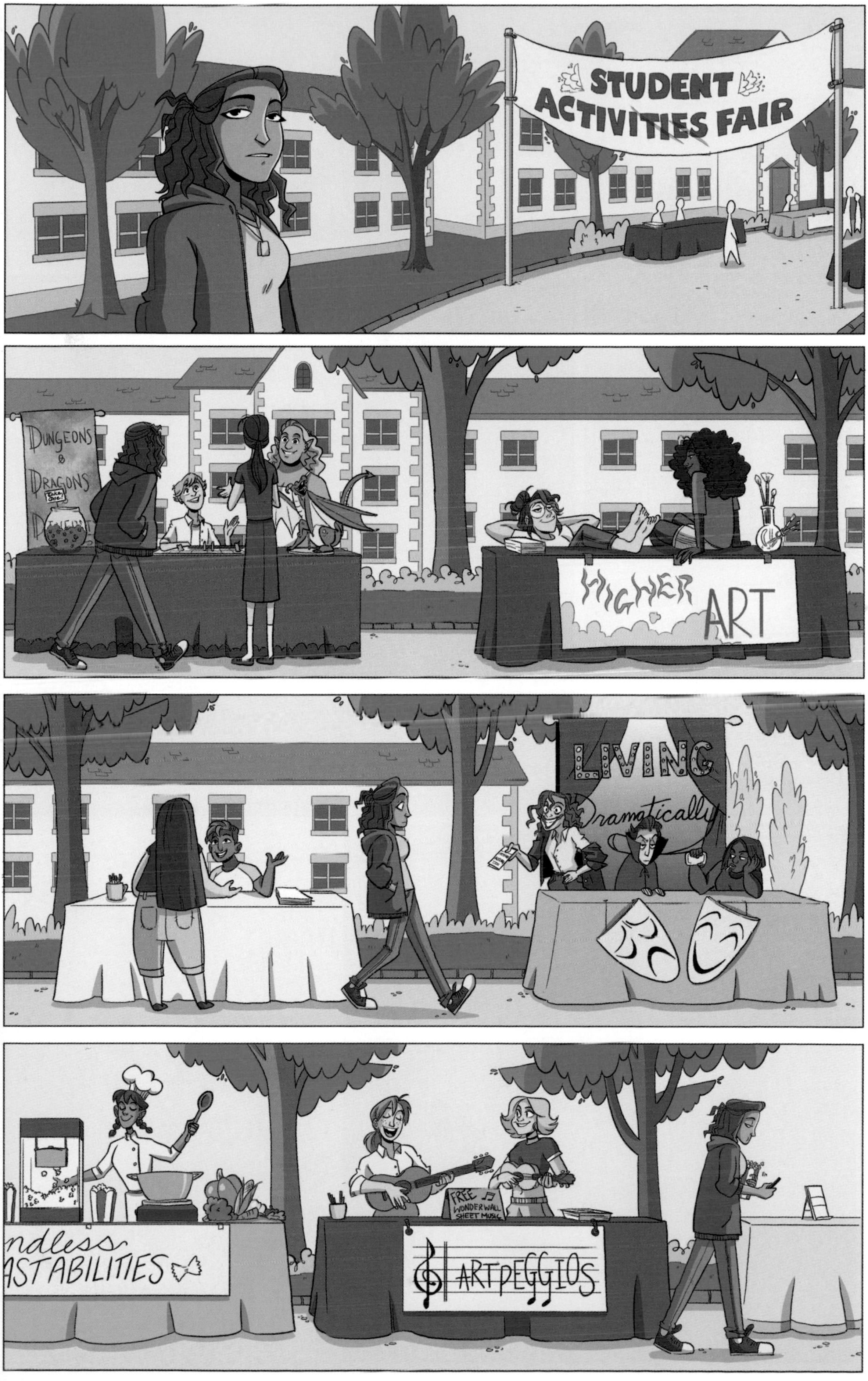
STUDENT ACTIVITIES FAIR
DUNGEONS & DRAGONS
Take One!
HIGHER ART
LIVING
Dramatically
ndless
ASTABILITIES
FREE WONDERWALL SHEET MUSIC
ARTPEGGIOS

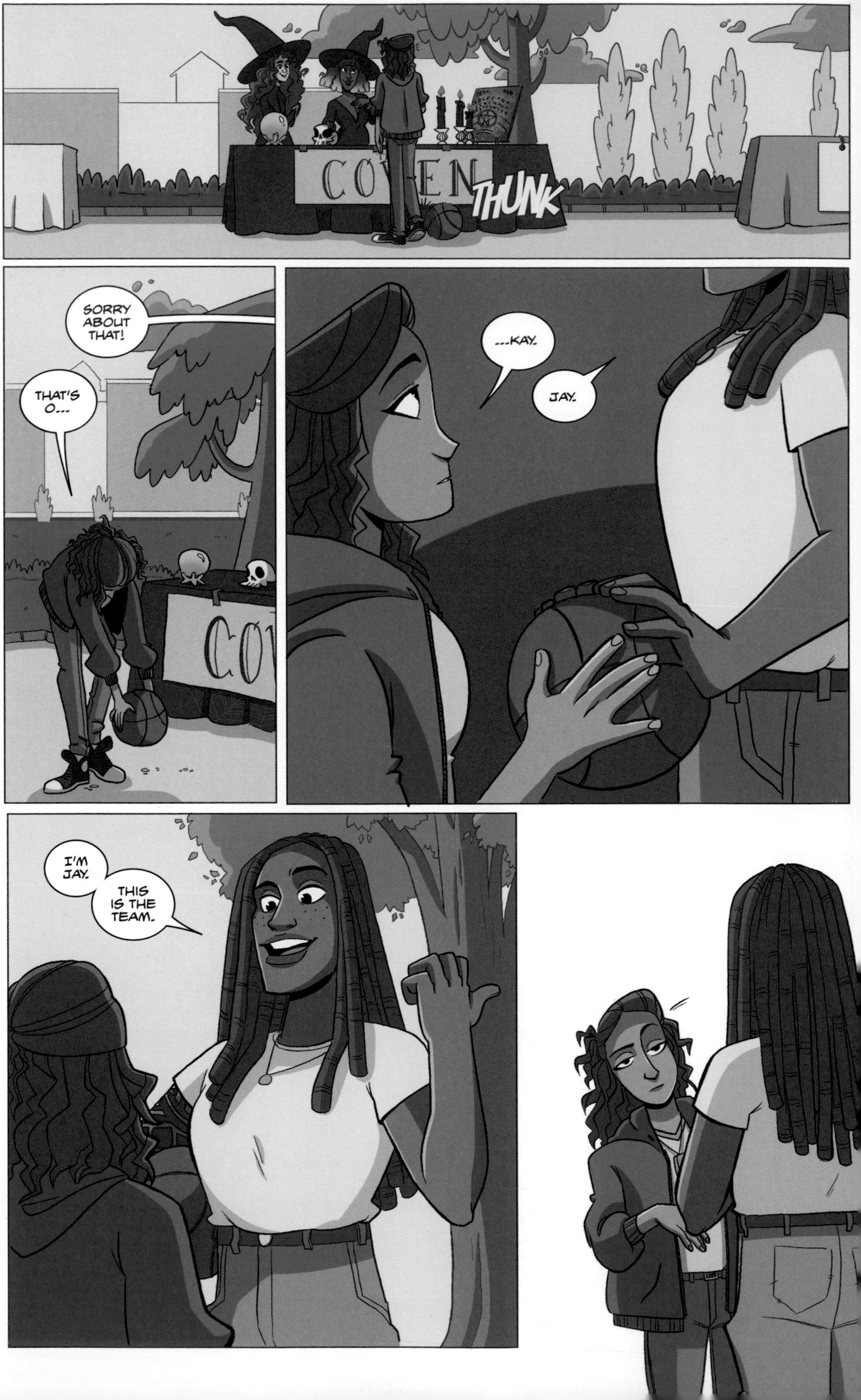
COVEN
THUNK
SORRY ABOUT THAT!
THAT'S O...
...KAY.
JAY.
I'M JAY.
THIS IS THE TEAM.

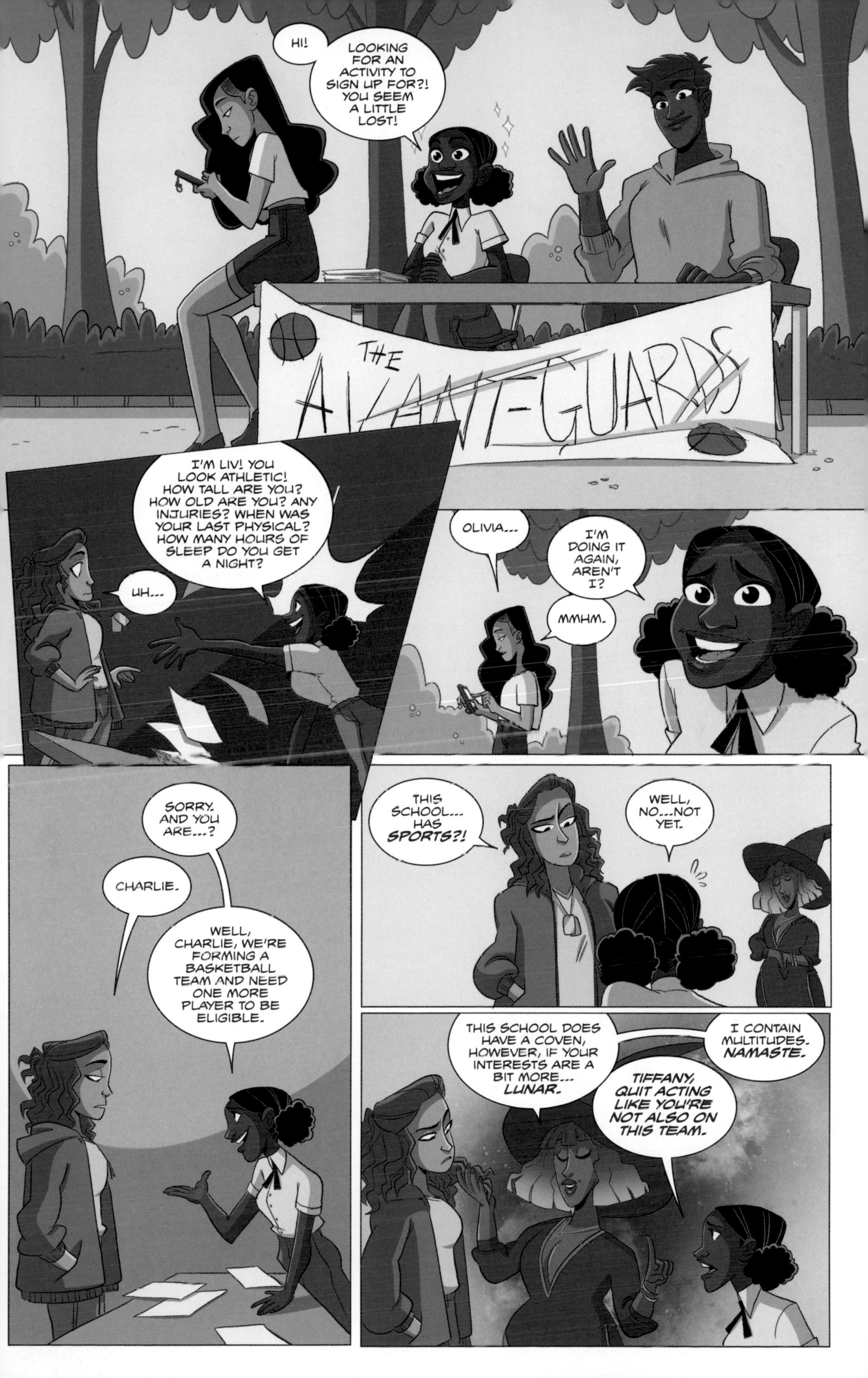
HI!
LOOKING FOR AN ACTIVITY TO SIGN UP FOR?! YOU SEEM A LITTLE LOST!
THE AVANT-GUARDS
I'M LIV! YOU LOOK ATHLETIC! HOW TALL ARE YOU? HOW OLD ARE YOU? ANY INJURIES? WHEN WAS YOUR LAST PHYSICAL? HOW MANY HOURS OF SLEEP DO YOU GET A NIGHT?
UH...
OLIVIA...
I'M DOING IT AGAIN, AREN'T I?
MMHM.
SORRY. AND YOU ARE...?
CHARLIE.
WELL, CHARLIE, WE'RE FORMING A BASKETBALL TEAM AND NEED ONE MORE PLAYER TO BE ELIGIBLE.
THIS SCHOOL... HAS SPORTS?!
WELL, NO...NOT YET.
THIS SCHOOL DOES HAVE A COVEN, HOWEVER, IF YOUR INTERESTS ARE A BIT MORE... LUNAR.
I CONTAIN MULTITUDES. NAMASTE.
TIFFANY, QUIT ACTING LIKE YOU'RE NOT ALSO ON THIS TEAM.

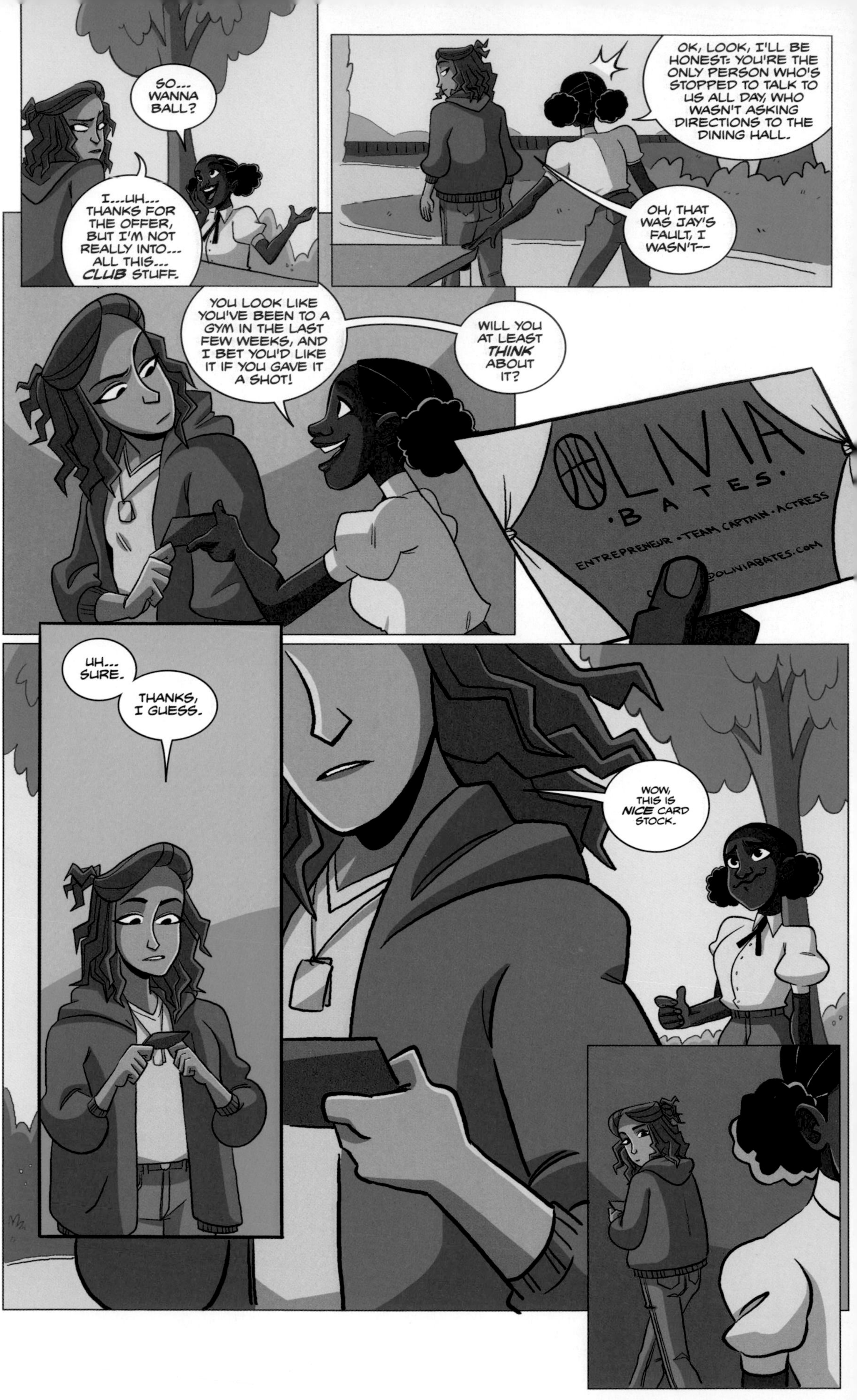
SO... WANNA BALL?
I...UH... THANKS FOR THE OFFER, BUT I'M NOT REALLY INTO... ALL THIS... CLUB STUFF.
OK, LOOK, I'LL BE HONEST: YOU'RE THE ONLY PERSON WHO'S STOPPED TO TALK TO US ALL DAY, WHO WASN'T ASKING DIRECTIONS TO THE DINING HALL.
OH, THAT WAS JAY'S FAULT, I WASN'T--
YOU LOOK LIKE YOU'VE BEEN TO A GYM IN THE LAST FEW WEEKS, AND I BET YOU'D LIKE IT IF YOU GAVE IT A SHOT!
WILL YOU AT LEAST THINK ABOUT IT?
OLIVIA BATES
ENTREPRENEUR • TEAM CAPTAIN • ACTRESS
@OLIVIABATES.COM
UH... SURE.
THANKS, I GUESS.
WOW, THIS IS NICE CARD STOCK.

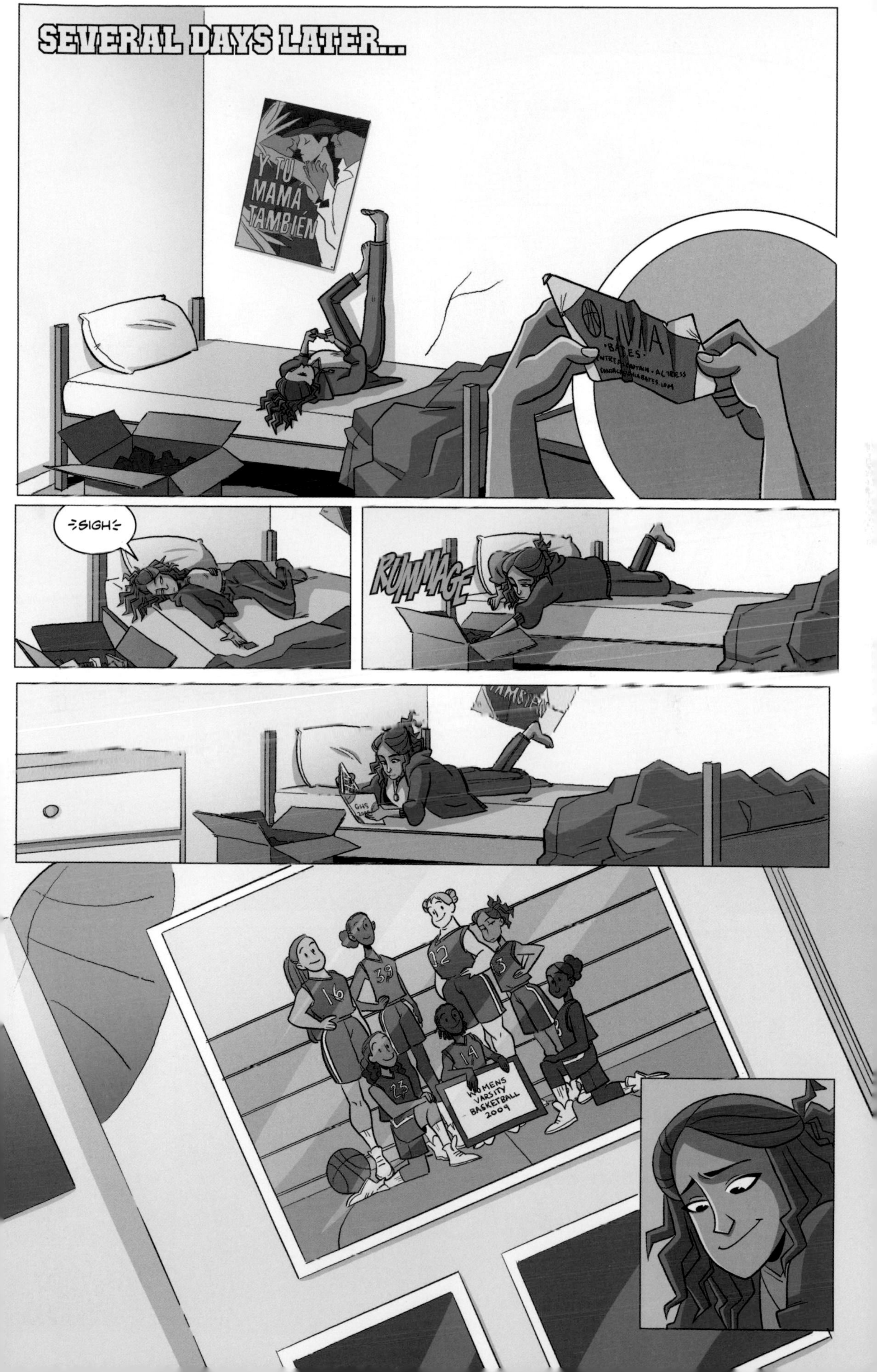
SEVERAL DAYS LATER...
Y TU MAMÁ TAMBIÉN
OLIVIA
BATES
SIGH
RUMMAGE
16
39
12
3
23
14
WOMENS VARSITY BASKETBALL 2009

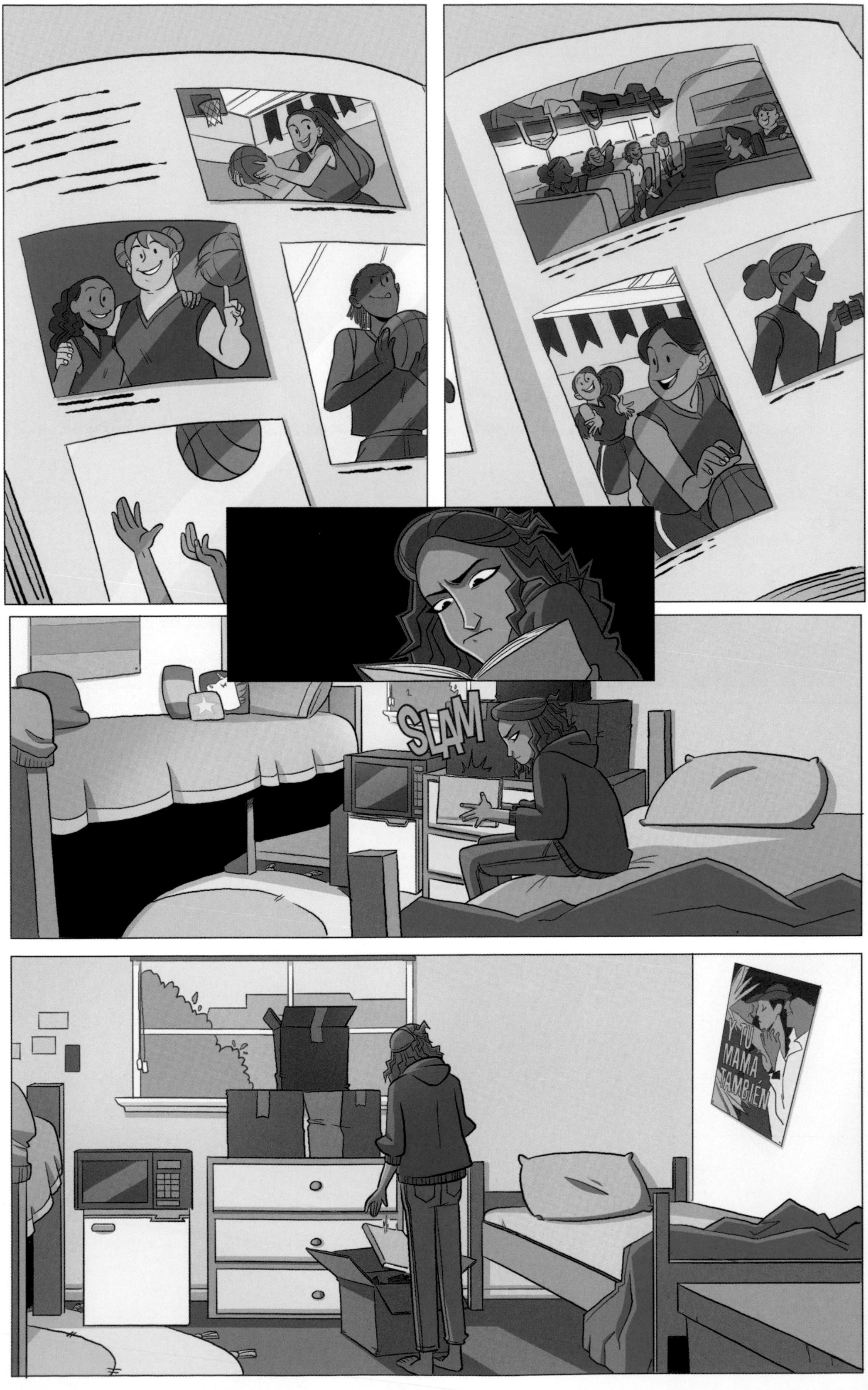
SLAM
Y TU MAMÁ TAMBIÉN

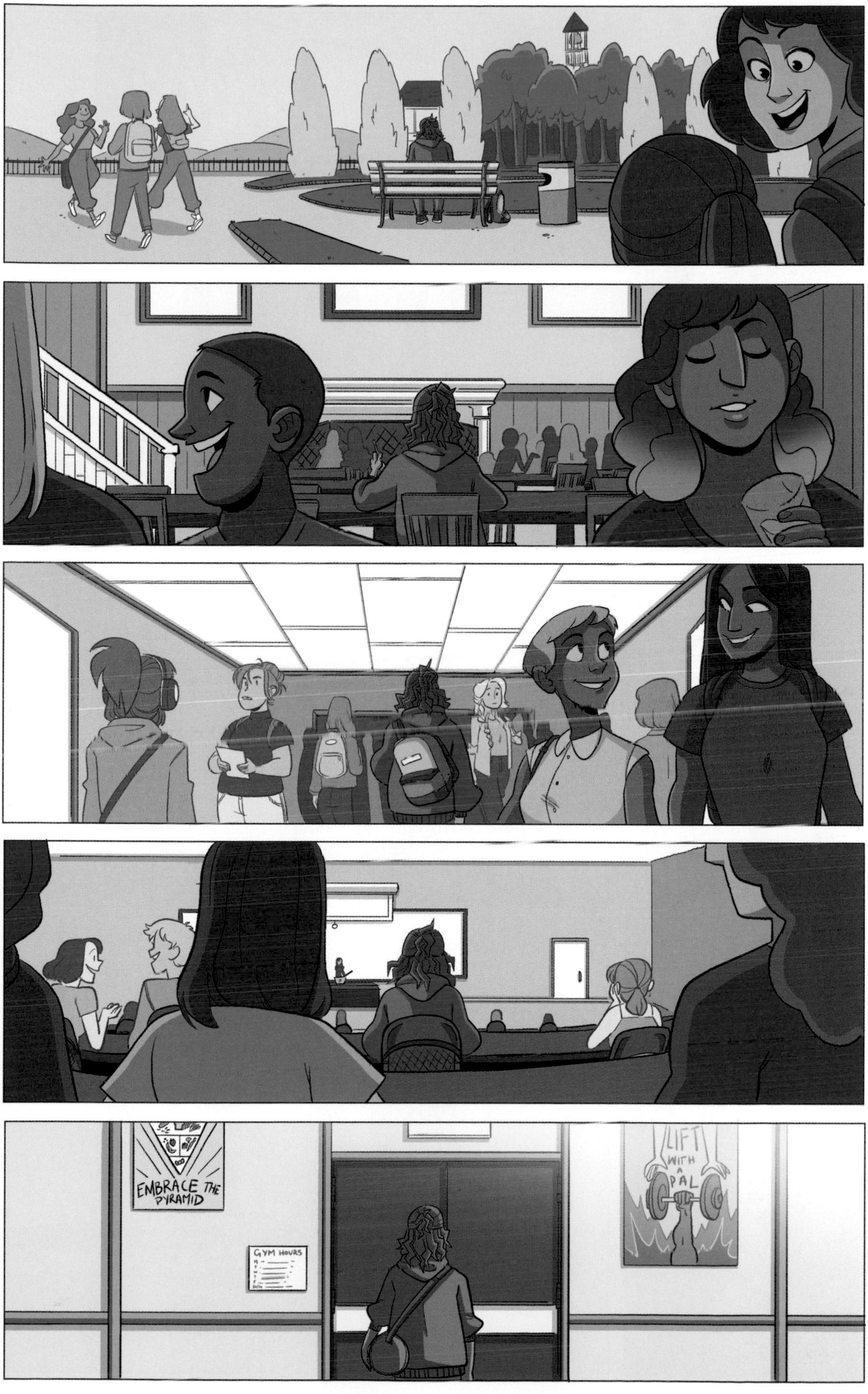
EMBRACE THE PYRAMID
GYM HOURS
LIFT WITH A PAL

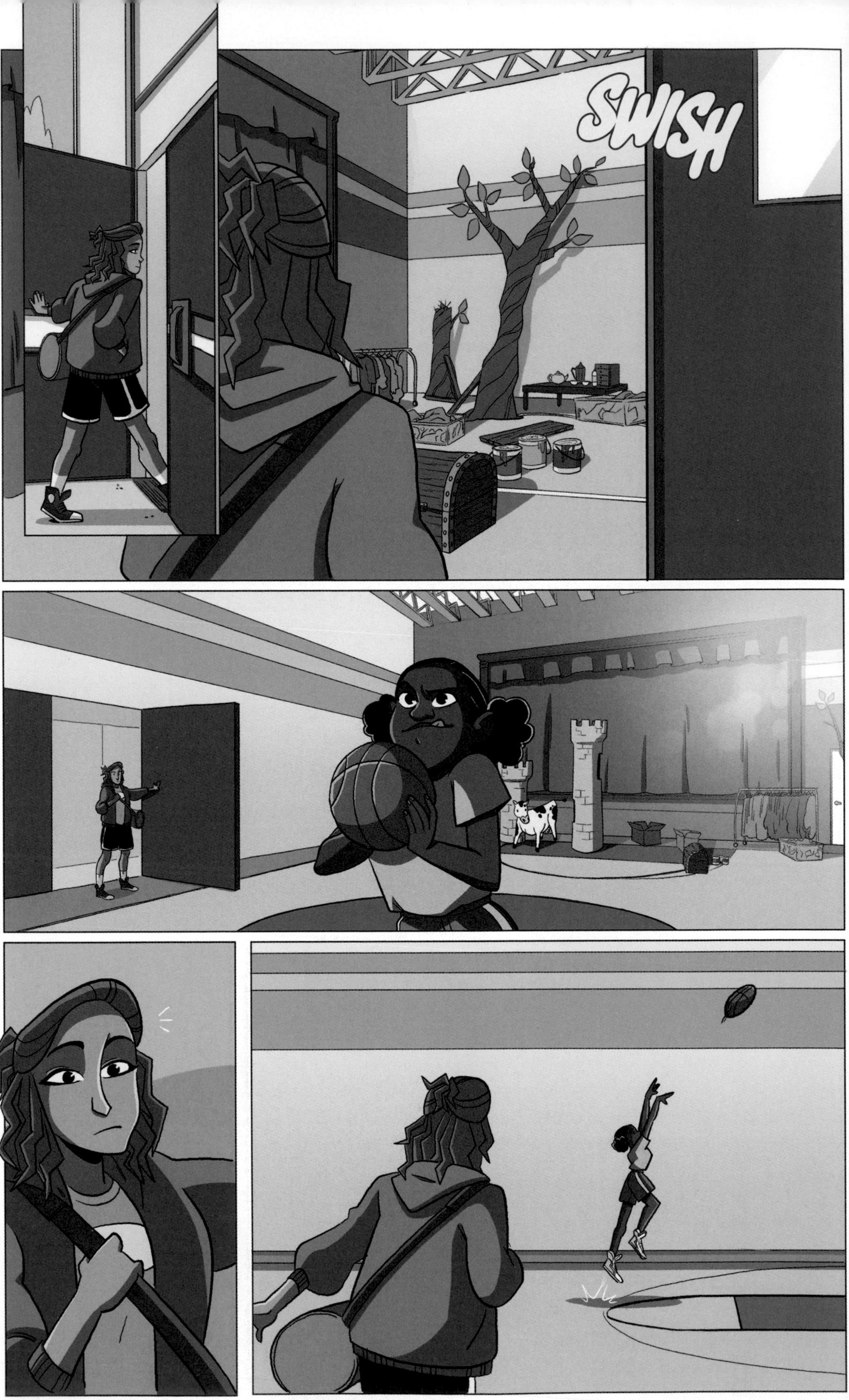
SWISH

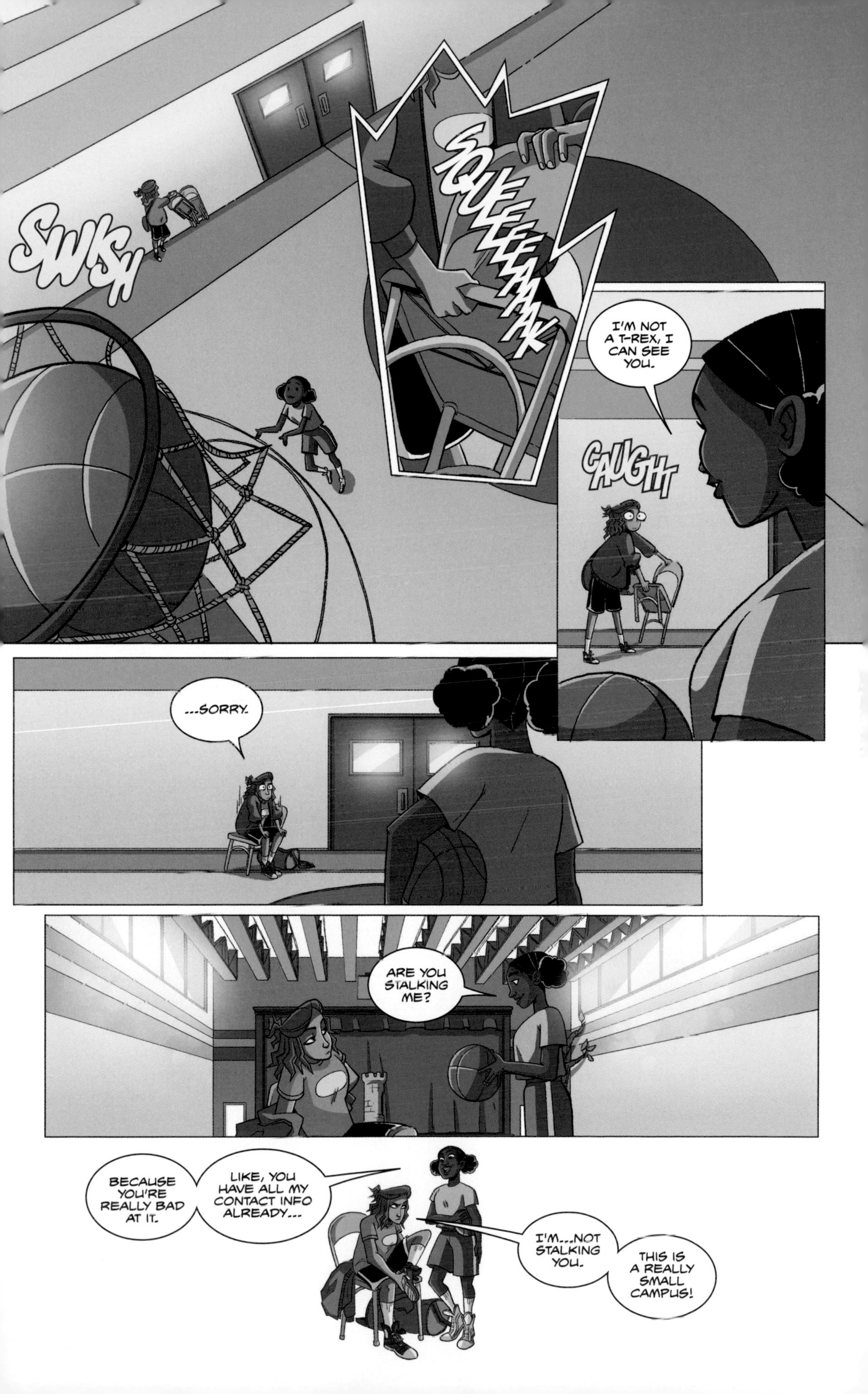
SWISH
SQUEEEEAAK
I'M NOT A T-REX, I CAN SEE YOU.
CAUGHT
...SORRY.
ARE YOU STALKING ME?
I'M...NOT STALKING YOU.
THIS IS A REALLY SMALL CAMPUS!
LIKE, YOU HAVE ALL MY CONTACT INFO ALREADY...
BECAUSE YOU'RE REALLY BAD AT IT.

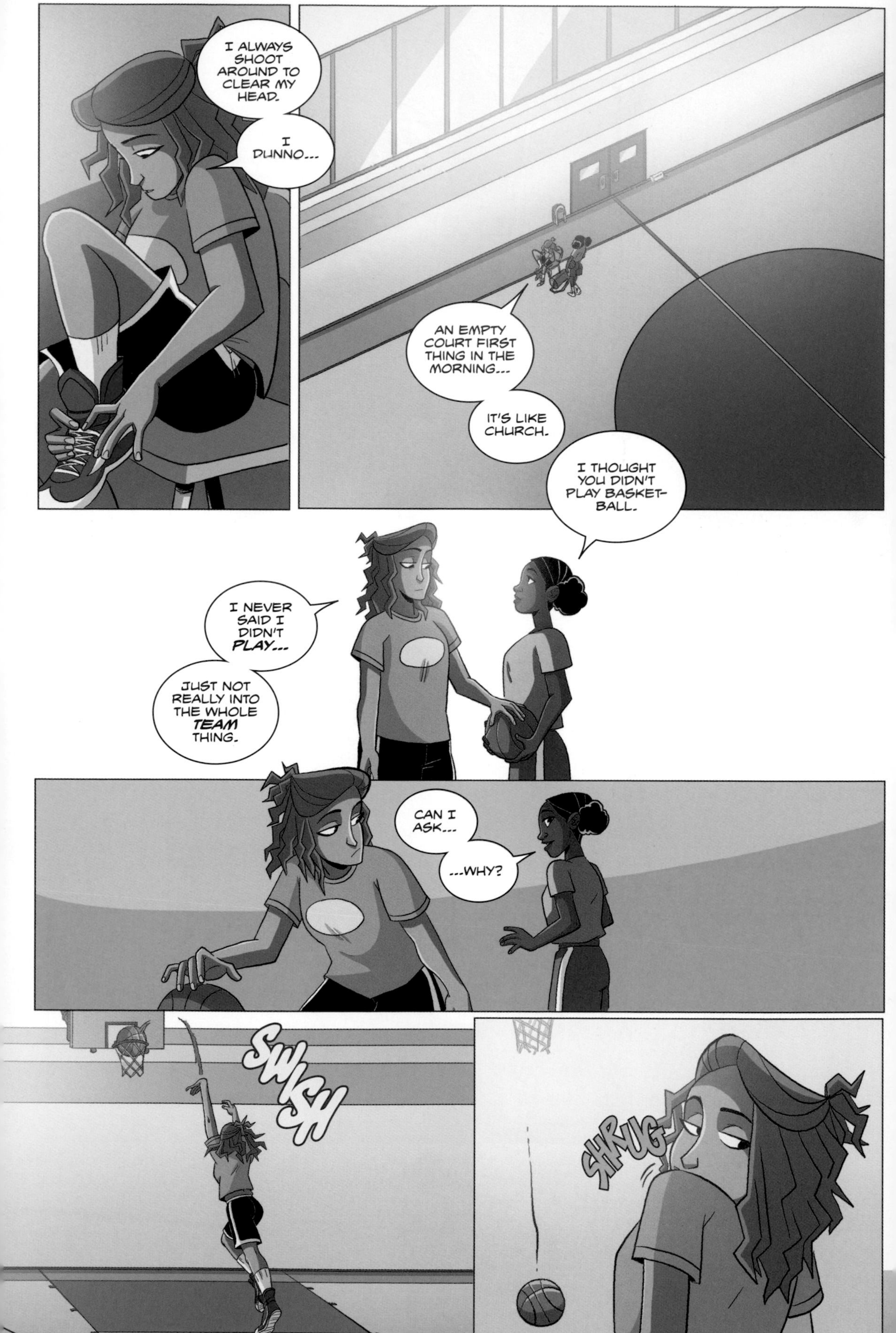
I ALWAYS SHOOT AROUND TO CLEAR MY HEAD.
I DUNNO...
AN EMPTY COURT FIRST THING IN THE MORNING...
IT'S LIKE CHURCH.
I THOUGHT YOU DIDN'T PLAY BASKET-BALL.
I NEVER SAID I DIDN'T *PLAY*...
JUST NOT REALLY INTO THE WHOLE *TEAM* THING.
CAN I ASK...
...WHY?
SWISH
SHRUG

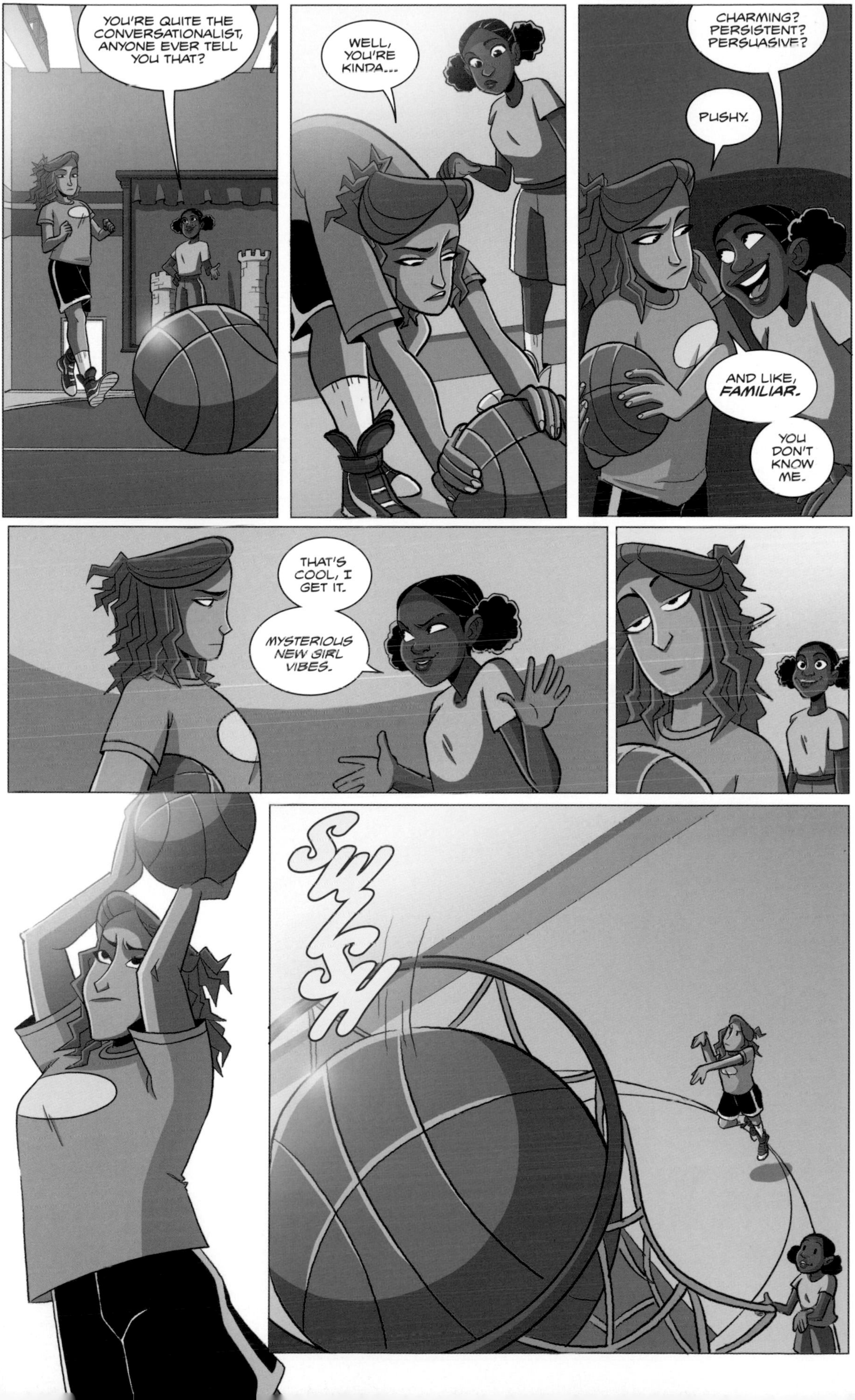
YOU'RE QUITE THE CONVERSATIONALIST, ANYONE EVER TELL YOU THAT?
WELL, YOU'RE KINDA...
CHARMING? PERSISTENT? PERSUASIVE?
PUSHY.
AND LIKE, FAMILIAR.
YOU DON'T KNOW ME.
THAT'S COOL, I GET IT.
MYSTERIOUS NEW GIRL VIBES.
SWISH

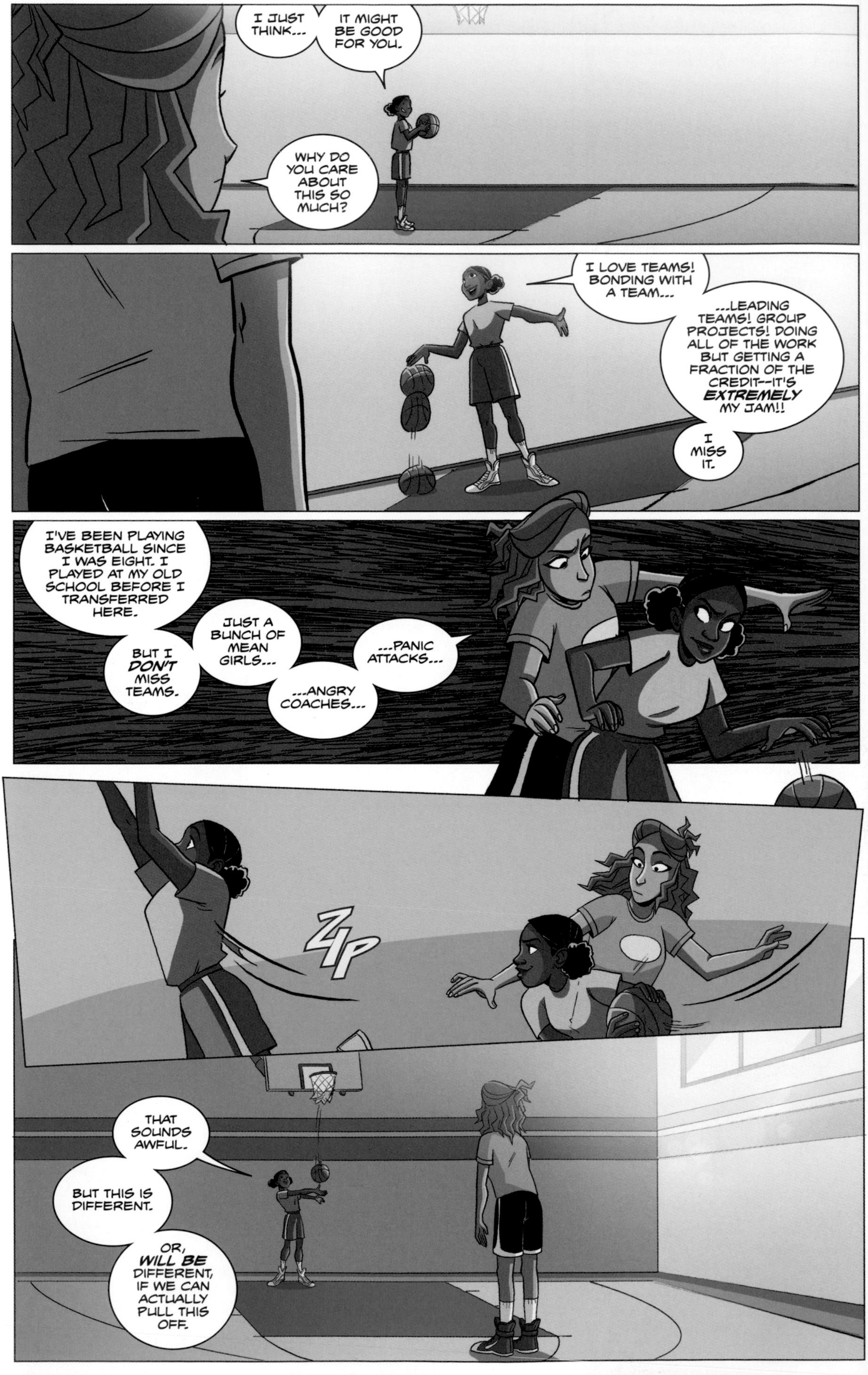
I JUST THINK...
IT MIGHT BE GOOD FOR YOU.
WHY DO YOU CARE ABOUT THIS SO MUCH?
I LOVE TEAMS! BONDING WITH A TEAM...
...LEADING TEAMS! GROUP PROJECTS! DOING ALL OF THE WORK BUT GETTING A FRACTION OF THE CREDIT--IT'S EXTREMELY MY JAM!!
I MISS IT.
I'VE BEEN PLAYING BASKETBALL SINCE I WAS EIGHT. I PLAYED AT MY OLD SCHOOL BEFORE I TRANSFERRED HERE.
BUT I DON'T MISS TEAMS.
JUST A BUNCH OF MEAN GIRLS...
...ANGRY COACHES...
...PANIC ATTACKS...
ZIP
THAT SOUNDS AWFUL.
BUT THIS IS DIFFERENT.
OR, WILL BE DIFFERENT, IF WE CAN ACTUALLY PULL THIS OFF.

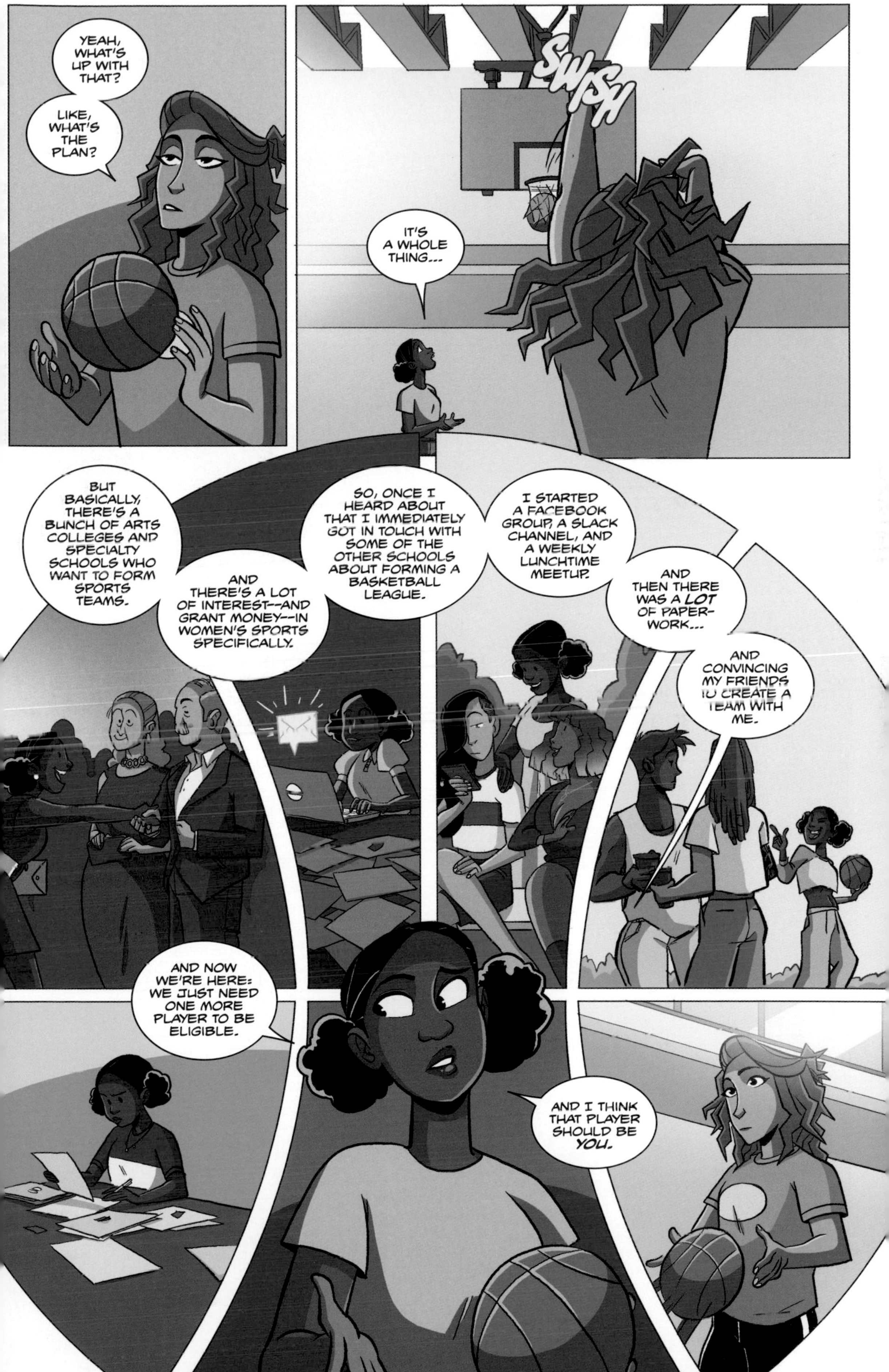
YEAH, WHAT'S UP WITH THAT?
LIKE, WHAT'S THE PLAN?
SWISH
IT'S A WHOLE THING...
BUT BASICALLY, THERE'S A BUNCH OF ARTS COLLEGES AND SPECIALTY SCHOOLS WHO WANT TO FORM SPORTS TEAMS.
AND THERE'S A LOT OF INTEREST--AND GRANT MONEY--IN WOMEN'S SPORTS SPECIFICALLY.
SO, ONCE I HEARD ABOUT THAT I IMMEDIATELY GOT IN TOUCH WITH SOME OF THE OTHER SCHOOLS ABOUT FORMING A BASKETBALL LEAGUE.
I STARTED A FACEBOOK GROUP, A SLACK CHANNEL, AND A WEEKLY LUNCHTIME MEETUP.
AND THEN THERE WAS A *LOT* OF PAPER-WORK...
AND CONVINCING MY FRIENDS TO CREATE A TEAM WITH ME.
AND NOW WE'RE HERE: WE JUST NEED ONE MORE PLAYER TO BE ELIGIBLE.
AND I THINK THAT PLAYER SHOULD BE *YOU*.

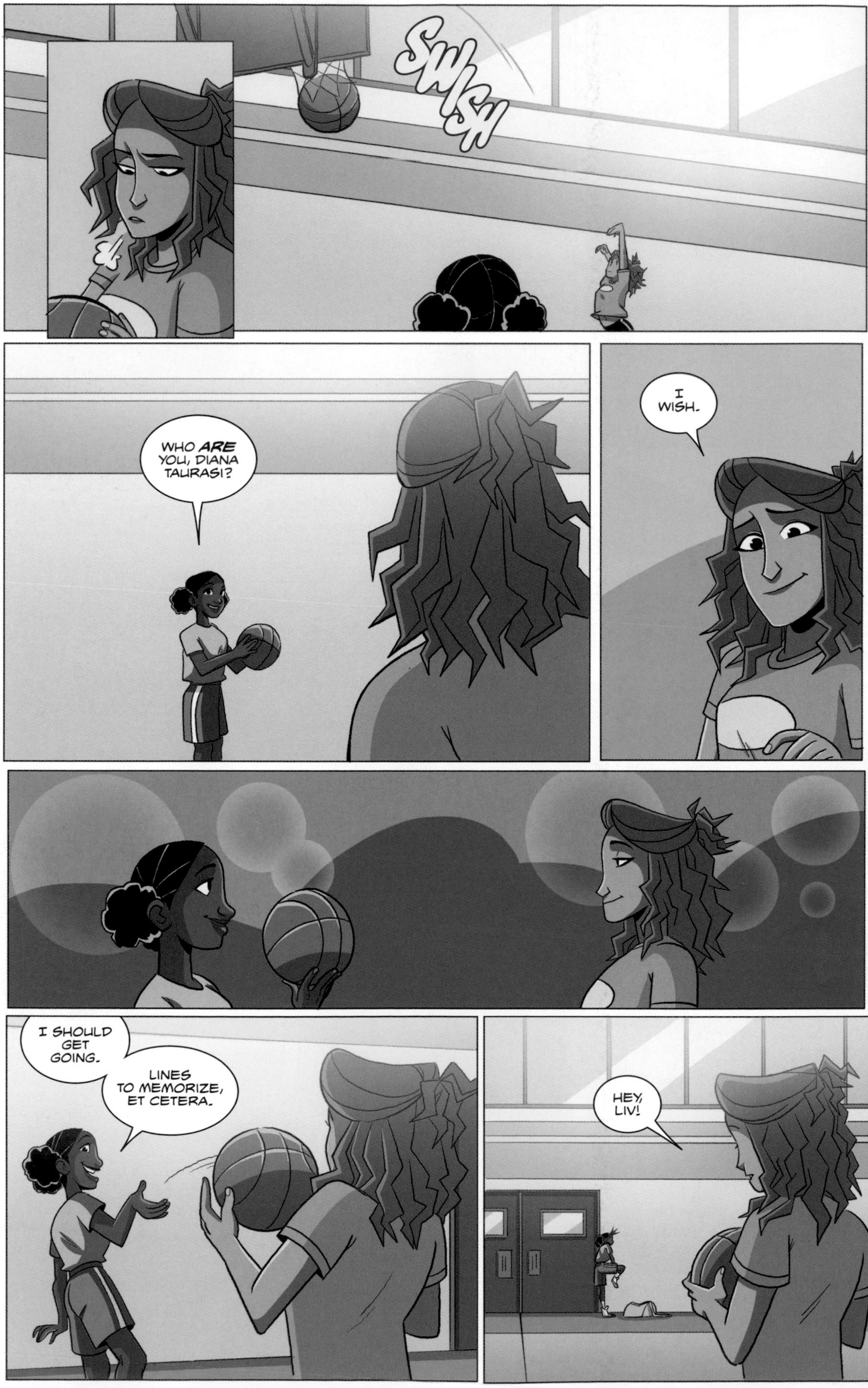
SWISH
WHO ARE YOU, DIANA TAURASI?
I WISH.
I SHOULD GET GOING.
LINES TO MEMORIZE, ET CETERA.
HEY, LIV!

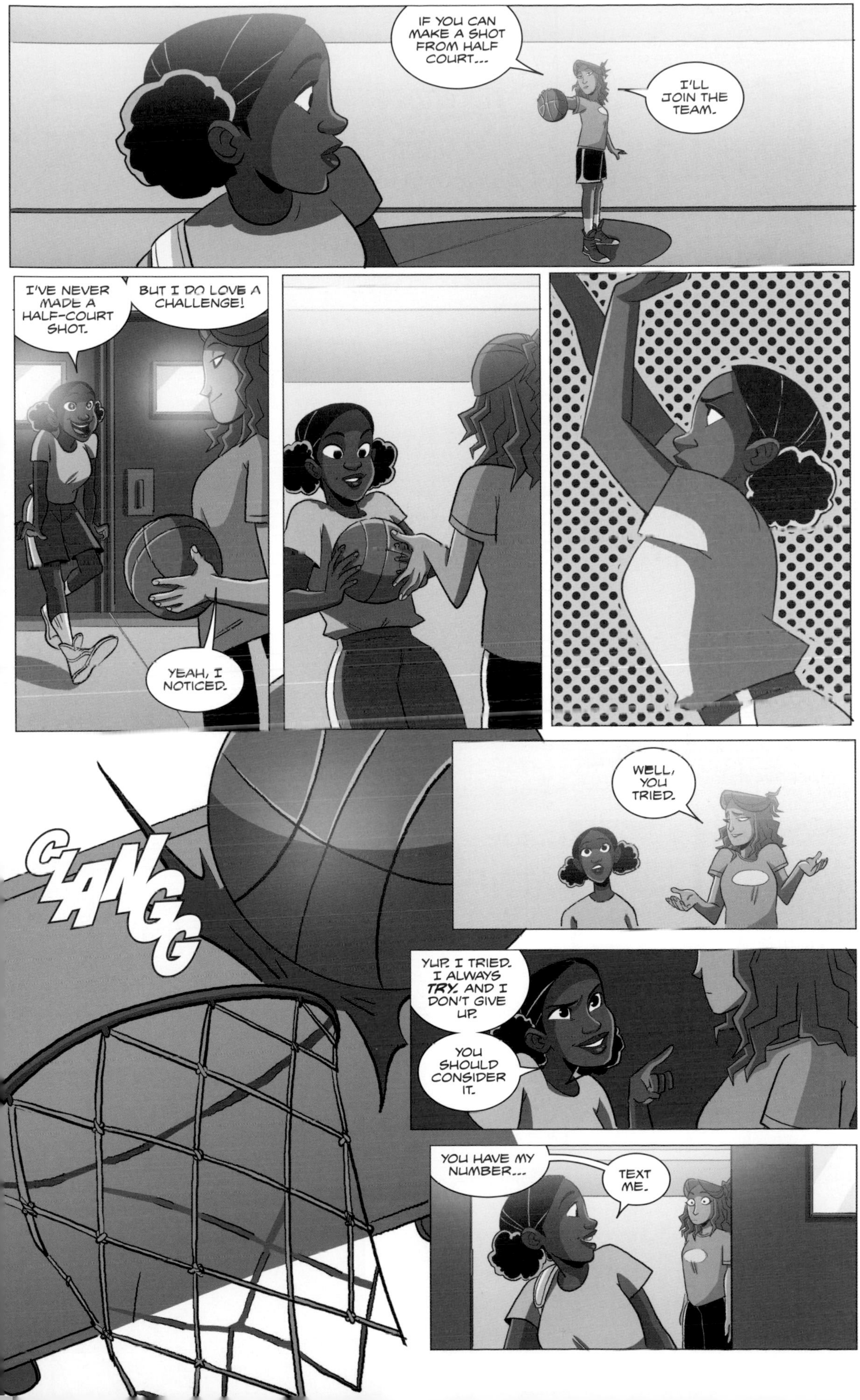
IF YOU CAN MAKE A SHOT FROM HALF COURT...
I'LL JOIN THE TEAM.
I'VE NEVER MADE A HALF-COURT SHOT.
BUT I DO LOVE A CHALLENGE!
YEAH, I NOTICED.
CLANGG
WELL, YOU TRIED.
YUP. I TRIED. I ALWAYS *TRY*. AND I DON'T GIVE UP.
YOU SHOULD CONSIDER IT.
YOU HAVE MY NUMBER...
TEXT ME.

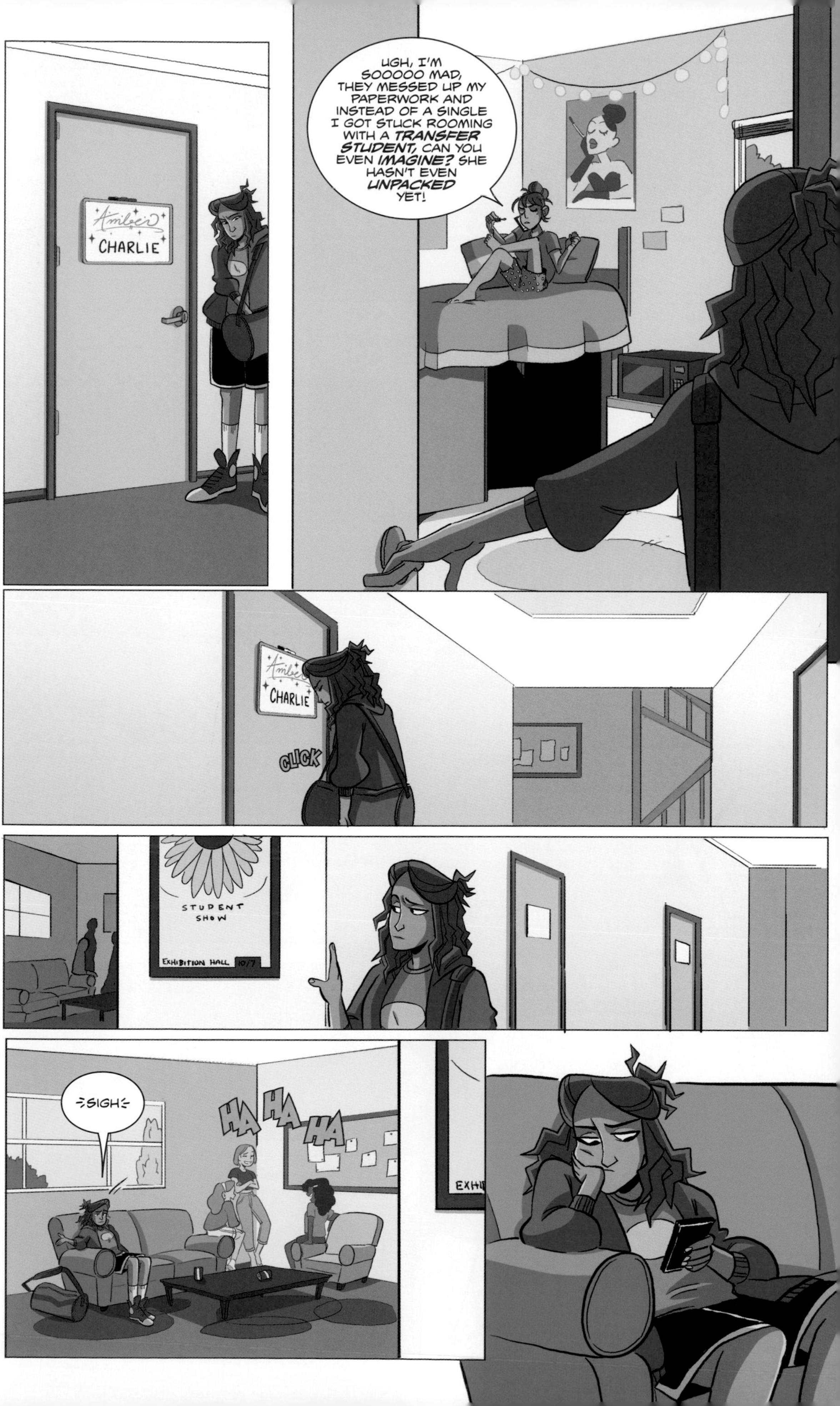
Amber
CHARLIE
UGH, I'M SOOOOO MAD, THEY MESSED UP MY PAPERWORK AND INSTEAD OF A SINGLE I GOT STUCK ROOMING WITH A TRANSFER STUDENT, CAN YOU EVEN IMAGINE? SHE HASN'T EVEN UNPACKED YET!
CLICK
STUDENT SHOW
EXHIBITION HALL 10/7
SIGH
HA HA HA
EXHI

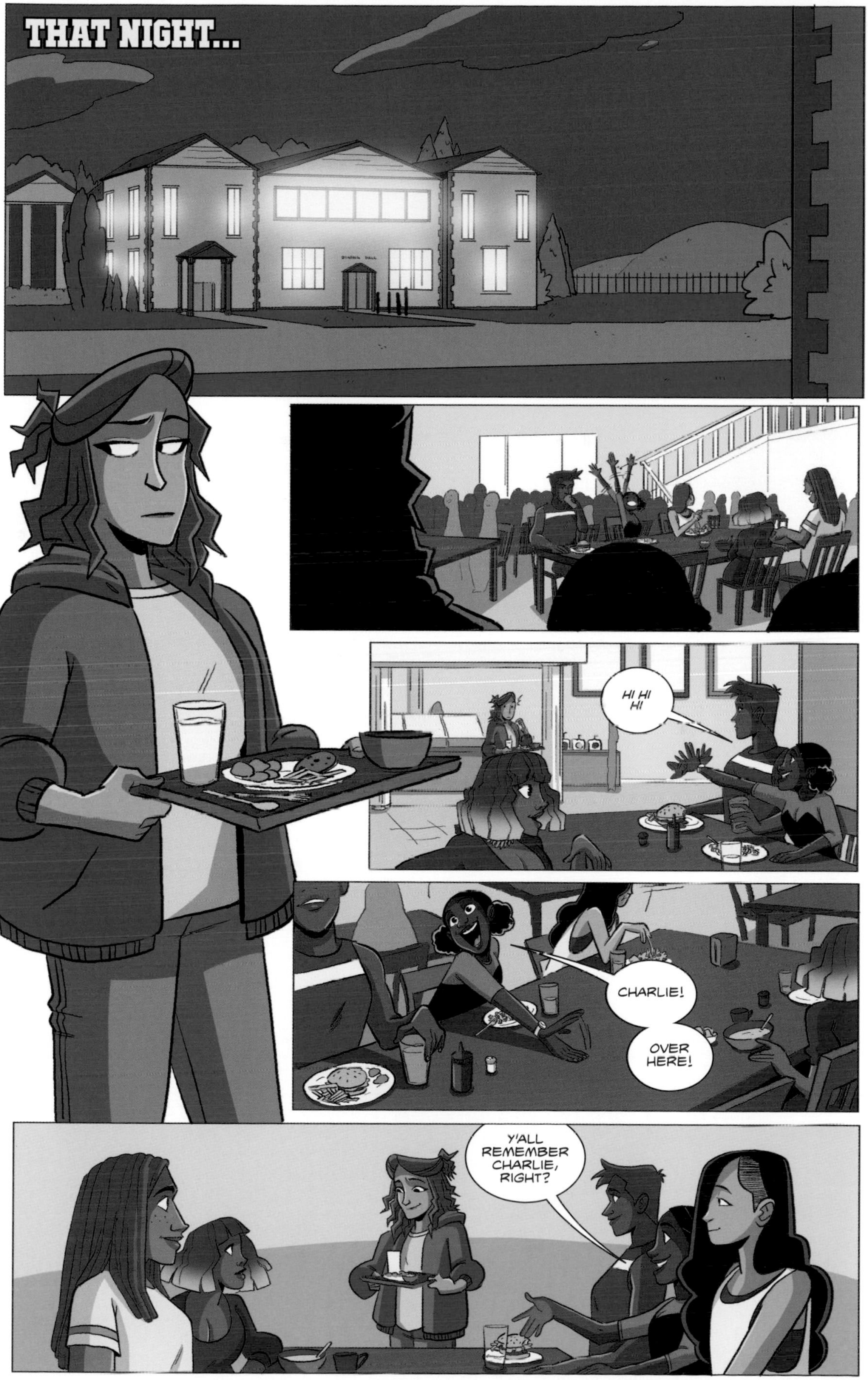
THAT NIGHT...
DINING HALL
HI HI HI
CHARLIE!
OVER HERE!
Y'ALL REMEMBER CHARLIE, RIGHT?

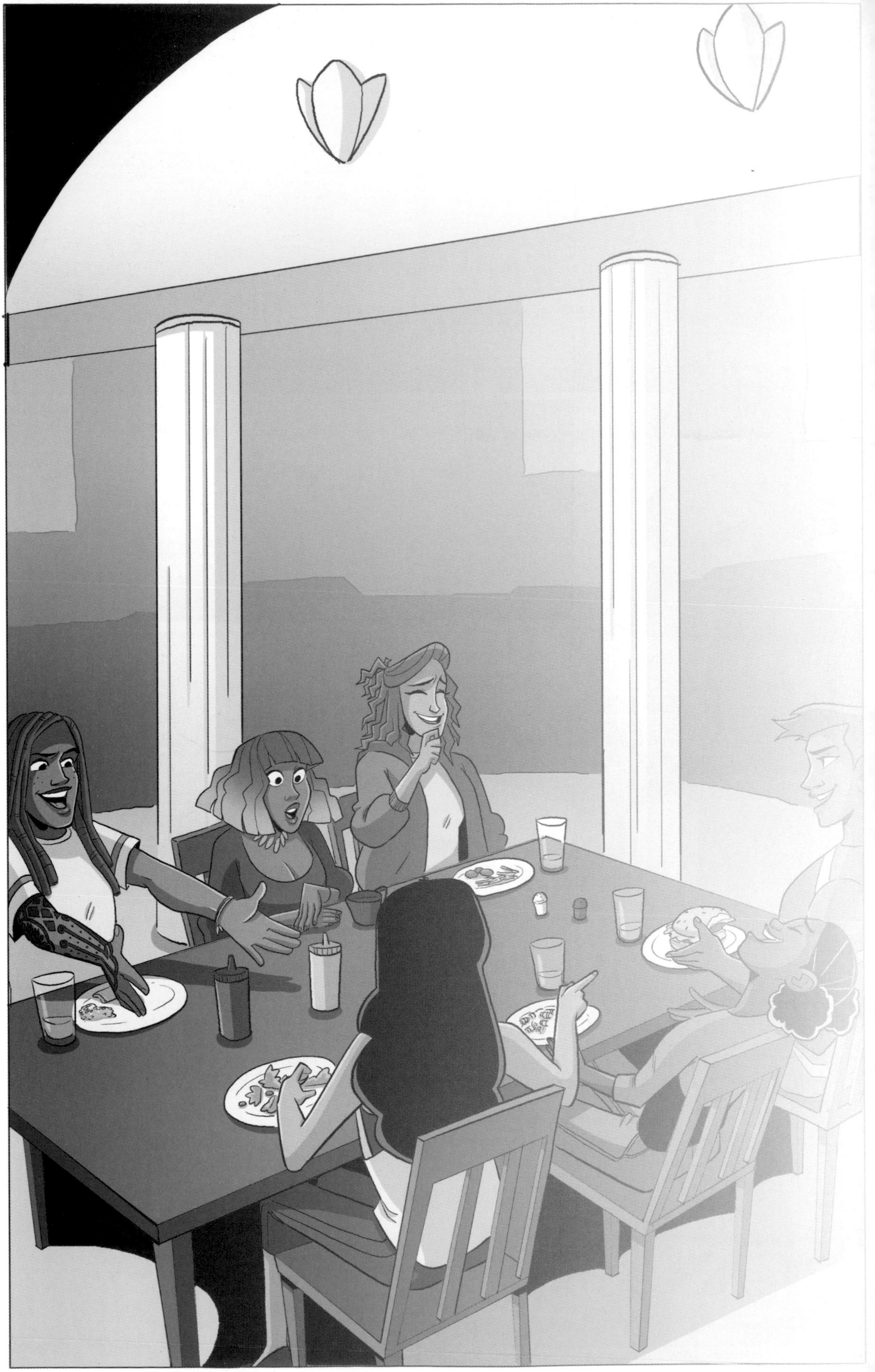

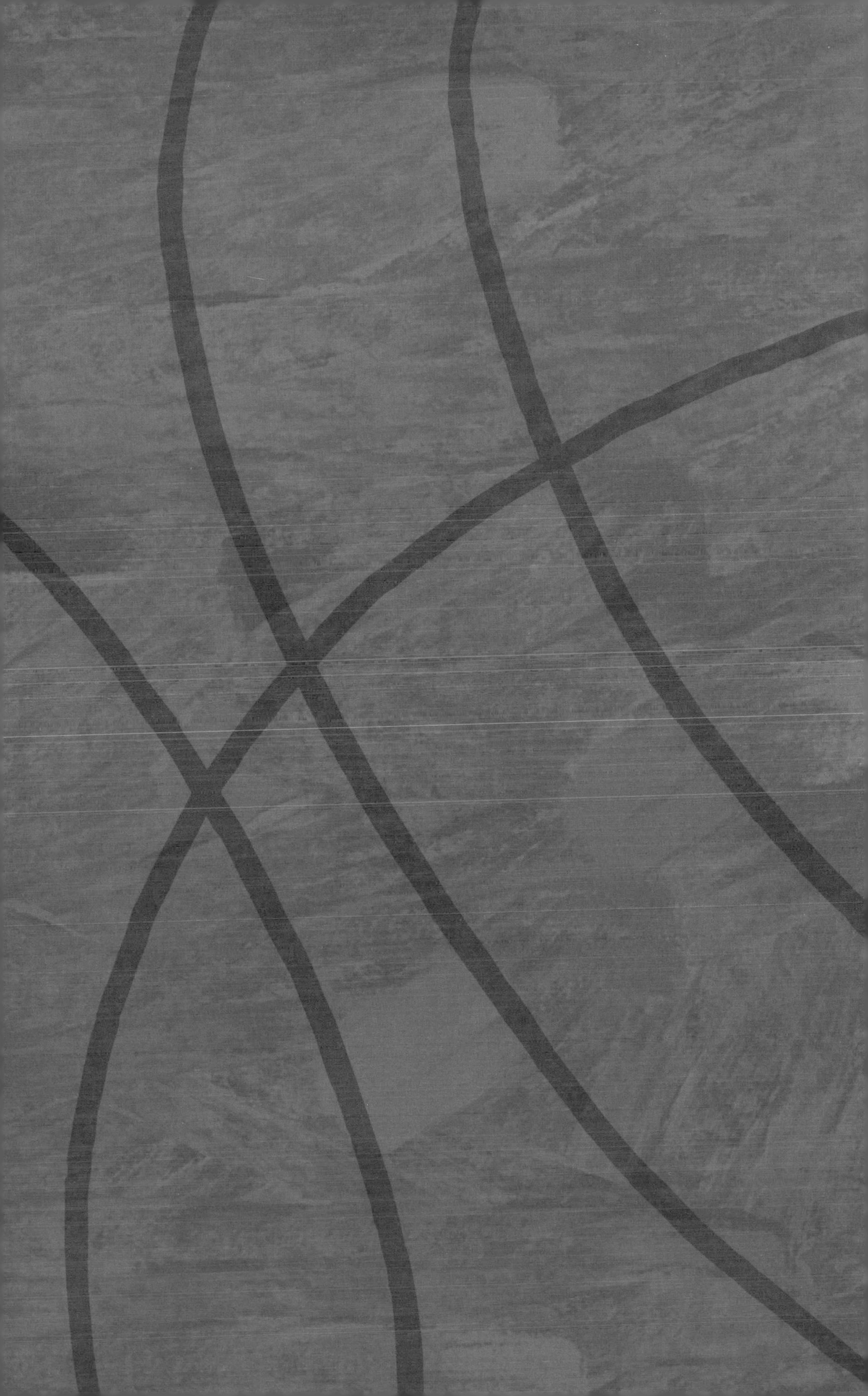

CHAPTER
TWO

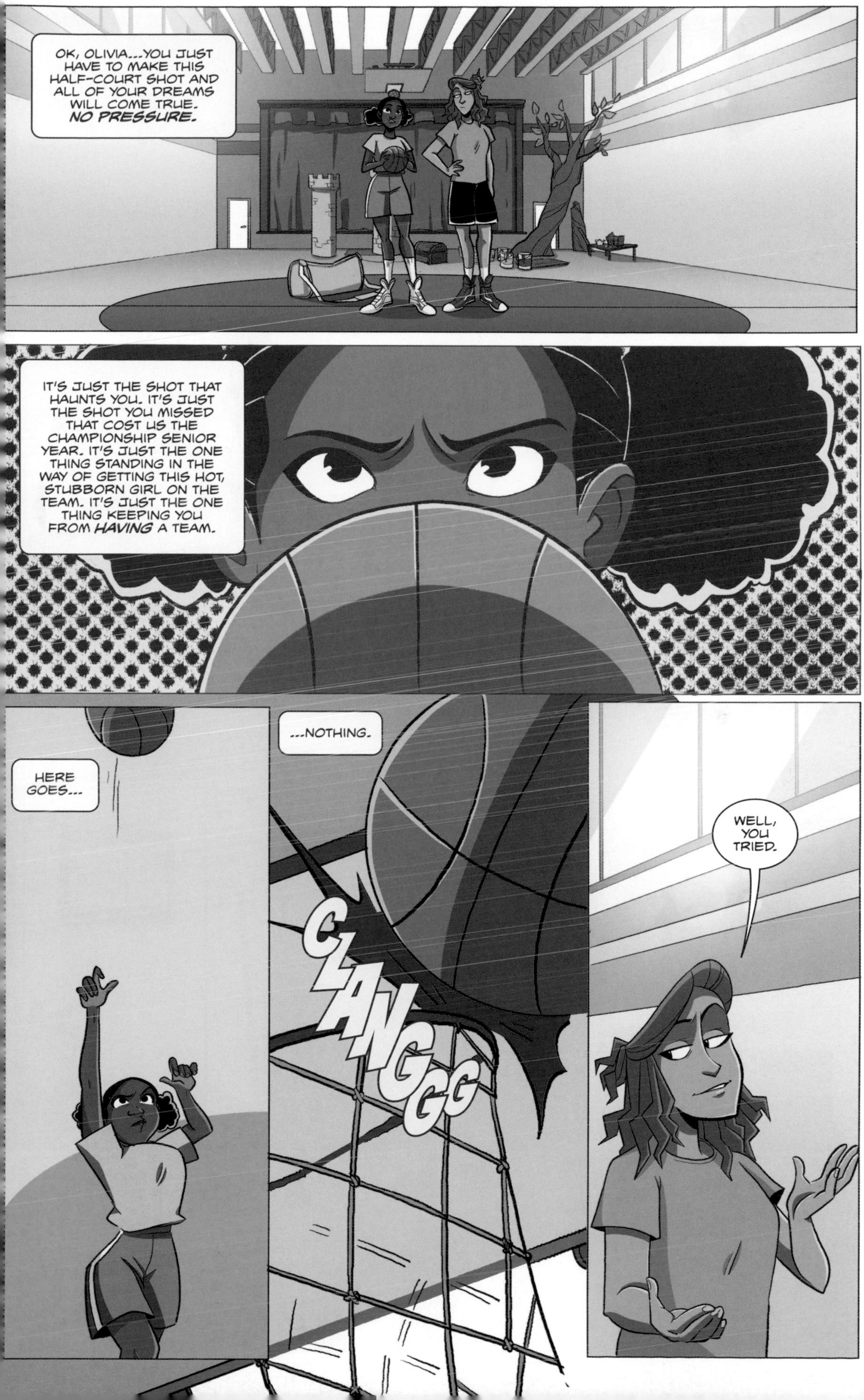
OK, OLIVIA...YOU JUST HAVE TO MAKE THIS HALF-COURT SHOT AND ALL OF YOUR DREAMS WILL COME TRUE. NO PRESSURE.
IT'S JUST THE SHOT THAT HAUNTS YOU. IT'S JUST THE SHOT YOU MISSED THAT COST US THE CHAMPIONSHIP SENIOR YEAR. IT'S JUST THE ONE THING STANDING IN THE WAY OF GETTING THIS HOT, STUBBORN GIRL ON THE TEAM. IT'S JUST THE ONE THING KEEPING YOU FROM HAVING A TEAM.
HERE GOES...
...NOTHING.
CLANGGG
WELL, YOU TRIED.

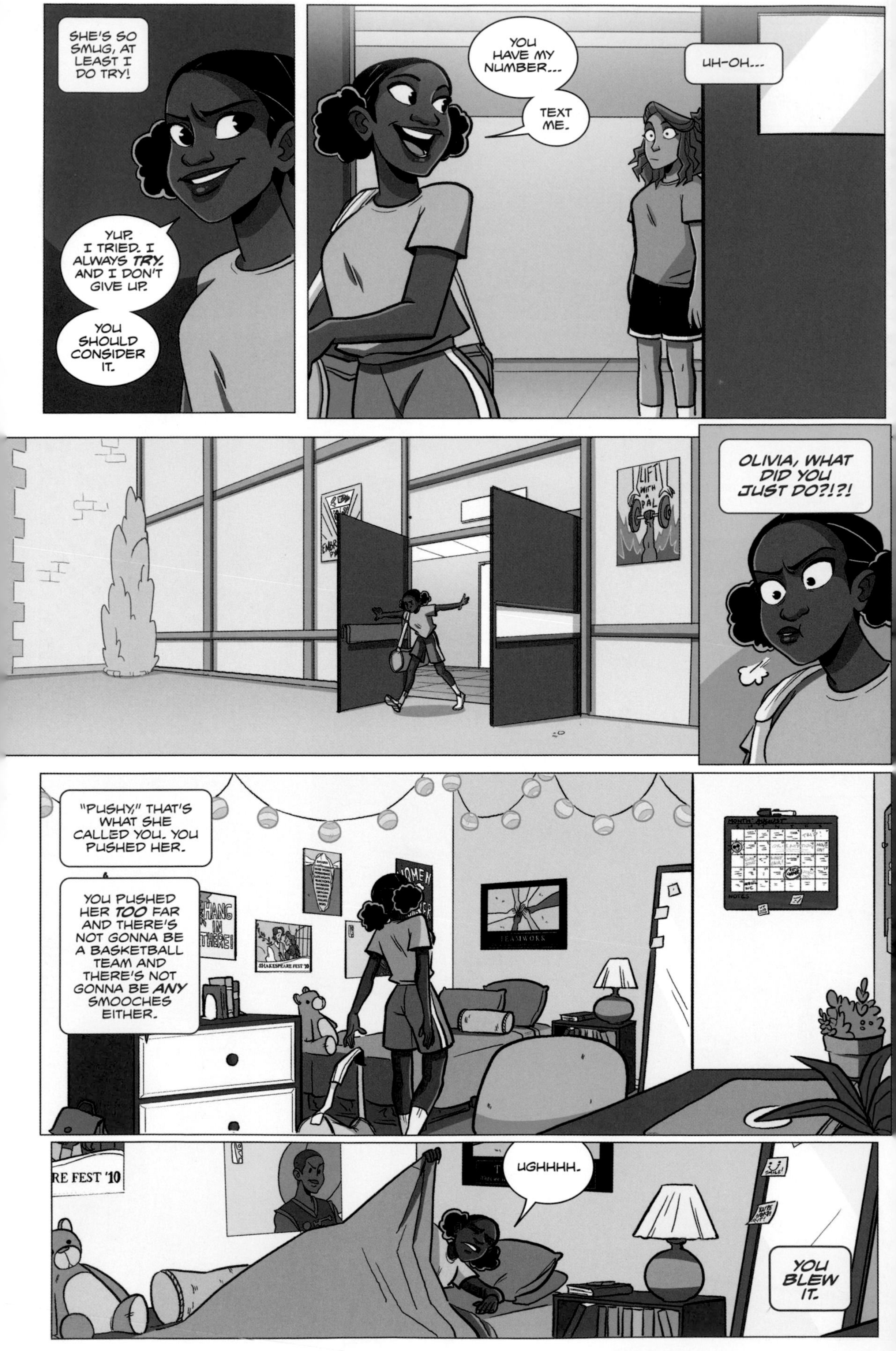
SHE'S SO SMUG, AT LEAST I DO TRY!
YUP. I TRIED. I ALWAYS TRY. AND I DON'T GIVE UP.
YOU SHOULD CONSIDER IT.
YOU HAVE MY NUMBER...
TEXT ME.
UH-OH...
LIFT WITH A PAL
OLIVIA, WHAT DID YOU JUST DO?!?!
"PUSHY," THAT'S WHAT SHE CALLED YOU. YOU PUSHED HER.
YOU PUSHED HER TOO FAR AND THERE'S NOT GONNA BE A BASKETBALL TEAM AND THERE'S NOT GONNA BE ANY SMOOCHES EITHER.
HANG IN THERE!
SHAKESPEARE FEST '10
TEAMWORK
UGHHHH.
RE FEST '10
YOU BLEW IT.

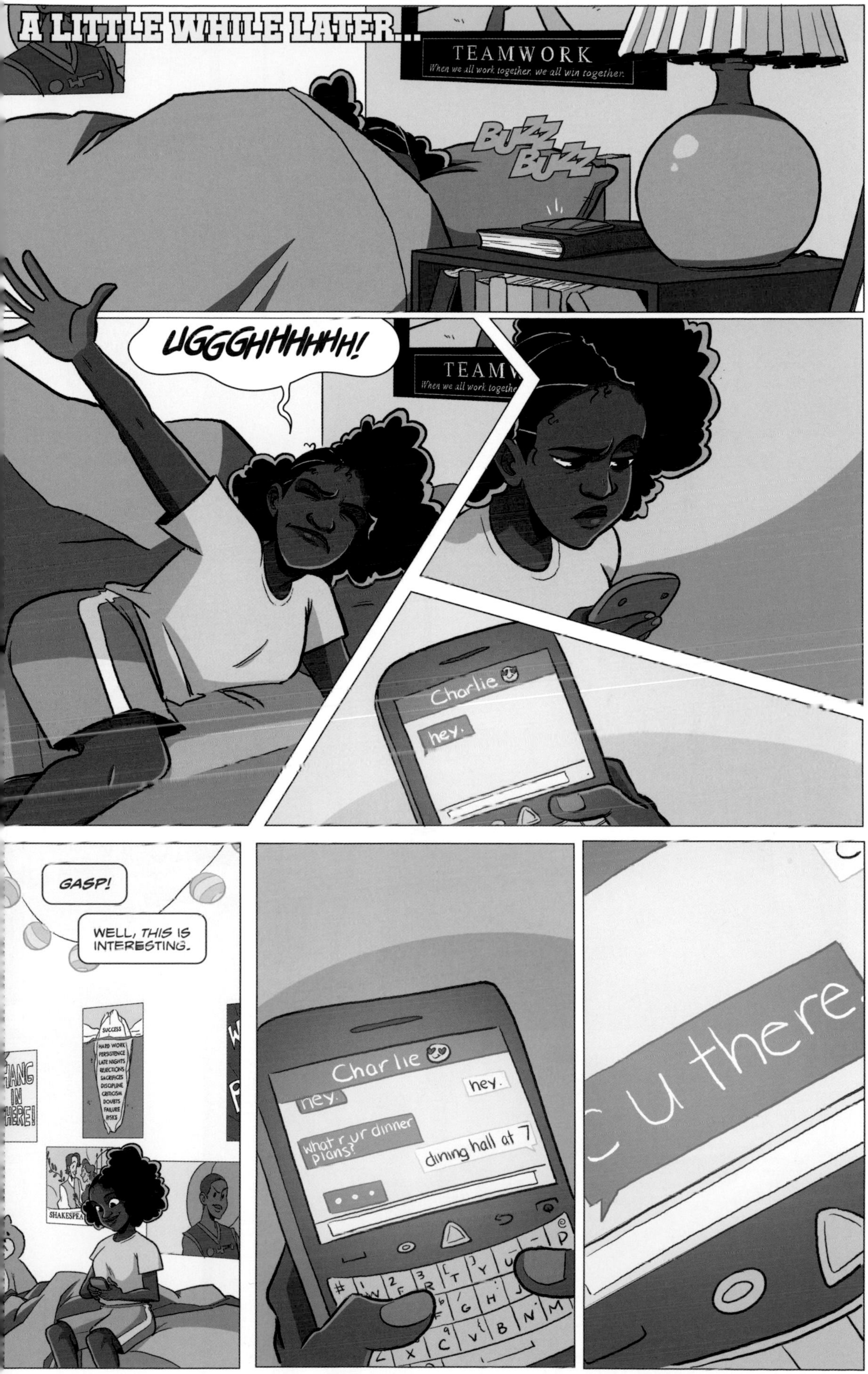
A LITTLE WHILE LATER...
TEAMWORK
When we all work together, we all win together.
BUZZ BUZZ
UGGGHHHHH!
Charlie
hey.
GASP!
WELL, THIS IS INTERESTING.
HANG IN THERE!
SUCCESS
HARD WORK
PERSISTENCE
LATE NIGHTS
REJECTIONS
SACRIFICES
DISCIPLINE
CRITICISM
DOUBTS
FAILURE
RISKS
SHAKESPEA
Charlie
hey.
hey.
what r ur dinner plans?
dining hall at 7
c u there.

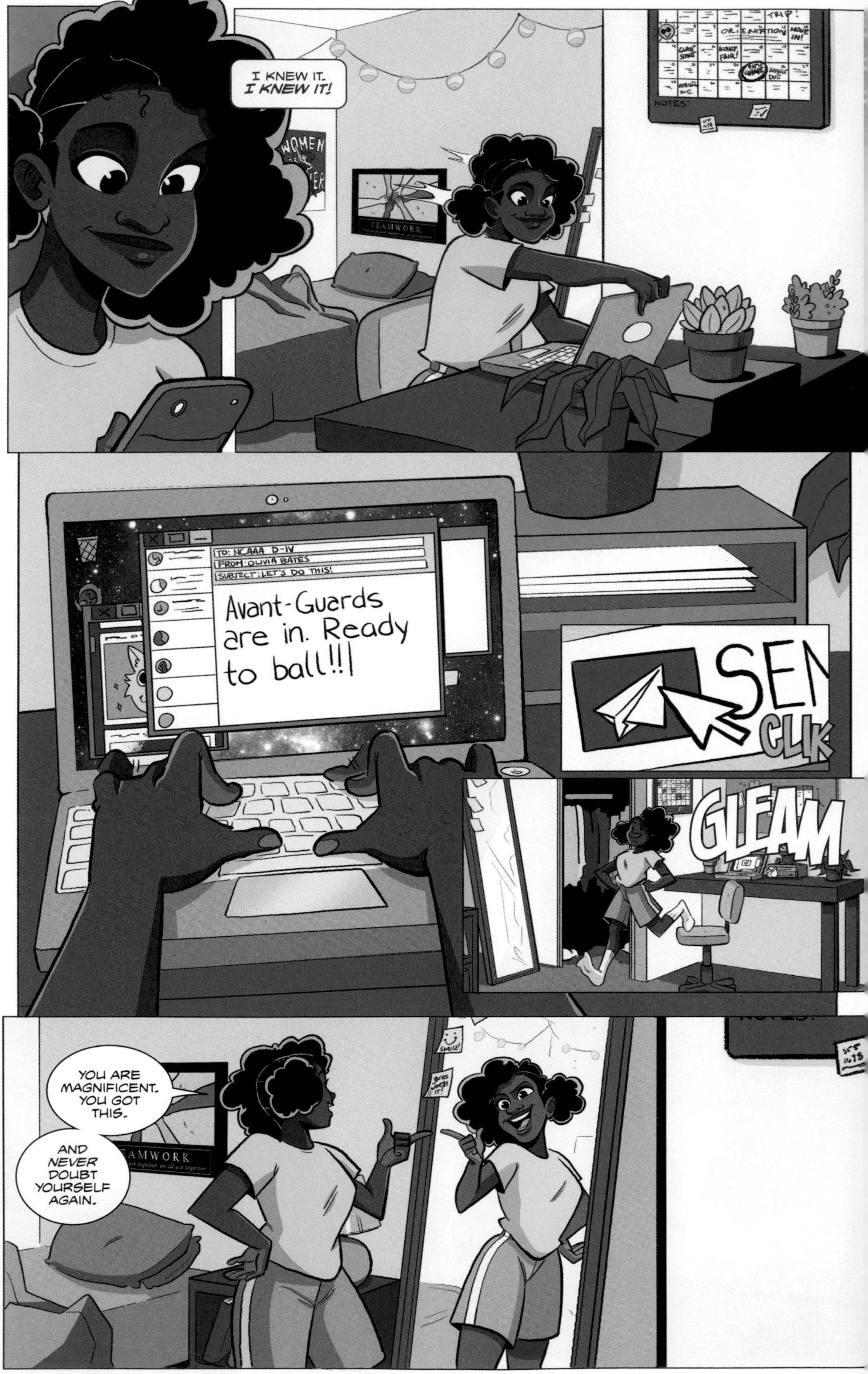
I KNEW IT. I KNEW IT!
TEAMWORK
TO: NCAAA D-IV
FROM: OLIVIA BATES
SUBJECT: LET'S DO THIS!
Avant-Guards are in. Ready to ball!!!
SEN
CLIK
GLEAM
YOU ARE MAGNIFICENT. YOU GOT THIS.
AND NEVER DOUBT YOURSELF AGAIN.
SMILE!
TEAMWORK

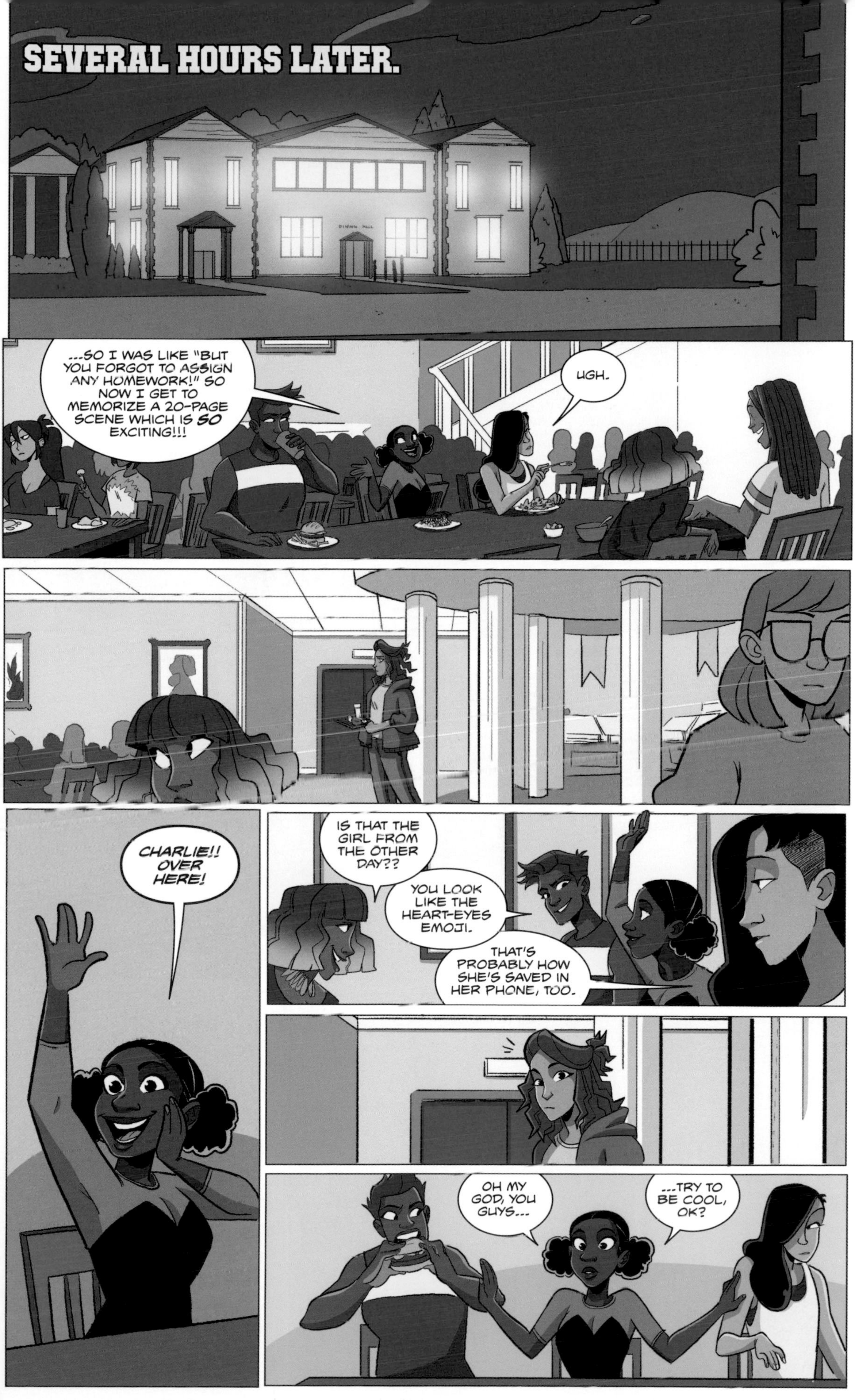
SEVERAL HOURS LATER.
DINING HALL
...SO I WAS LIKE "BUT YOU FORGOT TO ASSIGN ANY HOMEWORK!" SO NOW I GET TO MEMORIZE A 20-PAGE SCENE WHICH IS SO EXCITING!!!
UGH.
CHARLIE!! OVER HERE!
IS THAT THE GIRL FROM THE OTHER DAY??
YOU LOOK LIKE THE HEART-EYES EMOJI.
THAT'S PROBABLY HOW SHE'S SAVED IN HER PHONE, TOO.
OH MY GOD, YOU GUYS...
...TRY TO BE COOL, OK?

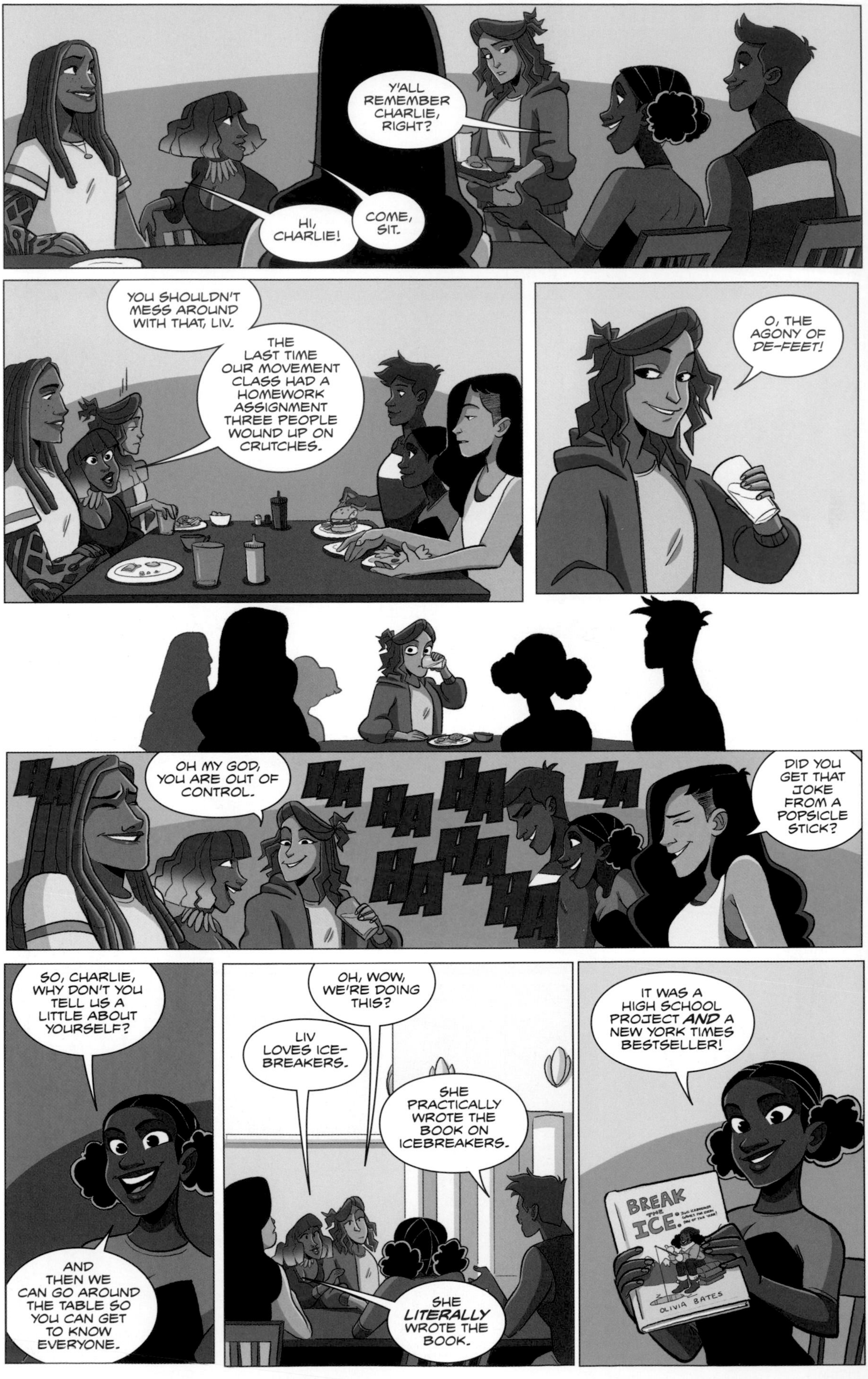
Y'ALL REMEMBER CHARLIE, RIGHT?
HI, CHARLIE!
COME, SIT.
YOU SHOULDN'T MESS AROUND WITH THAT, LIV.
THE LAST TIME OUR MOVEMENT CLASS HAD A HOMEWORK ASSIGNMENT THREE PEOPLE WOUND UP ON CRUTCHES.
O, THE AGONY OF *DE-FEET*!
HA HA HA HA HA HA HA HA HA
OH MY GOD, YOU ARE OUT OF CONTROL.
DID YOU GET THAT JOKE FROM A POPSICLE STICK?
SO, CHARLIE, WHY DON'T YOU TELL US A LITTLE ABOUT YOURSELF?
AND THEN WE CAN GO AROUND THE TABLE SO YOU CAN GET TO KNOW EVERYONE.
OH, WOW, WE'RE DOING THIS?
LIV LOVES ICE-BREAKERS.
SHE PRACTICALLY WROTE THE BOOK ON ICEBREAKERS.
SHE *LITERALLY* WROTE THE BOOK.
IT WAS A HIGH SCHOOL PROJECT ***AND*** A NEW YORK TIMES BESTSELLER!
BREAK THE ICE
OLIVIA BATES

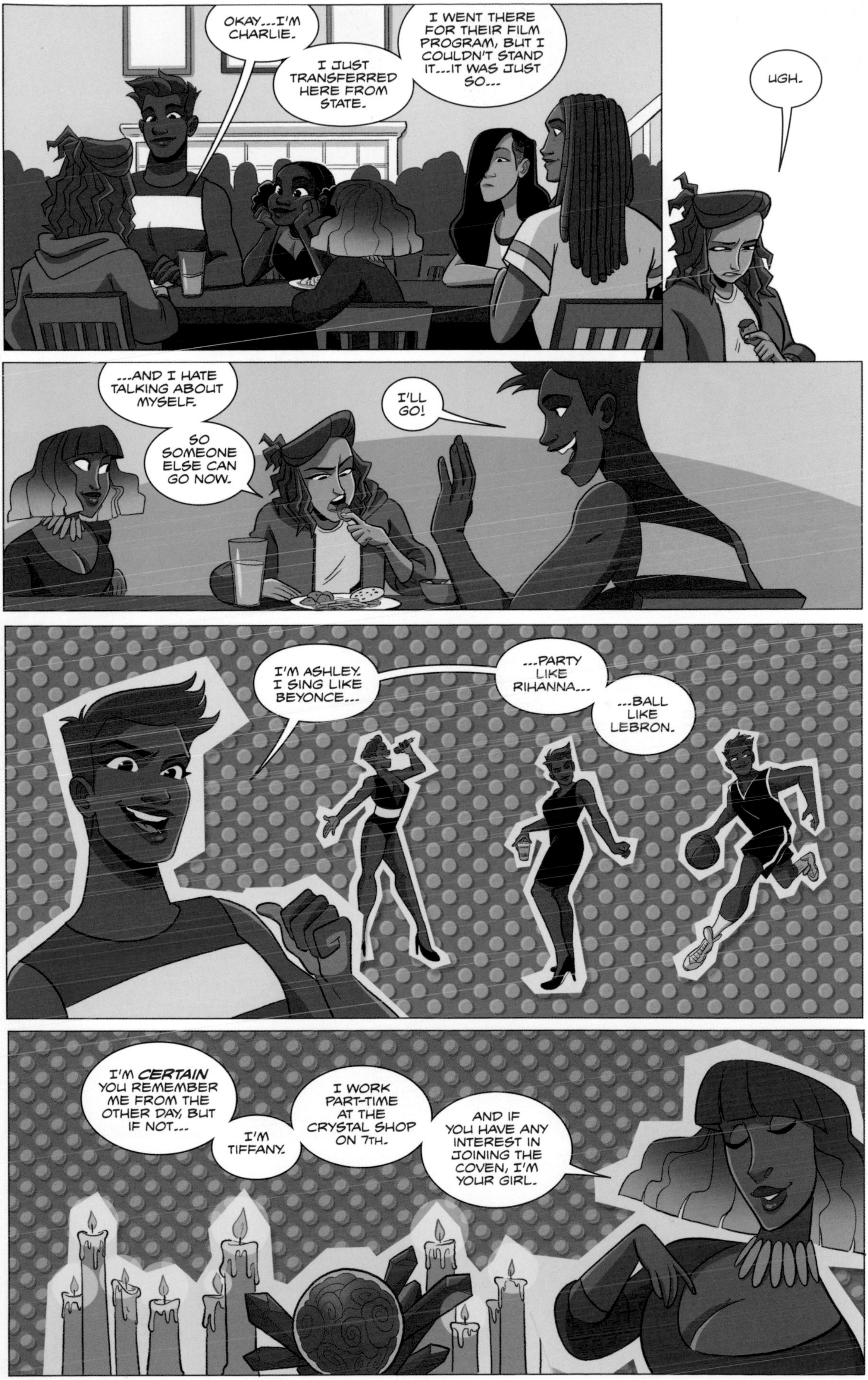
OKAY...I'M CHARLIE.
I JUST TRANSFERRED HERE FROM STATE.
I WENT THERE FOR THEIR FILM PROGRAM, BUT I COULDN'T STAND IT...IT WAS JUST SO...
UGH.
...AND I HATE TALKING ABOUT MYSELF.
SO SOMEONE ELSE CAN GO NOW.
I'LL GO!
I'M ASHLEY. I SING LIKE BEYONCE...
...PARTY LIKE RIHANNA...
...BALL LIKE LEBRON.
I'M *CERTAIN* YOU REMEMBER ME FROM THE OTHER DAY, BUT IF NOT...
I'M TIFFANY.
I WORK PART-TIME AT THE CRYSTAL SHOP ON 7TH.
AND IF YOU HAVE ANY INTEREST IN JOINING THE COVEN, I'M YOUR GIRL.

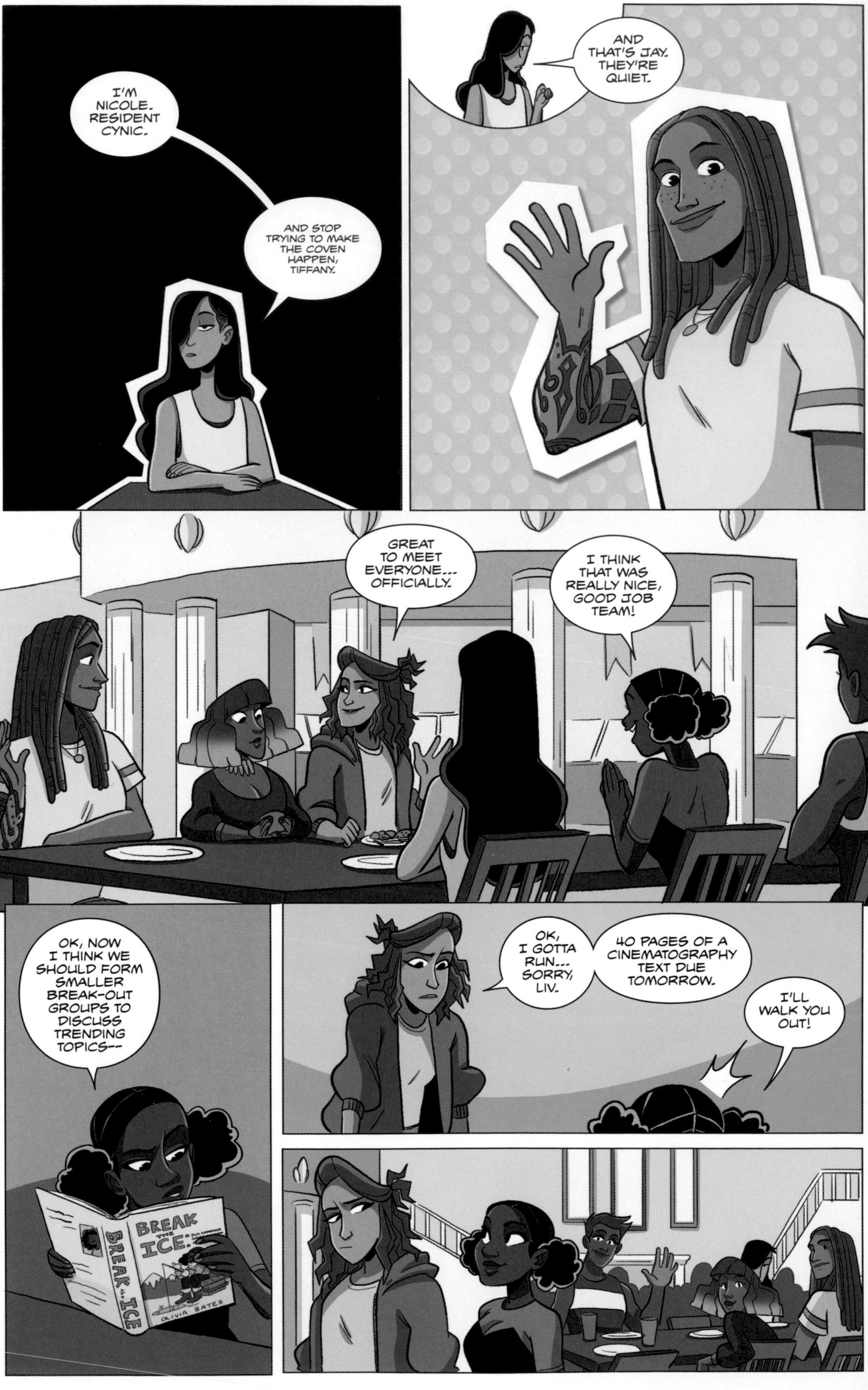
I'M NICOLE. RESIDENT CYNIC.
AND STOP TRYING TO MAKE THE COVEN HAPPEN, TIFFANY.
AND THAT'S JAY. THEY'RE QUIET.
GREAT TO MEET EVERYONE... OFFICIALLY.
I THINK THAT WAS REALLY NICE, GOOD JOB TEAM!
OK, NOW I THINK WE SHOULD FORM SMALLER BREAK-OUT GROUPS TO DISCUSS TRENDING TOPICS--
BREAK THE ICE
BREAK THE ICE
OLIVIA BATES
OK, I GOTTA RUN... SORRY, LIV.
40 PAGES OF A CINEMATOGRAPHY TEXT DUE TOMORROW.
I'LL WALK YOU OUT!

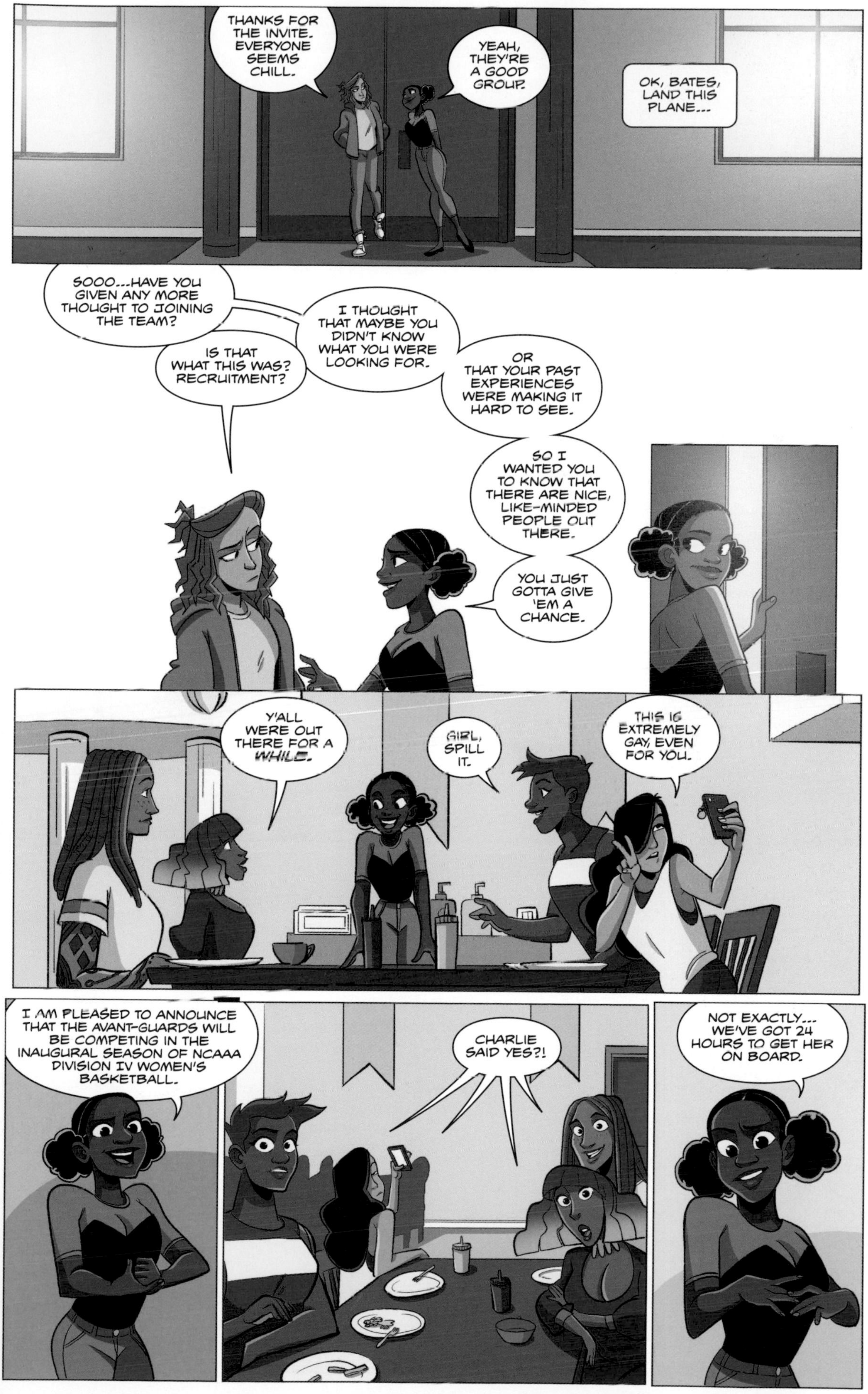
THANKS FOR THE INVITE. EVERYONE SEEMS CHILL.
YEAH, THEY'RE A GOOD GROUP.
OK, BATES, LAND THIS PLANE...
SOOO...HAVE YOU GIVEN ANY MORE THOUGHT TO JOINING THE TEAM?
IS THAT WHAT THIS WAS? RECRUITMENT?
I THOUGHT THAT MAYBE YOU DIDN'T KNOW WHAT YOU WERE LOOKING FOR.
OR THAT YOUR PAST EXPERIENCES WERE MAKING IT HARD TO SEE.
SO I WANTED YOU TO KNOW THAT THERE ARE NICE, LIKE-MINDED PEOPLE OUT THERE.
YOU JUST GOTTA GIVE 'EM A CHANCE.
Y'ALL WERE OUT THERE FOR A WHILE.
GIRL, SPILL IT.
THIS IS EXTREMELY GAY, EVEN FOR YOU.
I AM PLEASED TO ANNOUNCE THAT THE AVANT-GUARDS WILL BE COMPETING IN THE INAUGURAL SEASON OF NCAAA DIVISION IV WOMEN'S BASKETBALL.
CHARLIE SAID YES?!
NOT EXACTLY... WE'VE GOT 24 HOURS TO GET HER ON BOARD.

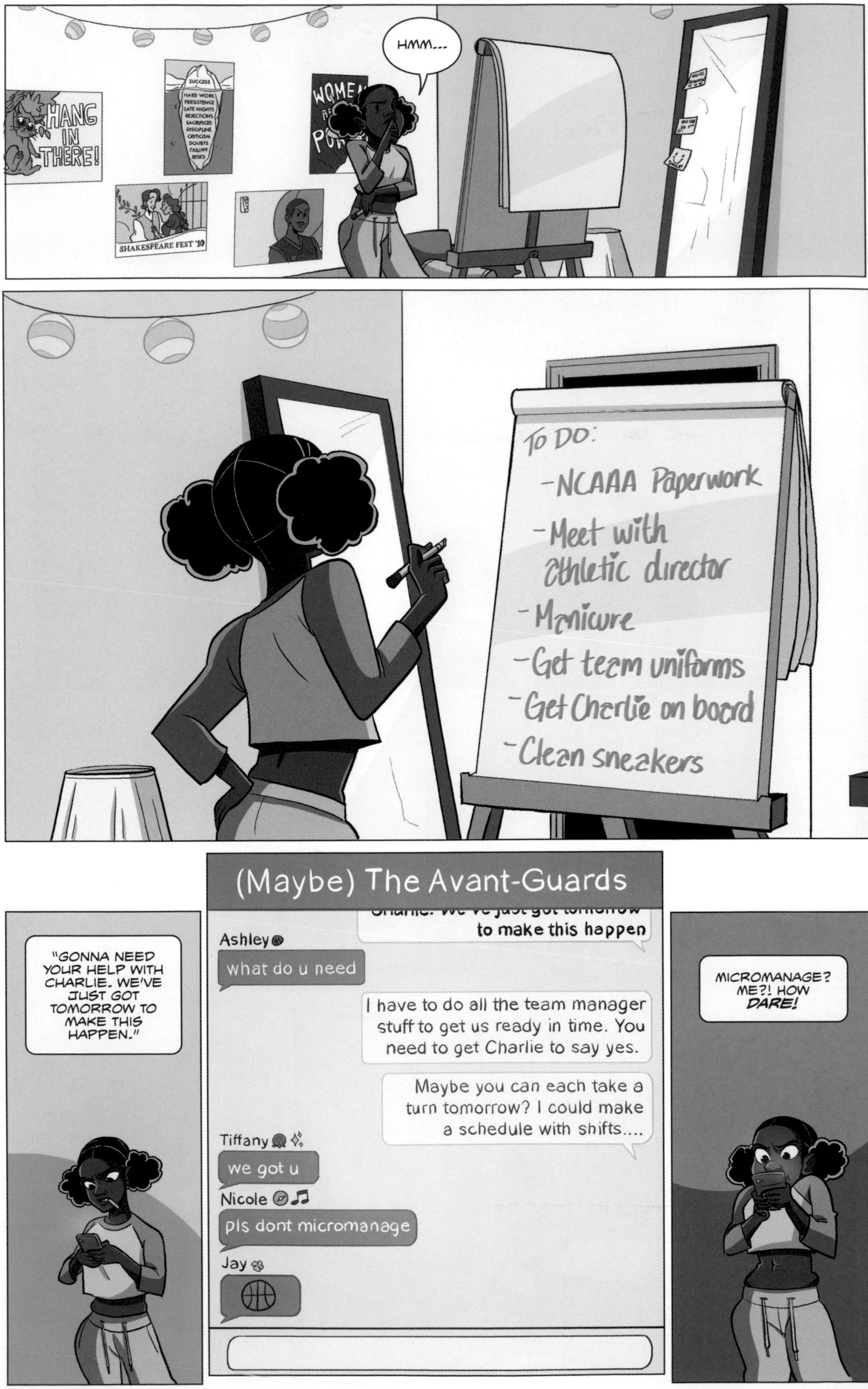
HANG IN THERE!
SUCCESS
HARD WORK
PERSISTENCE
LATE NIGHTS
REJECTIONS
SACRIFICES
DISCIPLINE
CRITICISM
DOUBTS
FAILURE
RISKS
SHAKESPEARE FEST '10
HMM...
TO DO:
-NCAAA Paperwork
-Meet with athletic director
-Manicure
-Get team uniforms
-Get Charlie on board
-Clean sneakers
"GONNA NEED YOUR HELP WITH CHARLIE. WE'VE JUST GOT TOMORROW TO MAKE THIS HAPPEN."
(Maybe) The Avant-Guards
to make this happen
Ashley
what do u need
I have to do all the team manager stuff to get us ready in time. You need to get Charlie to say yes.
Maybe you can each take a turn tomorrow? I could make a schedule with shifts....
Tiffany
we got u
Nicole
pls dont micromanage
Jay
MICROMANAGE? ME?! HOW *DARE!*

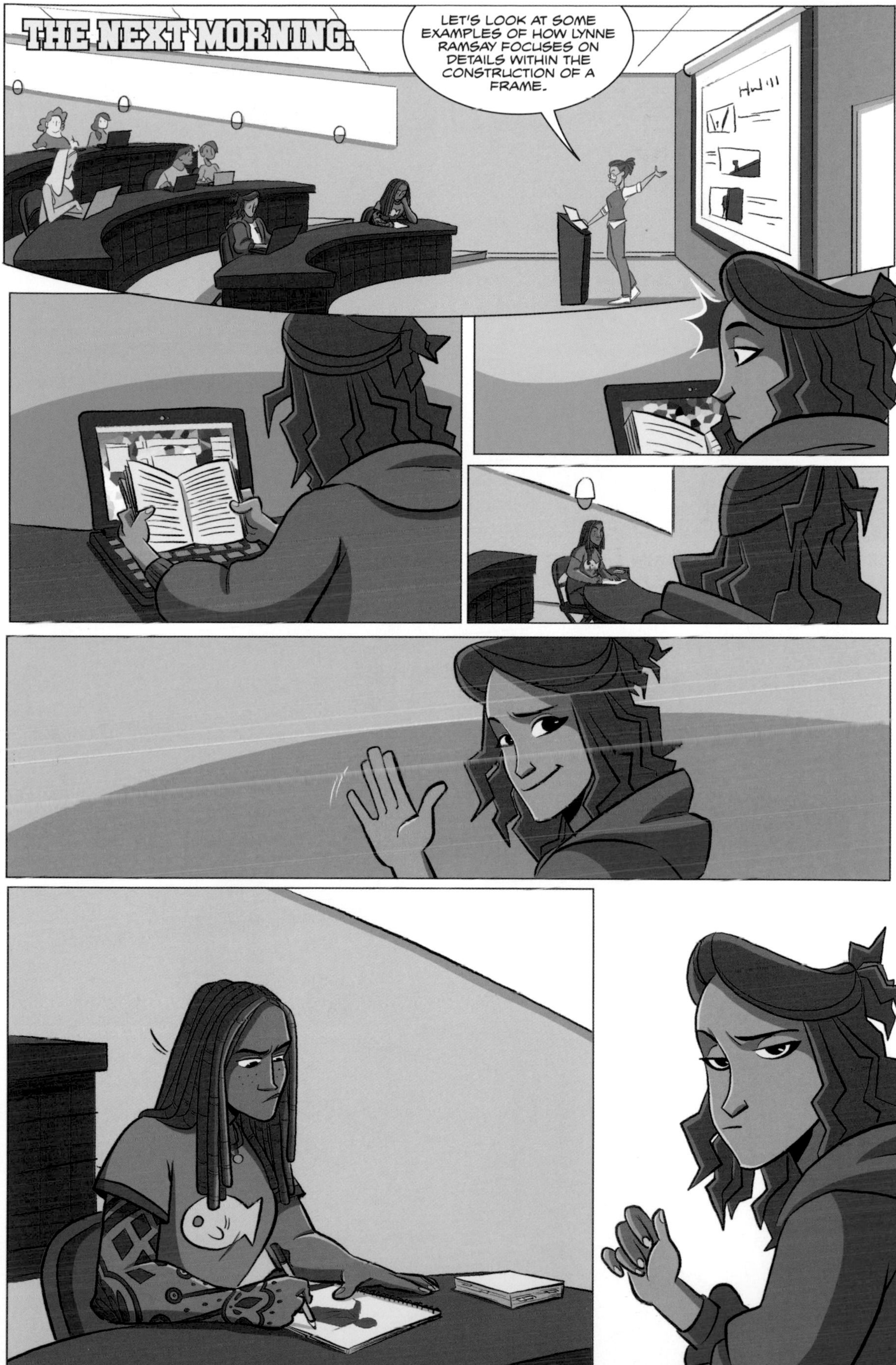
THE NEXT MORNING.
LET'S LOOK AT SOME EXAMPLES OF HOW LYNNE RAMSAY FOCUSES ON DETAILS WITHIN THE CONSTRUCTION OF A FRAME.

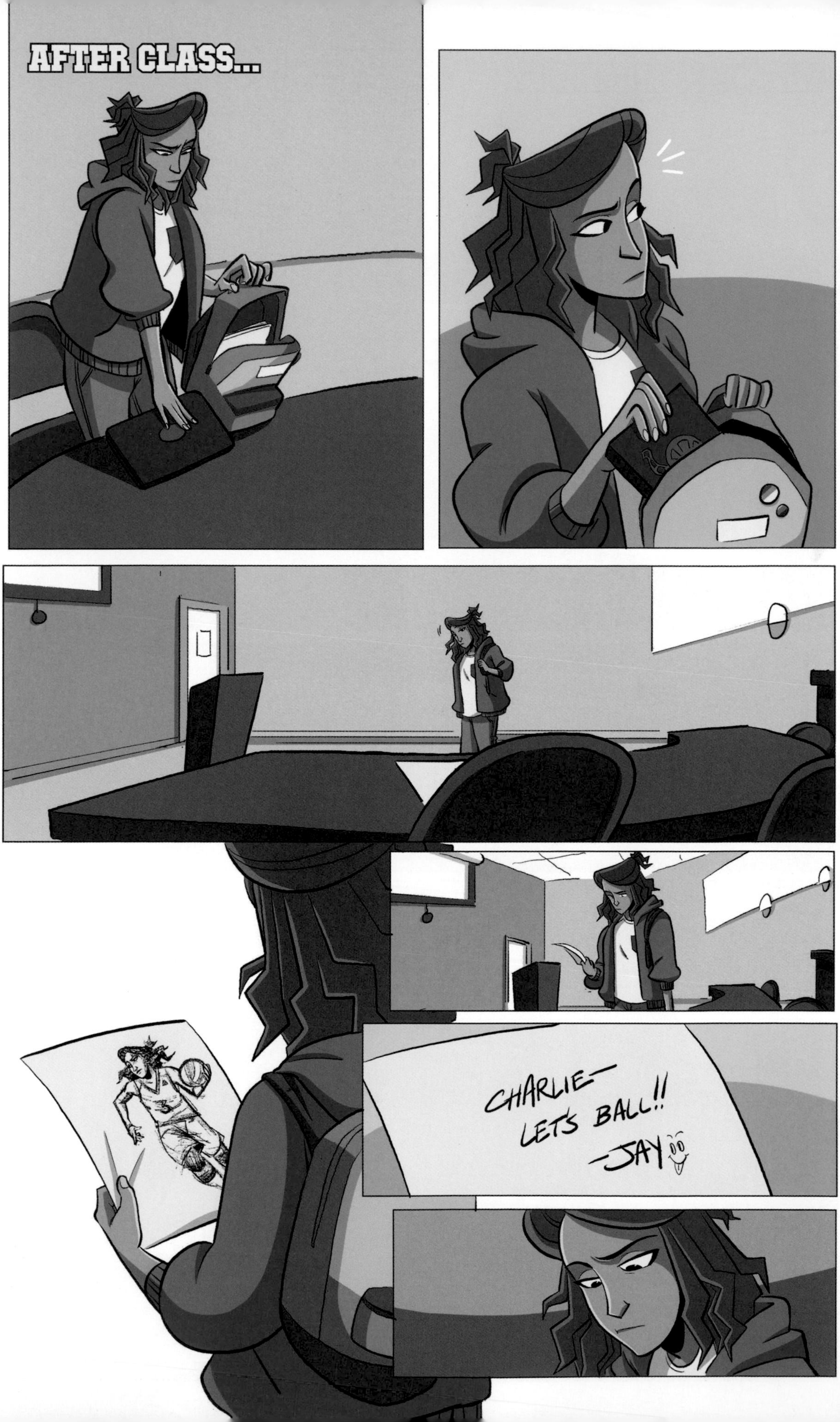
AFTER CLASS...
CHARLIE—
LETS BALL!!
—JAY

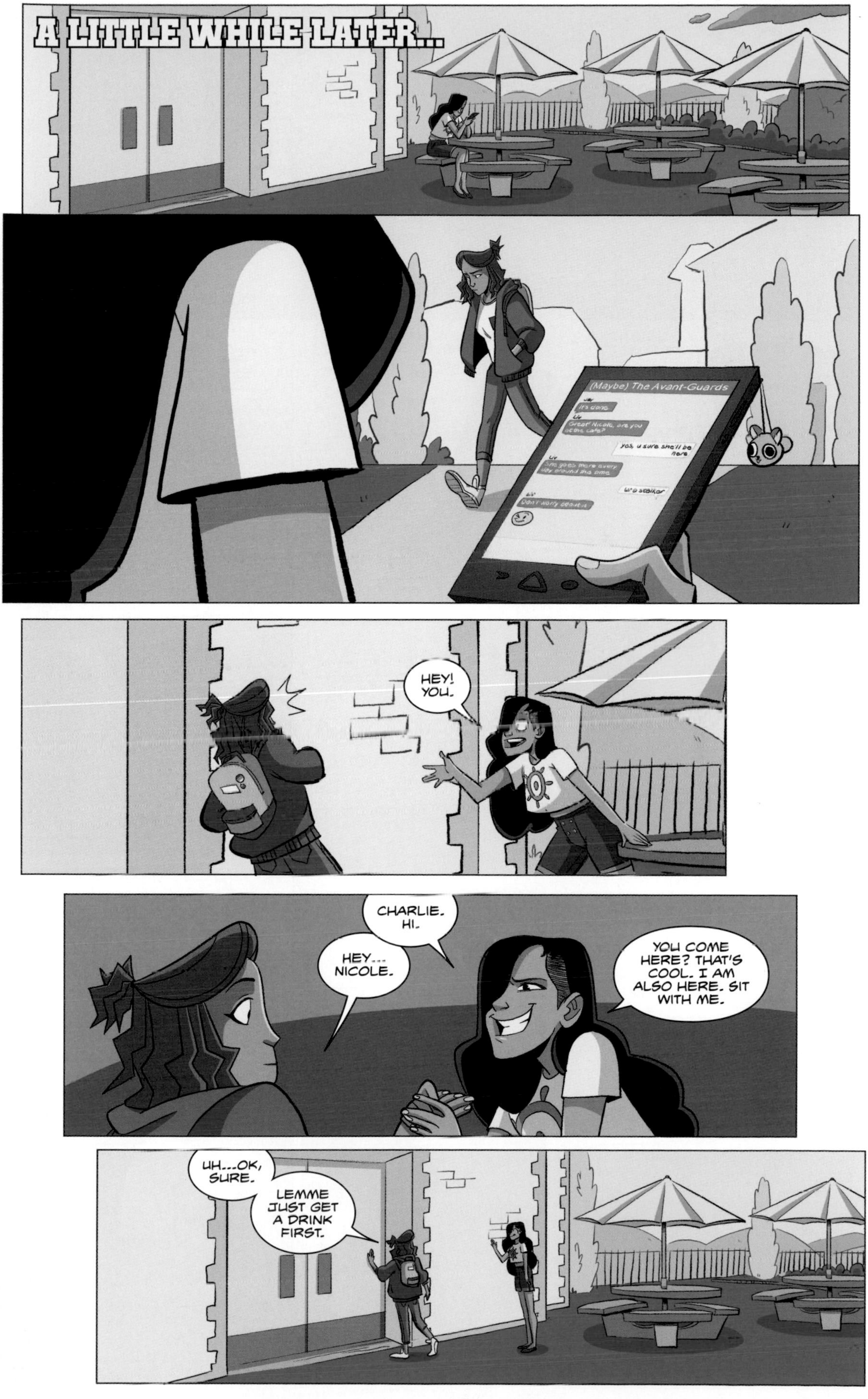
A LITTLE WHILE LATER...
(Maybe) The Avant-Guards
It's done.
Great! Nicole, are you at the cafe?
yes, u sure she'll be here
HEY! YOU.
CHARLIE. HI.
HEY... NICOLE.
YOU COME HERE? THAT'S COOL. I AM ALSO HERE. SIT WITH ME.
UH...OK, SURE.
LEMME JUST GET A DRINK FIRST.

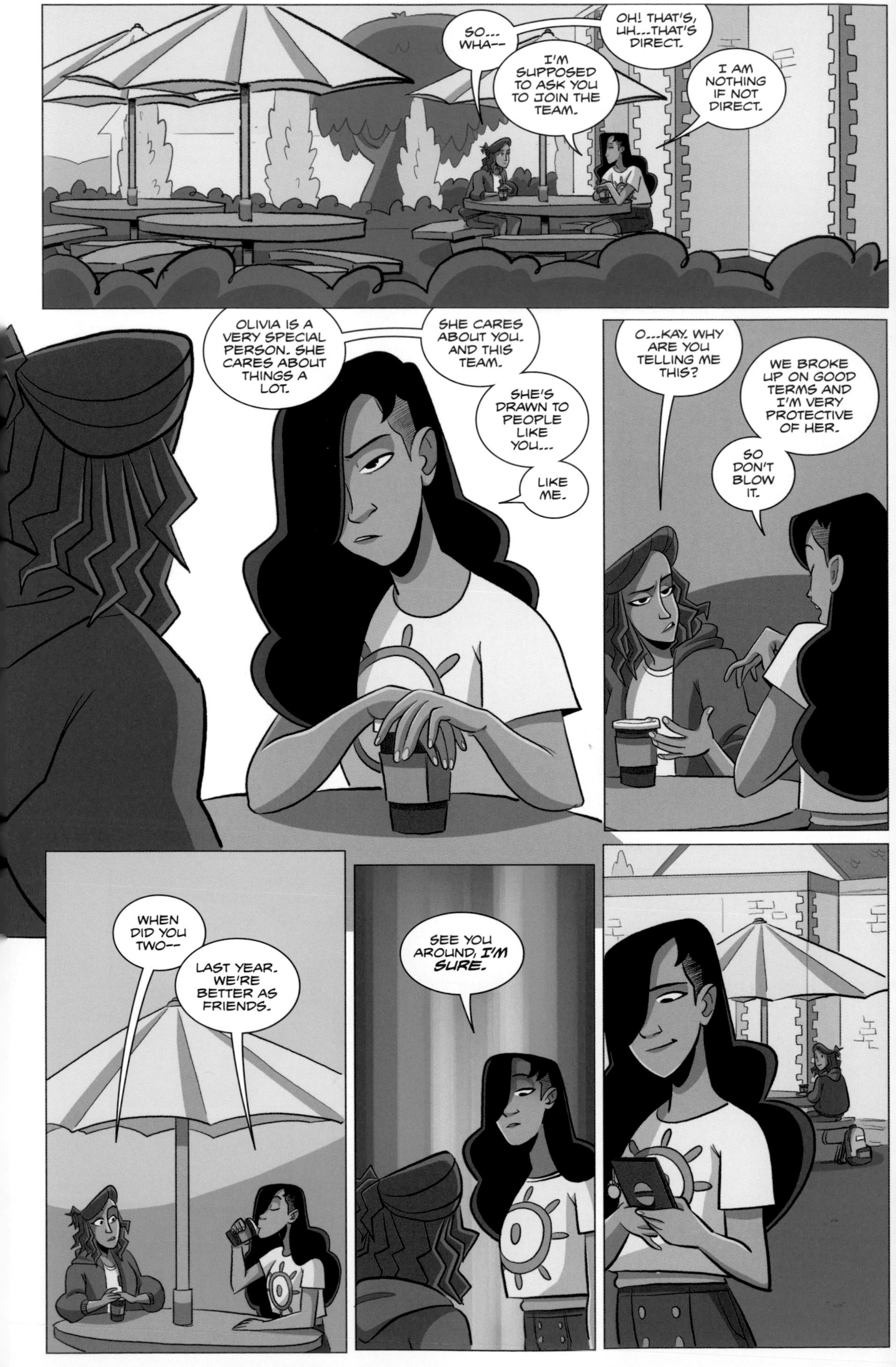
SO... WHA--
I'M SUPPOSED TO ASK YOU TO JOIN THE TEAM.
OH! THAT'S, UH...THAT'S DIRECT.
I AM NOTHING IF NOT DIRECT.
OLIVIA IS A VERY SPECIAL PERSON. SHE CARES ABOUT THINGS A LOT.
SHE CARES ABOUT YOU. AND THIS TEAM.
SHE'S DRAWN TO PEOPLE LIKE YOU...
LIKE ME.
O...KAY. WHY ARE YOU TELLING ME THIS?
WE BROKE UP ON GOOD TERMS AND I'M VERY PROTECTIVE OF HER.
SO DON'T BLOW IT.
WHEN DID YOU TWO--
LAST YEAR. WE'RE BETTER AS FRIENDS.
SEE YOU AROUND, *I'M SURE.*

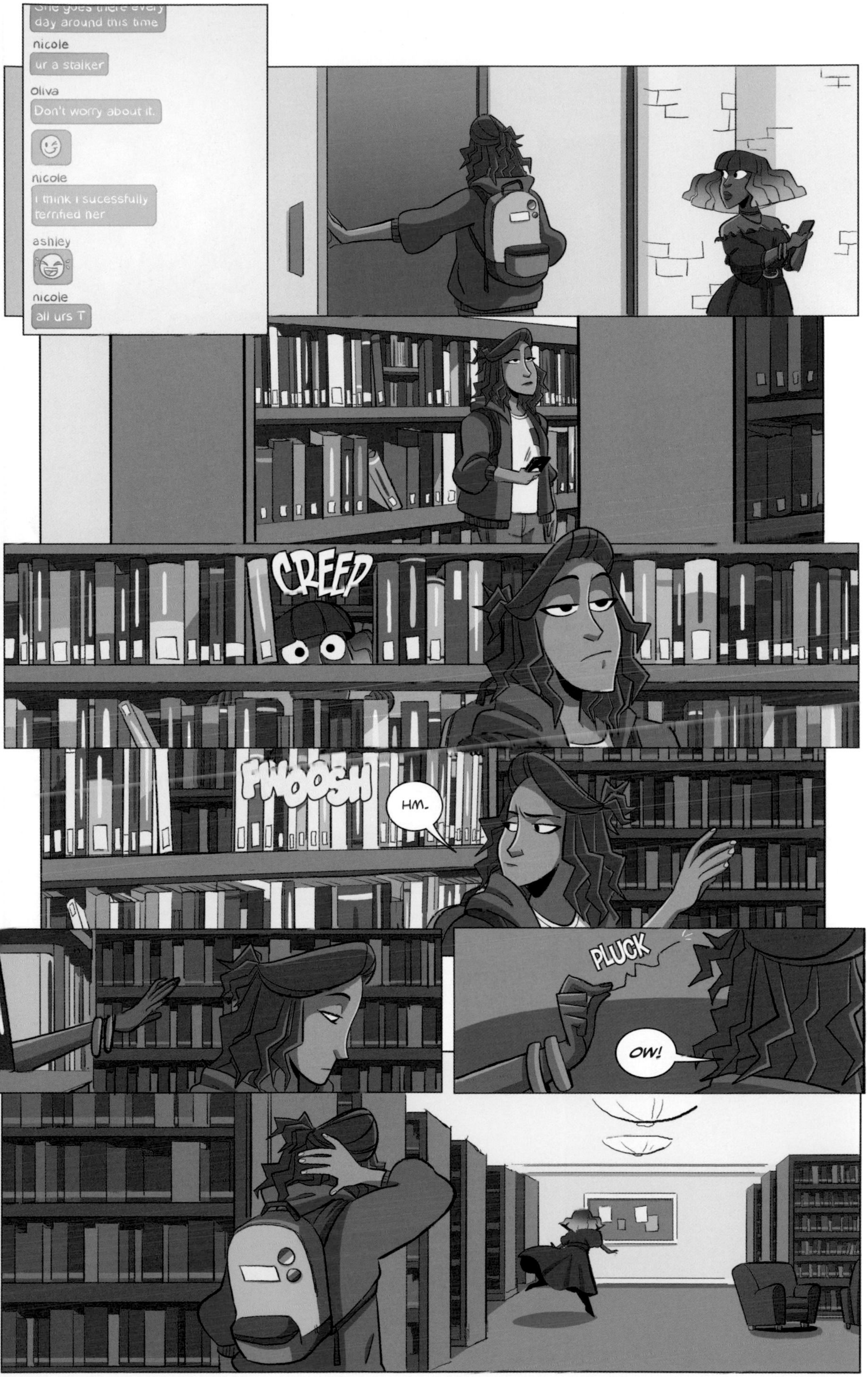

She goes there every day around this time
nicole
ur a stalker
oliva
Don't worry about it.
nicole
i think i sucessfully terrified her
ashley
nicole
all urs T
CREEP
FWOOSH
HM.
PLUCK
OW!

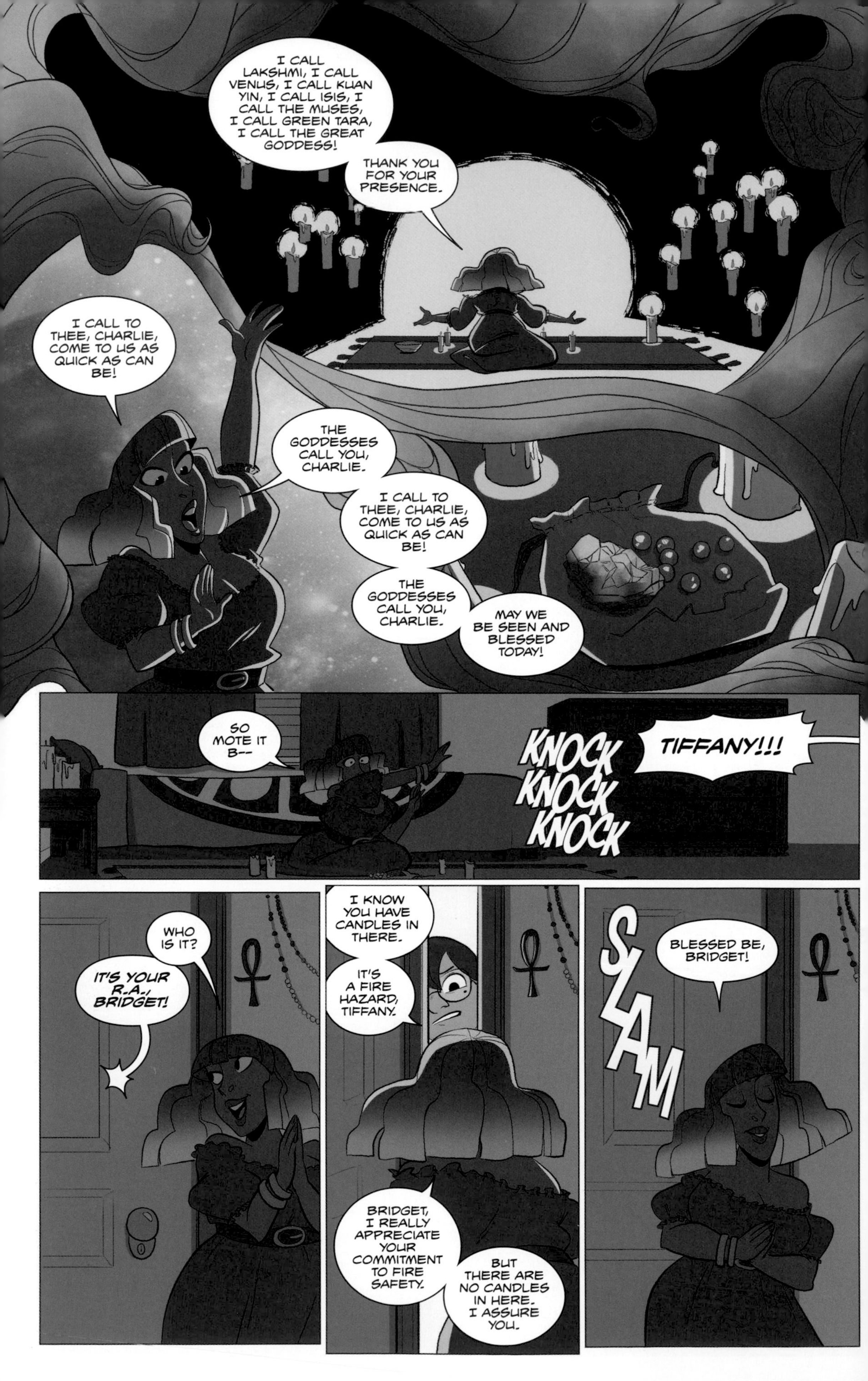
I CALL LAKSHMI, I CALL VENUS, I CALL KUAN YIN, I CALL ISIS, I CALL THE MUSES, I CALL GREEN TARA, I CALL THE GREAT GODDESS!
THANK YOU FOR YOUR PRESENCE.
I CALL TO THEE, CHARLIE, COME TO US AS QUICK AS CAN BE!
THE GODDESSES CALL YOU, CHARLIE.
I CALL TO THEE, CHARLIE, COME TO US AS QUICK AS CAN BE!
THE GODDESSES CALL YOU, CHARLIE.
MAY WE BE SEEN AND BLESSED TODAY!
SO MOTE IT B--
KNOCK KNOCK KNOCK
TIFFANY!!!
WHO IS IT?
IT'S YOUR R.A., BRIDGET!
I KNOW YOU HAVE CANDLES IN THERE.
IT'S A FIRE HAZARD, TIFFANY.
BRIDGET, I REALLY APPRECIATE YOUR COMMITMENT TO FIRE SAFETY.
BUT THERE ARE NO CANDLES IN HERE. I ASSURE YOU.
SLAM
BLESSED BE, BRIDGET!

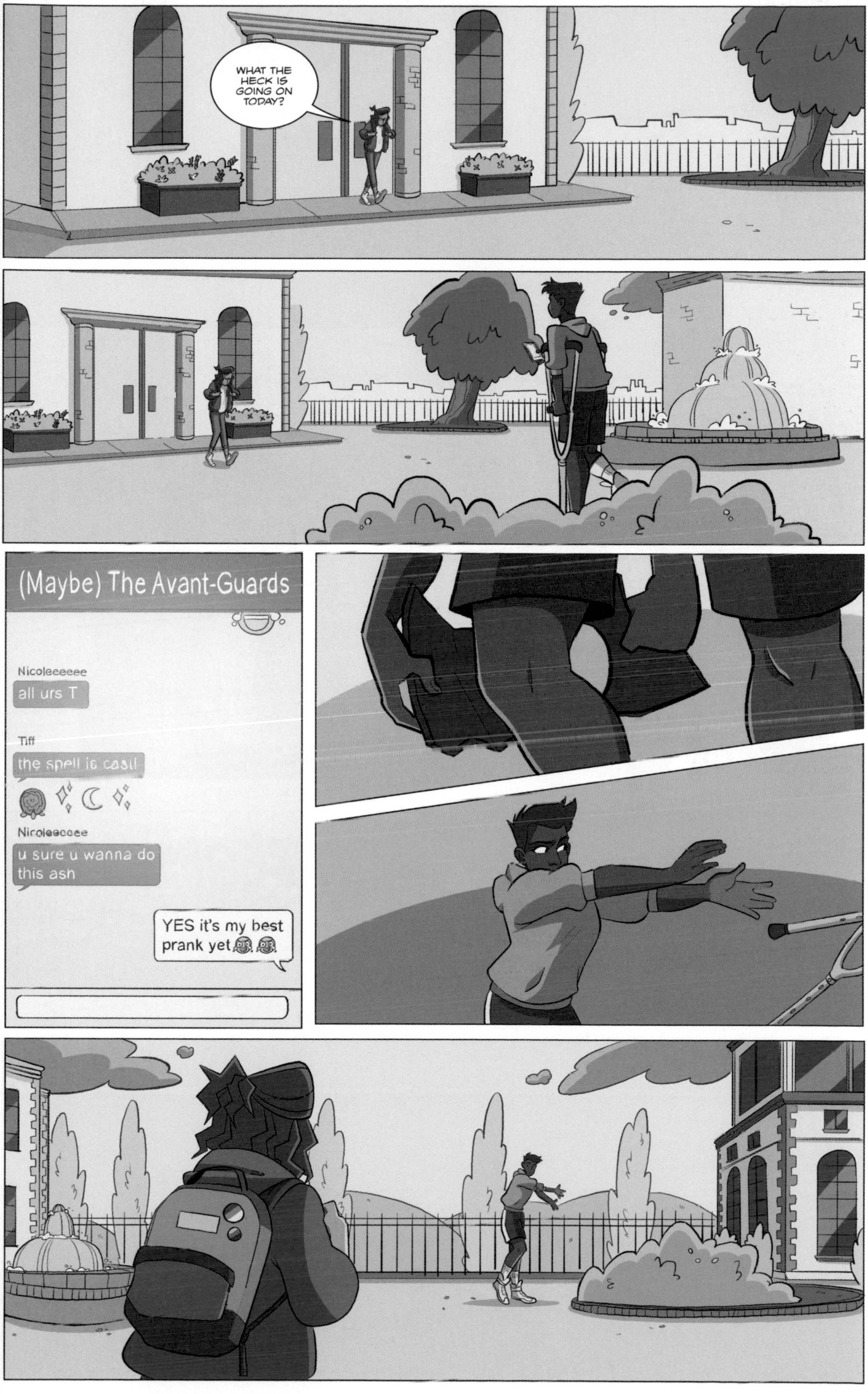
WHAT THE HECK IS GOING ON TODAY?
(Maybe) The Avant-Guards
Nicoleeeeee
all urs T
Tiff
the spell is cast!
Nicoleeeeee
u sure u wanna do this ash
YES it's my best prank yet

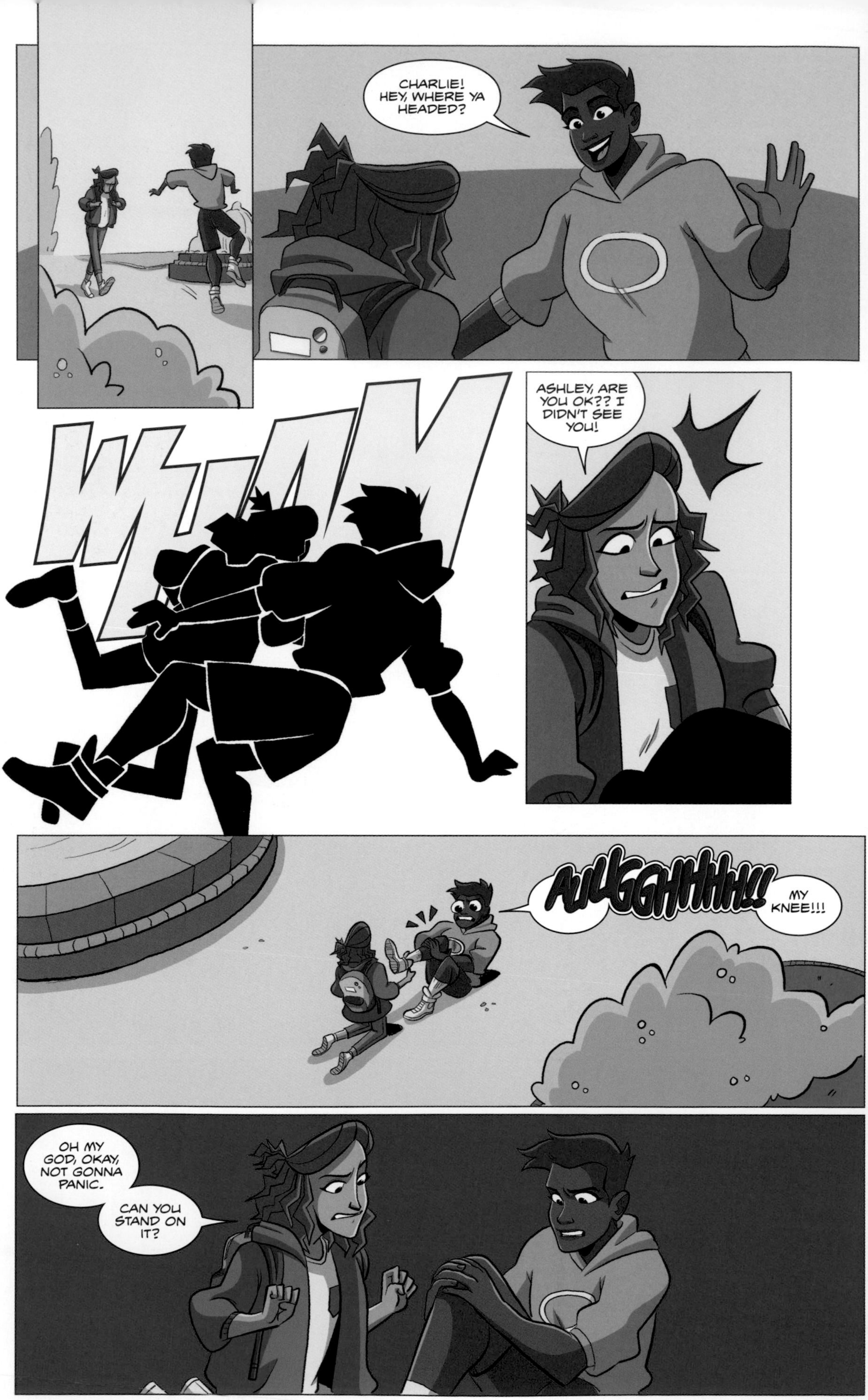
CHARLIE! HEY, WHERE YA HEADED?
WHAM
ASHLEY, ARE YOU OK?? I DIDN'T SEE YOU!
AUUGGHHHH!!
MY KNEE!!!
OH MY GOD, OKAY, NOT GONNA PANIC.
CAN YOU STAND ON IT?

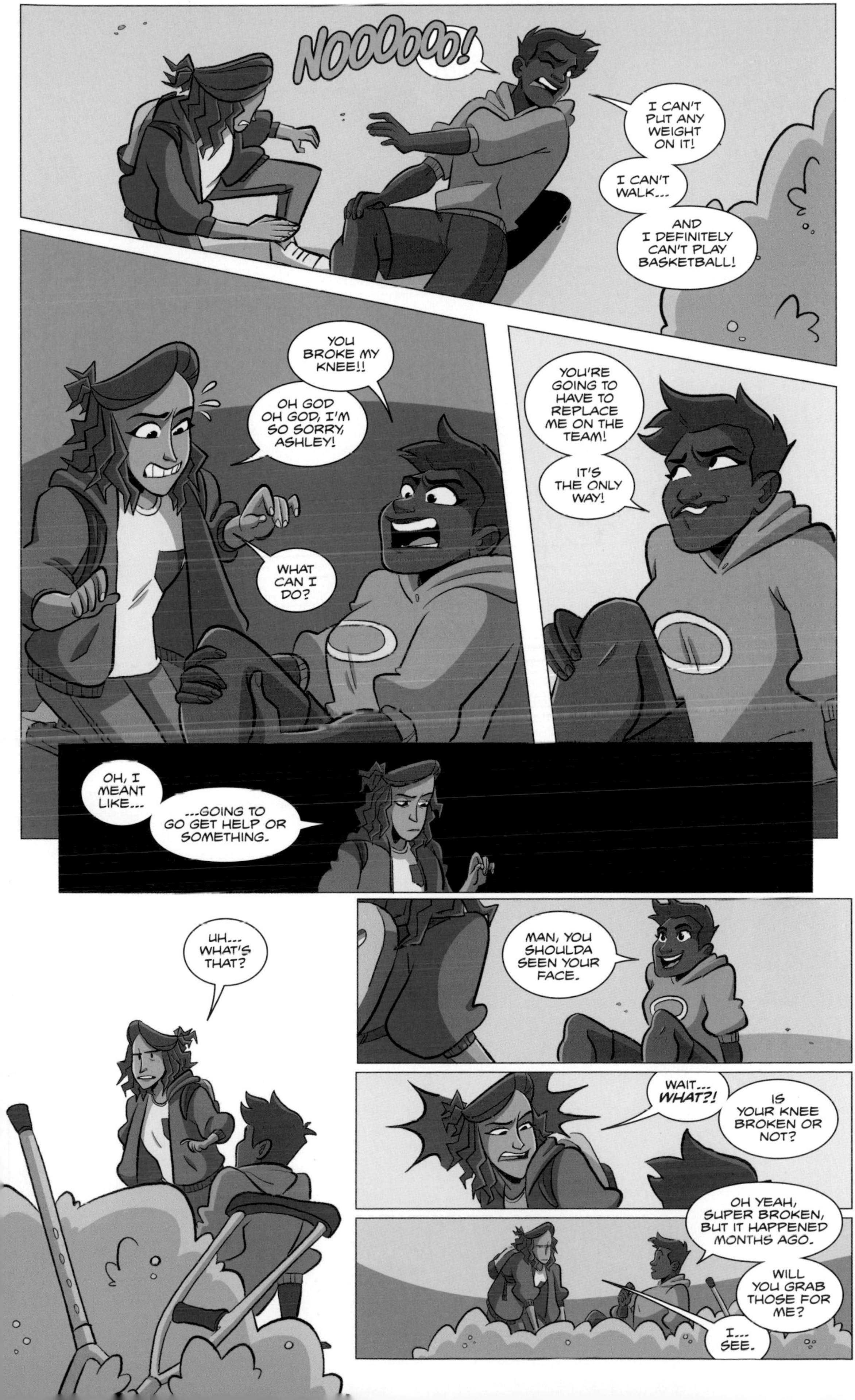
NOOOOOO!
I CAN'T PUT ANY WEIGHT ON IT!
I CAN'T WALK...
AND I DEFINITELY CAN'T PLAY BASKETBALL!
YOU BROKE MY KNEE!!
OH GOD OH GOD, I'M SO SORRY, ASHLEY!
WHAT CAN I DO?
YOU'RE GOING TO HAVE TO REPLACE ME ON THE TEAM!
IT'S THE ONLY WAY!
OH, I MEANT LIKE...
...GOING TO GO GET HELP OR SOMETHING.
UH... WHAT'S THAT?
MAN, YOU SHOULDA SEEN YOUR FACE.
WAIT... WHAT?!
IS YOUR KNEE BROKEN OR NOT?
OH YEAH, SUPER BROKEN, BUT IT HAPPENED MONTHS AGO.
WILL YOU GRAB THOSE FOR ME?
I... SEE.

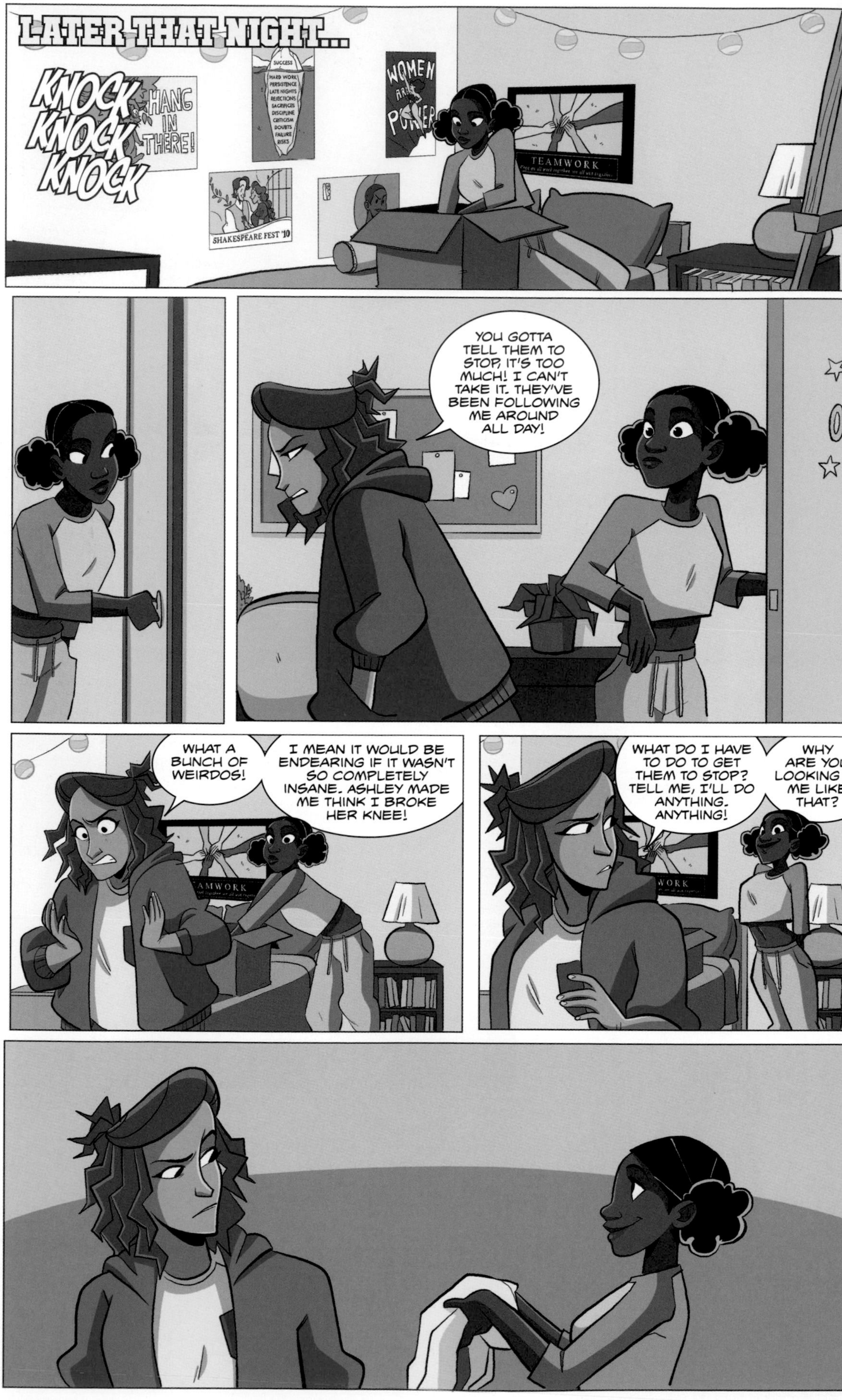
LATER THAT NIGHT...
KNOCK KNOCK KNOCK
HANG IN THERE!
SUCCESS
HARD WORK
PERSISTENCE
LATE NIGHTS
REJECTIONS
SACRIFICES
DISCIPLINE
CRITICISM
DOUBTS
FAILURE
RISKS
WOMEN ARE POWER
TEAMWORK
SHAKESPEARE FEST '10
YOU GOTTA TELL THEM TO STOP, IT'S TOO MUCH! I CAN'T TAKE IT. THEY'VE BEEN FOLLOWING ME AROUND ALL DAY!
WHAT A BUNCH OF WEIRDOS!
I MEAN IT WOULD BE ENDEARING IF IT WASN'T SO COMPLETELY INSANE. ASHLEY MADE ME THINK I BROKE HER KNEE!
WHAT DO I HAVE TO DO TO GET THEM TO STOP? TELL ME, I'LL DO ANYTHING. ANYTHING!
WHY ARE YOU LOOKING AT ME LIKE THAT?

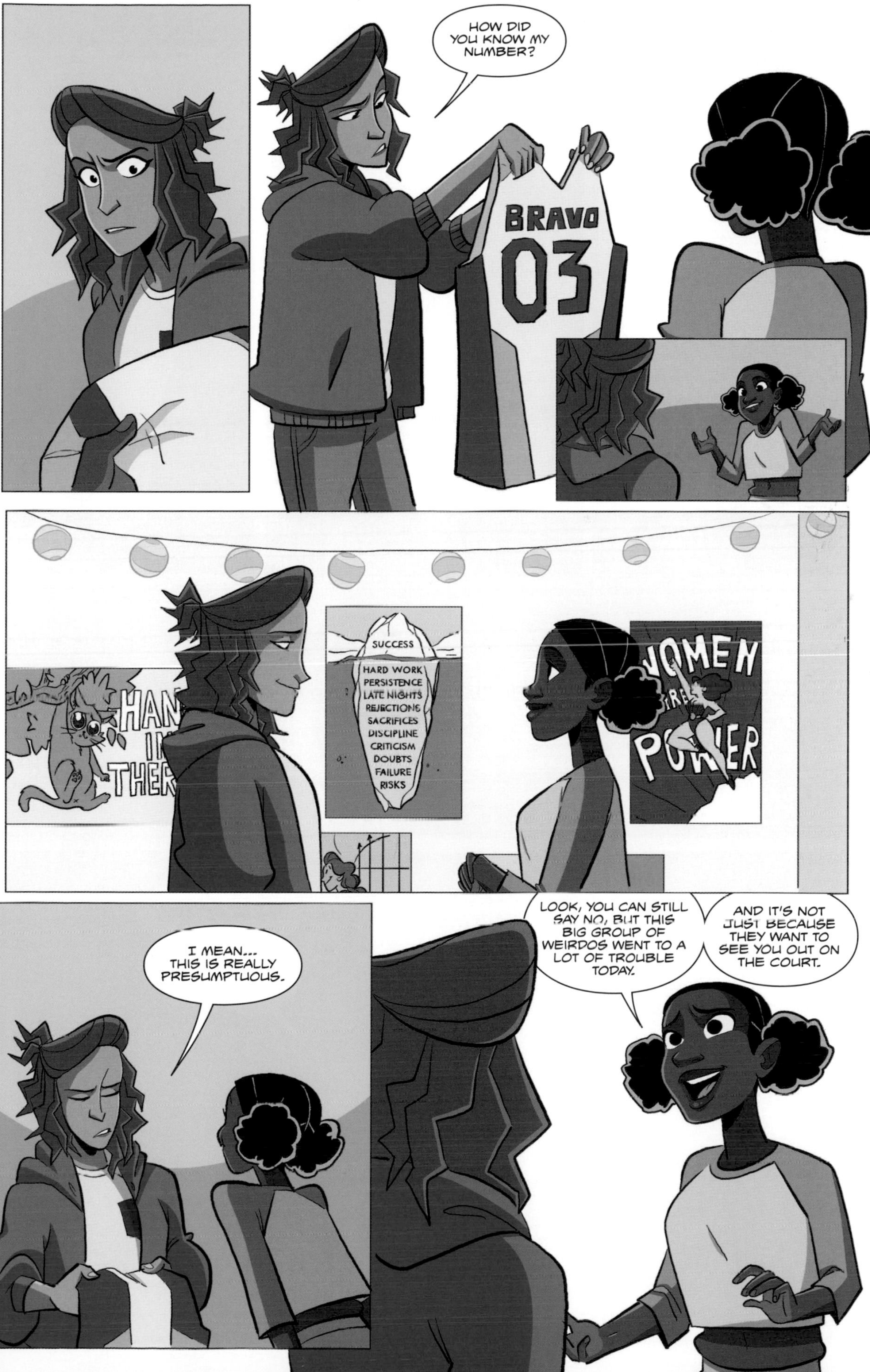
HOW DID YOU KNOW MY NUMBER?
BRAVO
03
SUCCESS
HARD WORK
PERSISTENCE
LATE NIGHTS
REJECTIONS
SACRIFICES
DISCIPLINE
CRITICISM
DOUBTS
FAILURE
RISKS
I MEAN... THIS IS REALLY PRESUMPTUOUS.
LOOK, YOU CAN STILL SAY NO, BUT THIS BIG GROUP OF WEIRDOS WENT TO A LOT OF TROUBLE TODAY.
AND IT'S NOT JUST BECAUSE THEY WANT TO SEE YOU OUT ON THE COURT.

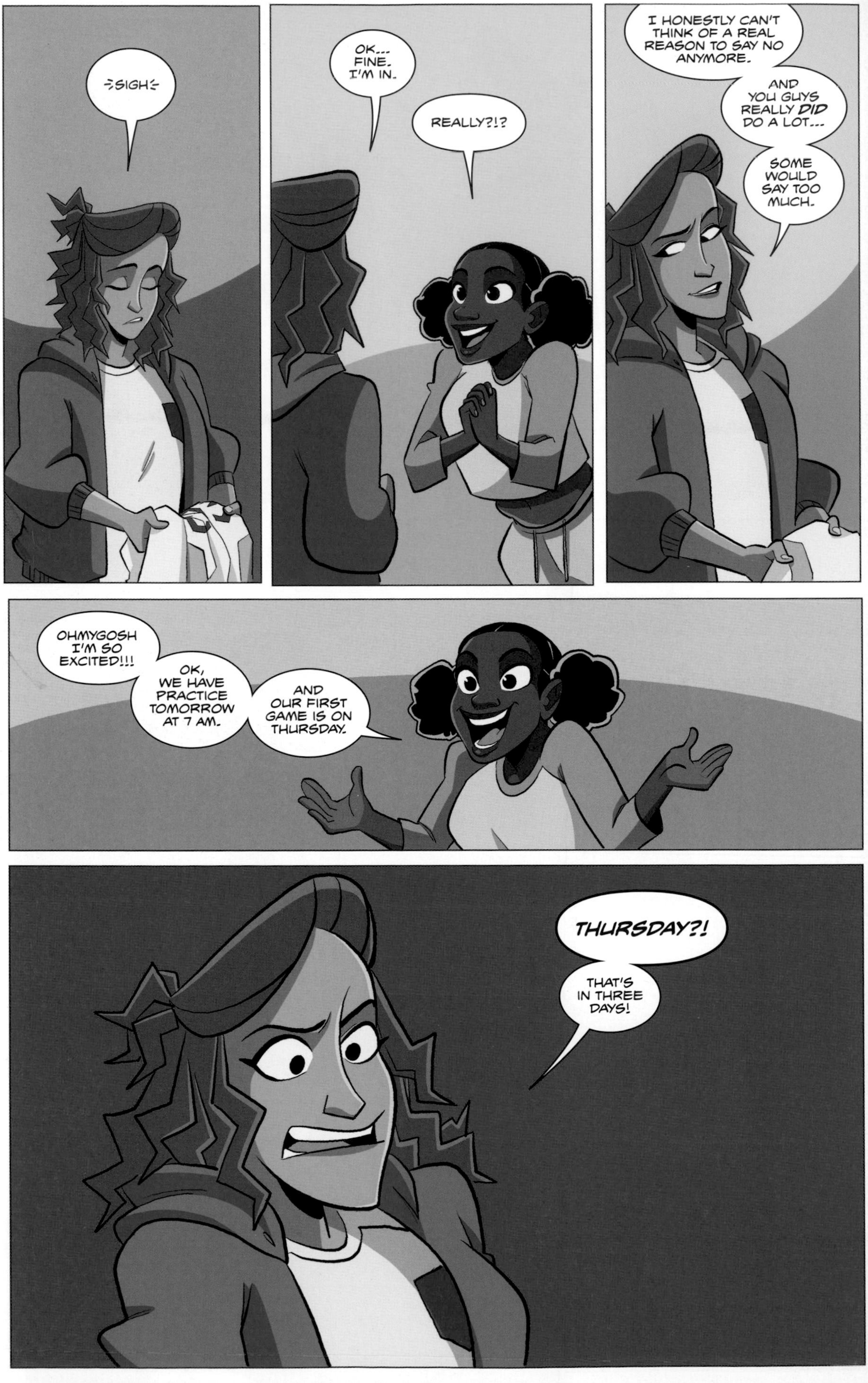

-SIGH-
OK... FINE. I'M IN.
REALLY?!?
I HONESTLY CAN'T THINK OF A REAL REASON TO SAY NO ANYMORE.
AND YOU GUYS REALLY *DID* DO A LOT...
SOME WOULD SAY TOO MUCH.
OHMYGOSH I'M SO EXCITED!!!
OK, WE HAVE PRACTICE TOMORROW AT 7 AM.
AND OUR FIRST GAME IS ON THURSDAY.
THURSDAY?!
THAT'S IN THREE DAYS!

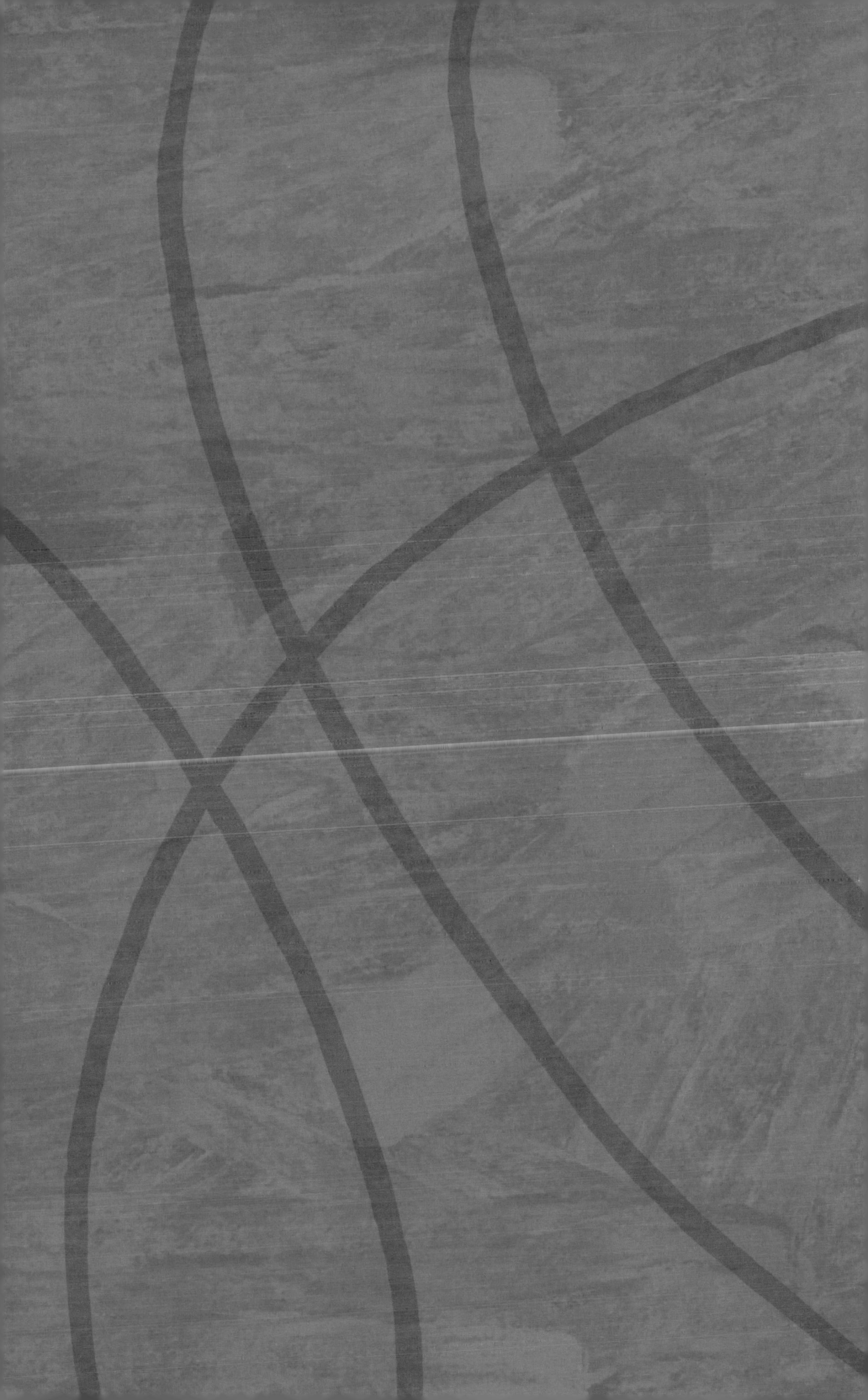

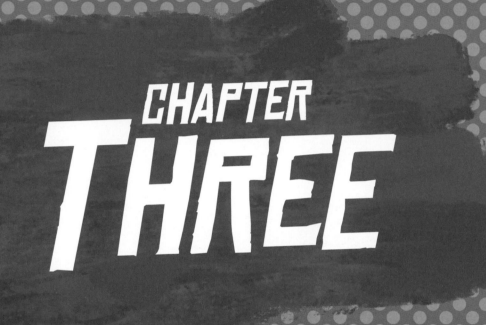

CHAPTER THREE

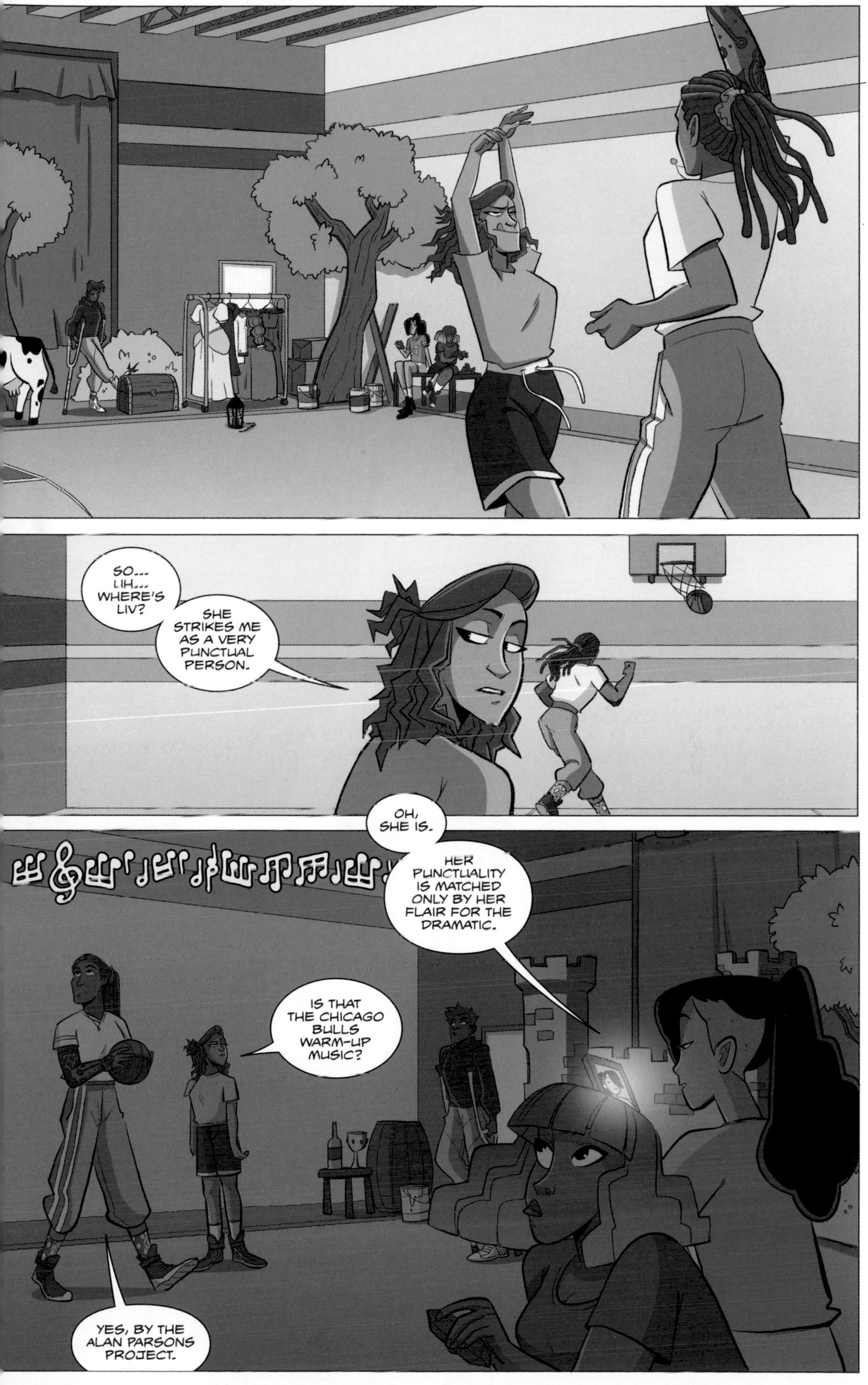
SO... UH... WHERE'S LIV?
SHE STRIKES ME AS A VERY PUNCTUAL PERSON.
OH, SHE IS.
HER PUNCTUALITY IS MATCHED ONLY BY HER FLAIR FOR THE DRAMATIC.
IS THAT THE CHICAGO BULLS WARM-UP MUSIC?
YES, BY THE ALAN PARSONS PROJECT.

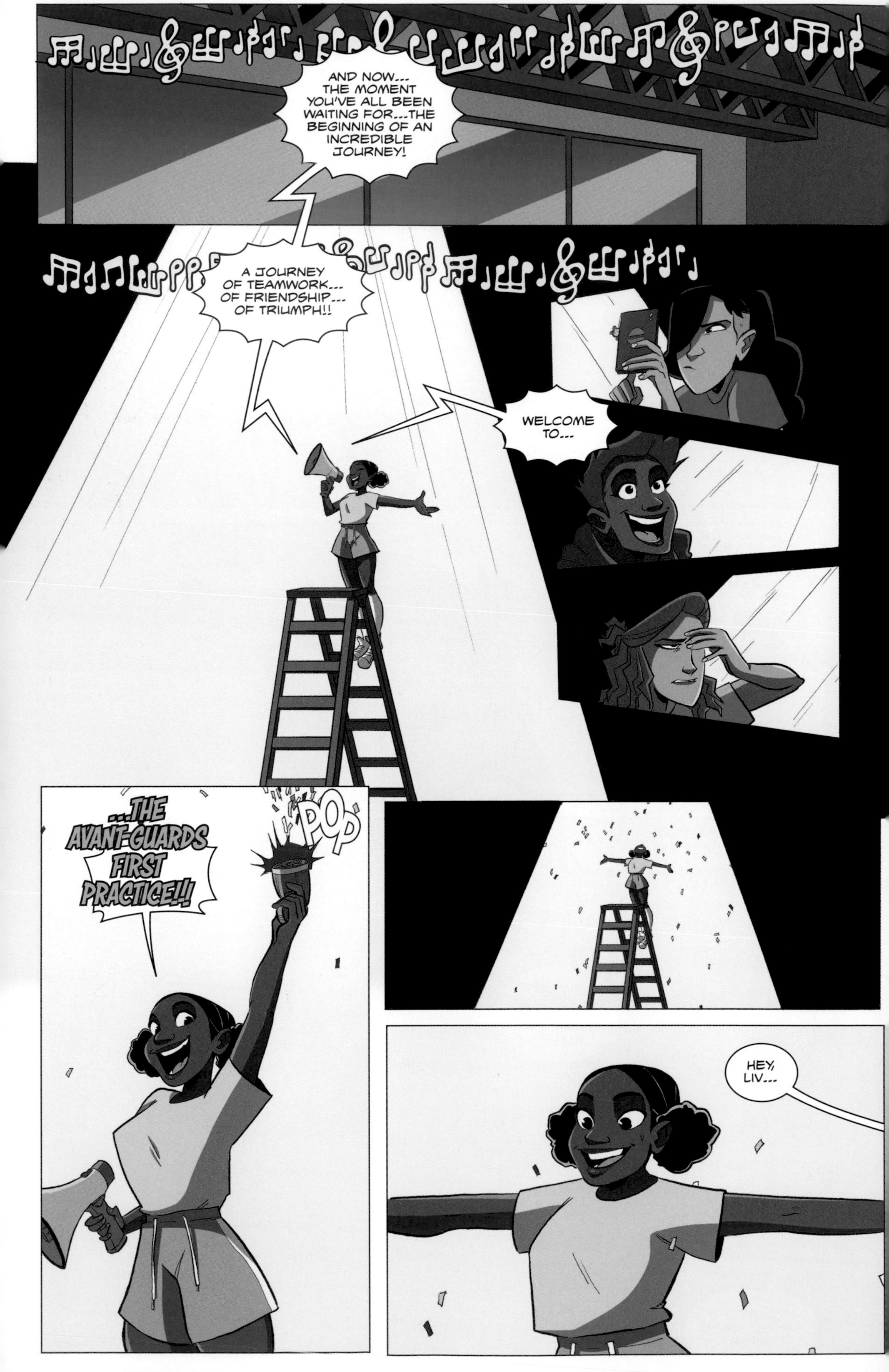

AND NOW... THE MOMENT YOU'VE ALL BEEN WAITING FOR...THE BEGINNING OF AN INCREDIBLE JOURNEY!
A JOURNEY OF TEAMWORK... OF FRIENDSHIP... OF TRIUMPH!!
WELCOME TO...
...THE AVANT-GUARDS FIRST PRACTICE!!
POP
HEY, LIV...

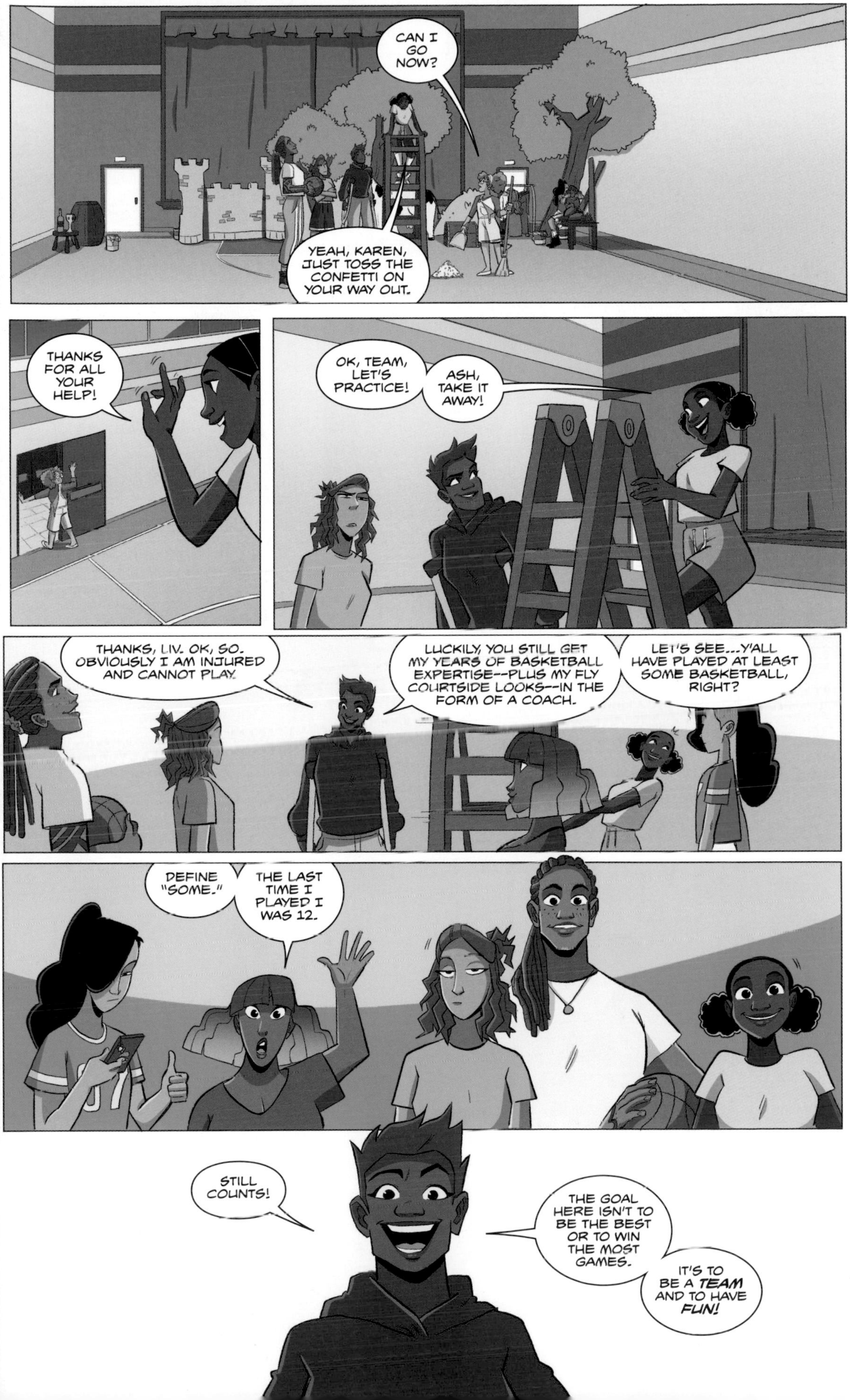
CAN I GO NOW?
YEAH, KAREN, JUST TOSS THE CONFETTI ON YOUR WAY OUT.
THANKS FOR ALL YOUR HELP!
OK, TEAM, LET'S PRACTICE!
ASH, TAKE IT AWAY!
THANKS, LIV. OK, SO. OBVIOUSLY I AM INJURED AND CANNOT PLAY.
LUCKILY, YOU STILL GET MY YEARS OF BASKETBALL EXPERTISE--PLUS MY FLY COURTSIDE LOOKS--IN THE FORM OF A COACH.
LET'S SEE...Y'ALL HAVE PLAYED AT LEAST SOME BASKETBALL, RIGHT?
DEFINE "SOME."
THE LAST TIME I PLAYED I WAS 12.
STILL COUNTS!
THE GOAL HERE ISN'T TO BE THE BEST OR TO WIN THE MOST GAMES.
IT'S TO BE A *TEAM* AND TO HAVE *FUN!*

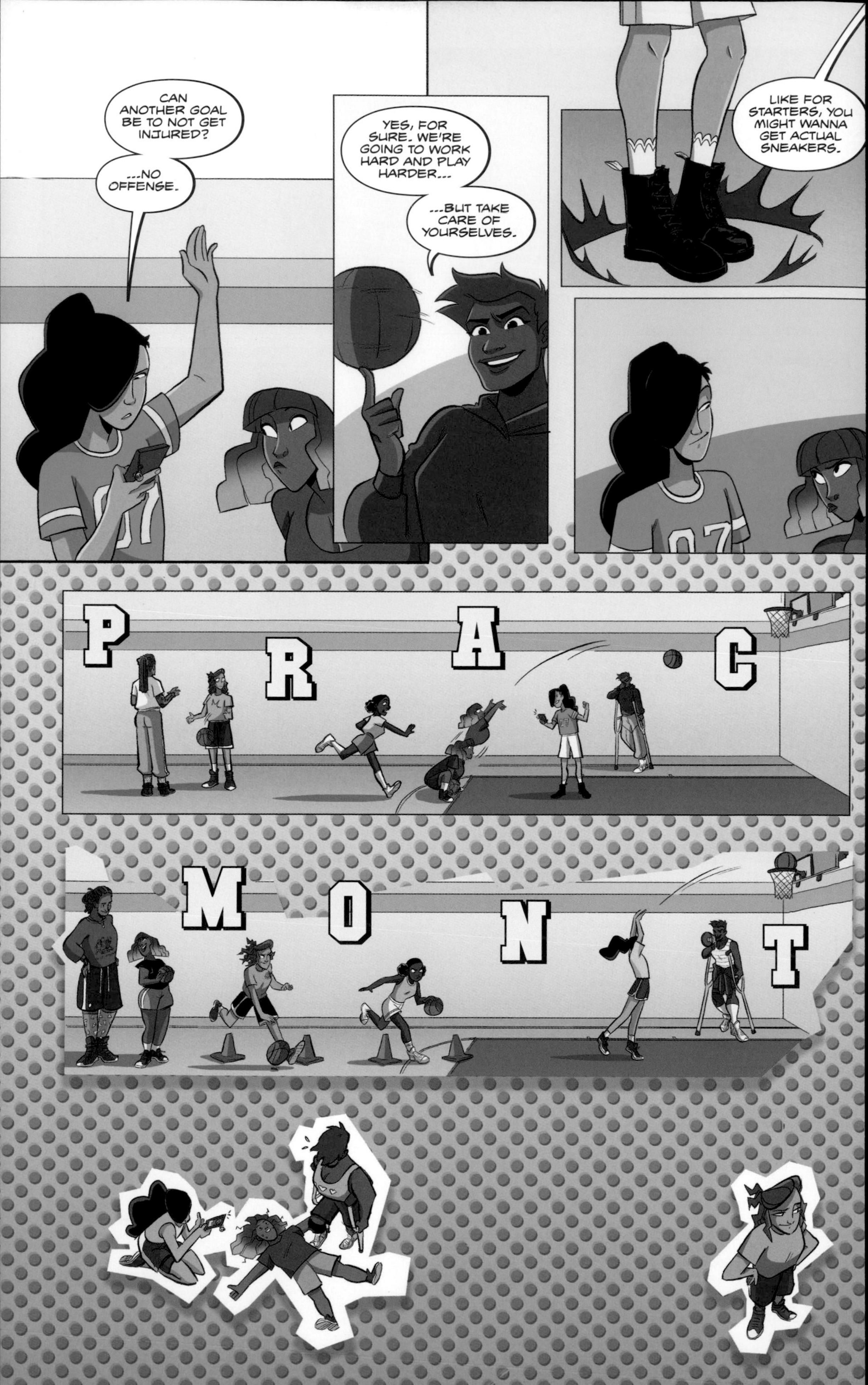
CAN ANOTHER GOAL BE TO NOT GET INJURED?
...NO OFFENSE.
YES, FOR SURE. WE'RE GOING TO WORK HARD AND PLAY HARDER...
...BUT TAKE CARE OF YOURSELVES.
LIKE FOR STARTERS, YOU MIGHT WANNA GET ACTUAL SNEAKERS.
P R A C
M O N T

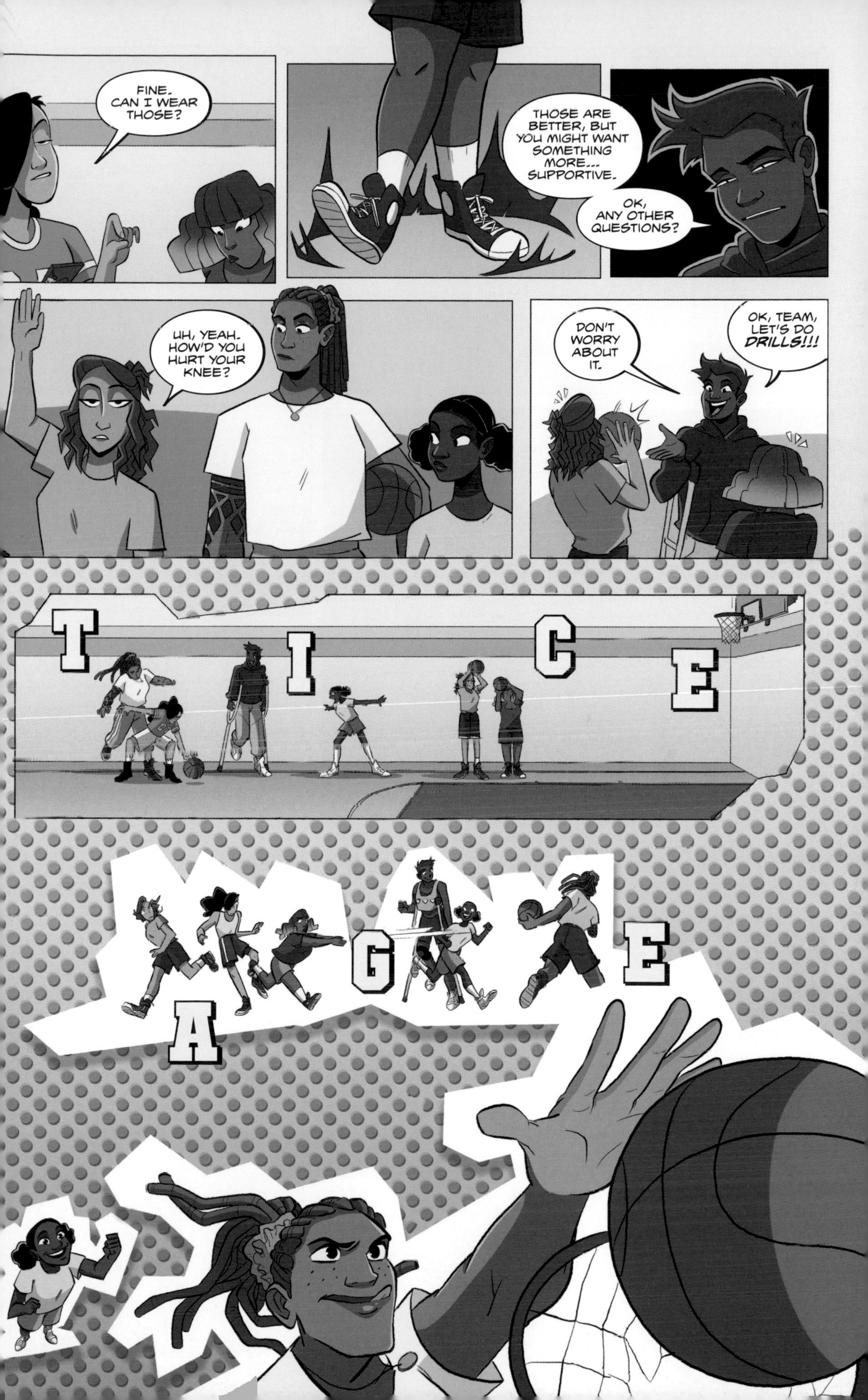
FINE. CAN I WEAR THOSE?
THOSE ARE BETTER, BUT YOU MIGHT WANT SOMETHING MORE... SUPPORTIVE.
OK, ANY OTHER QUESTIONS?
UH, YEAH. HOW'D YOU HURT YOUR KNEE?
DON'T WORRY ABOUT IT.
OK, TEAM, LET'S DO DRILLS!!!
T I C E
A G E

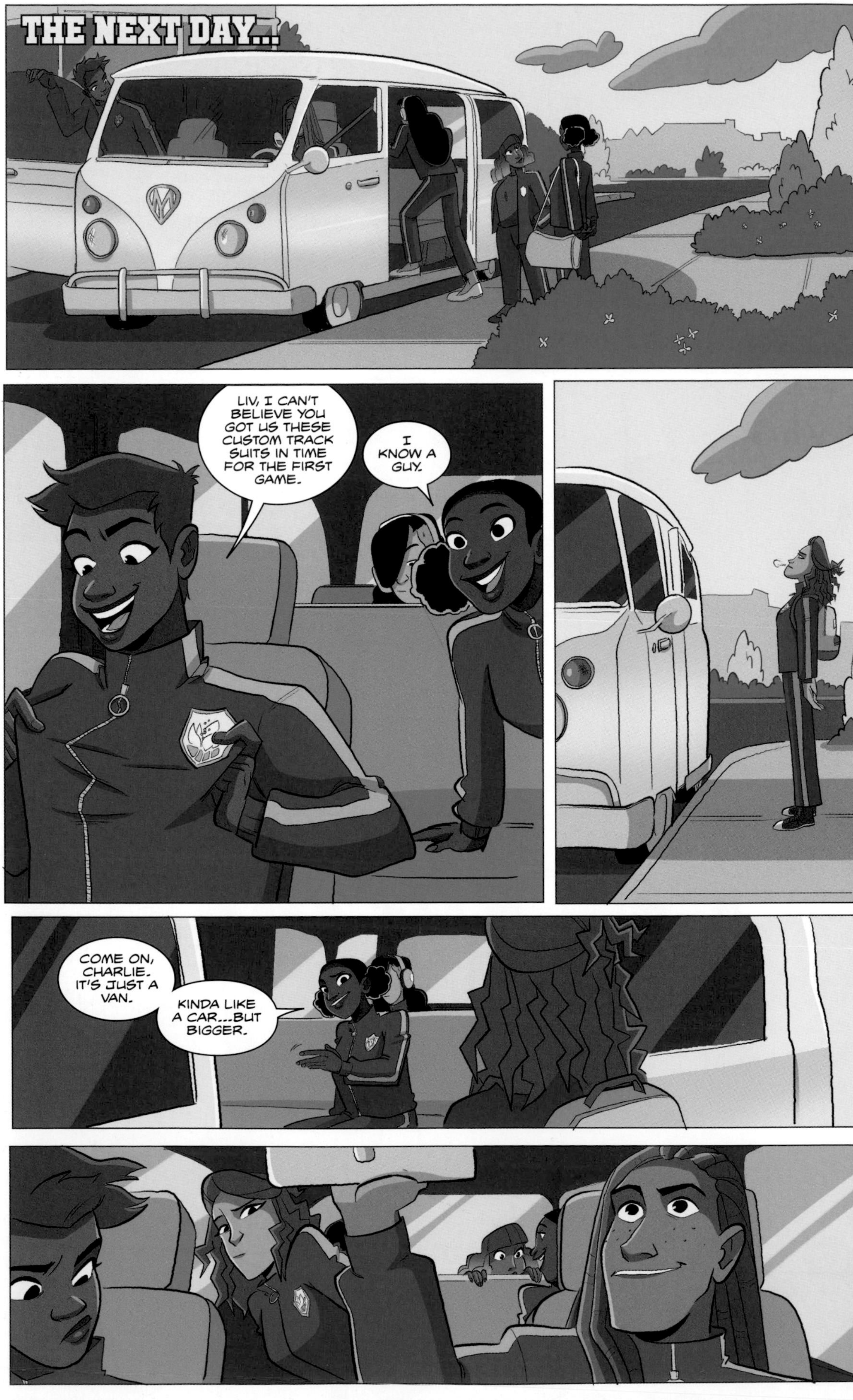
THE NEXT DAY...
LIV, I CAN'T BELIEVE YOU GOT US THESE CUSTOM TRACK SUITS IN TIME FOR THE FIRST GAME.
I KNOW A GUY.
COME ON, CHARLIE. IT'S JUST A VAN.
KINDA LIKE A CAR...BUT BIGGER.

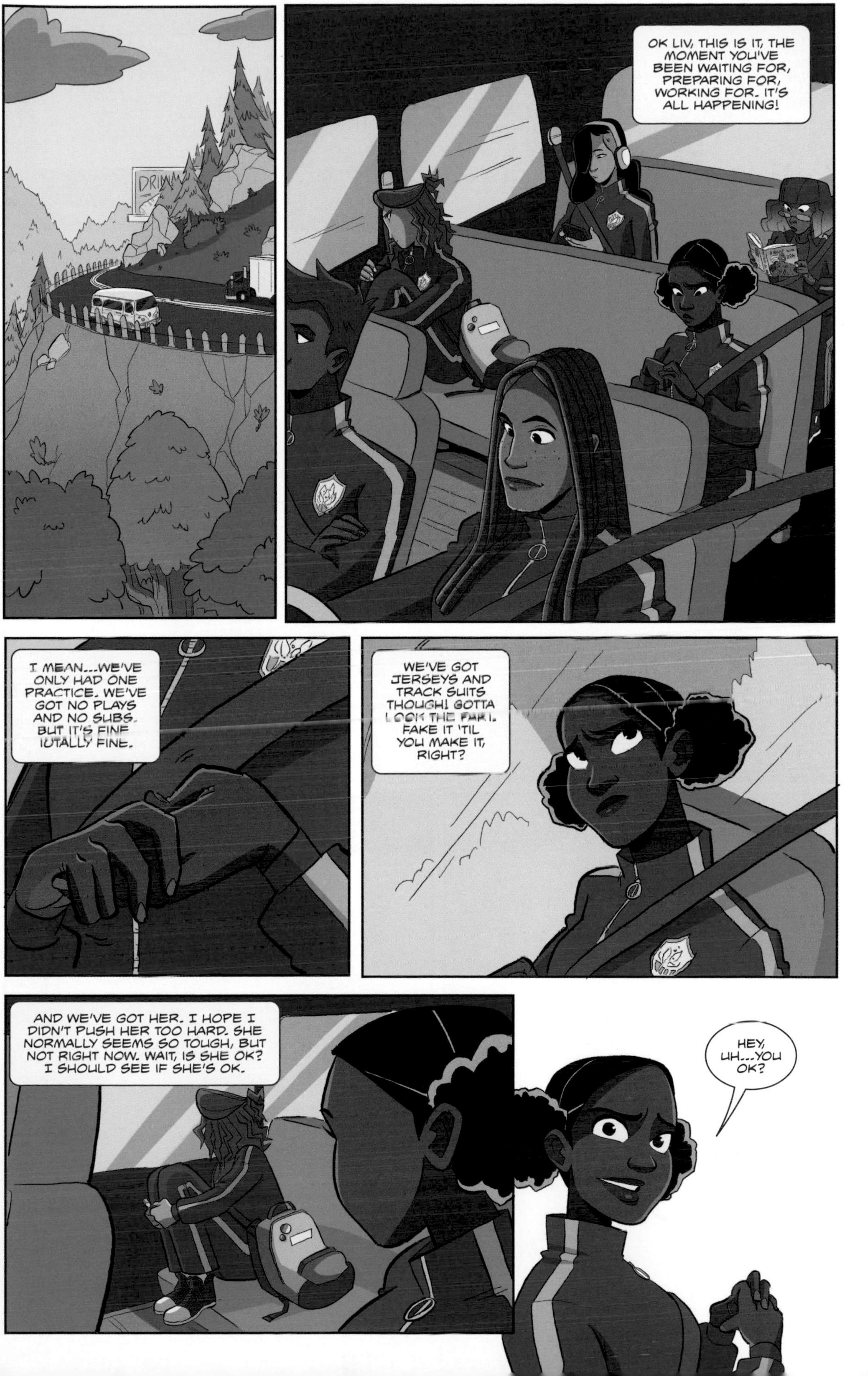
OK LIV, THIS IS IT, THE MOMENT YOU'VE BEEN WAITING FOR, PREPARING FOR, WORKING FOR. IT'S ALL HAPPENING!
I MEAN...WE'VE ONLY HAD ONE PRACTICE. WE'VE GOT NO PLAYS AND NO SUBS. BUT IT'S FINE. TOTALLY FINE.
WE'VE GOT JERSEYS AND TRACK SUITS THOUGH! GOTTA LOOK THE PART. FAKE IT 'TIL YOU MAKE IT, RIGHT?
AND WE'VE GOT HER. I HOPE I DIDN'T PUSH HER TOO HARD. SHE NORMALLY SEEMS SO TOUGH, BUT NOT RIGHT NOW. WAIT, IS SHE OK? I SHOULD SEE IF SHE'S OK.
HEY, UH...YOU OK?

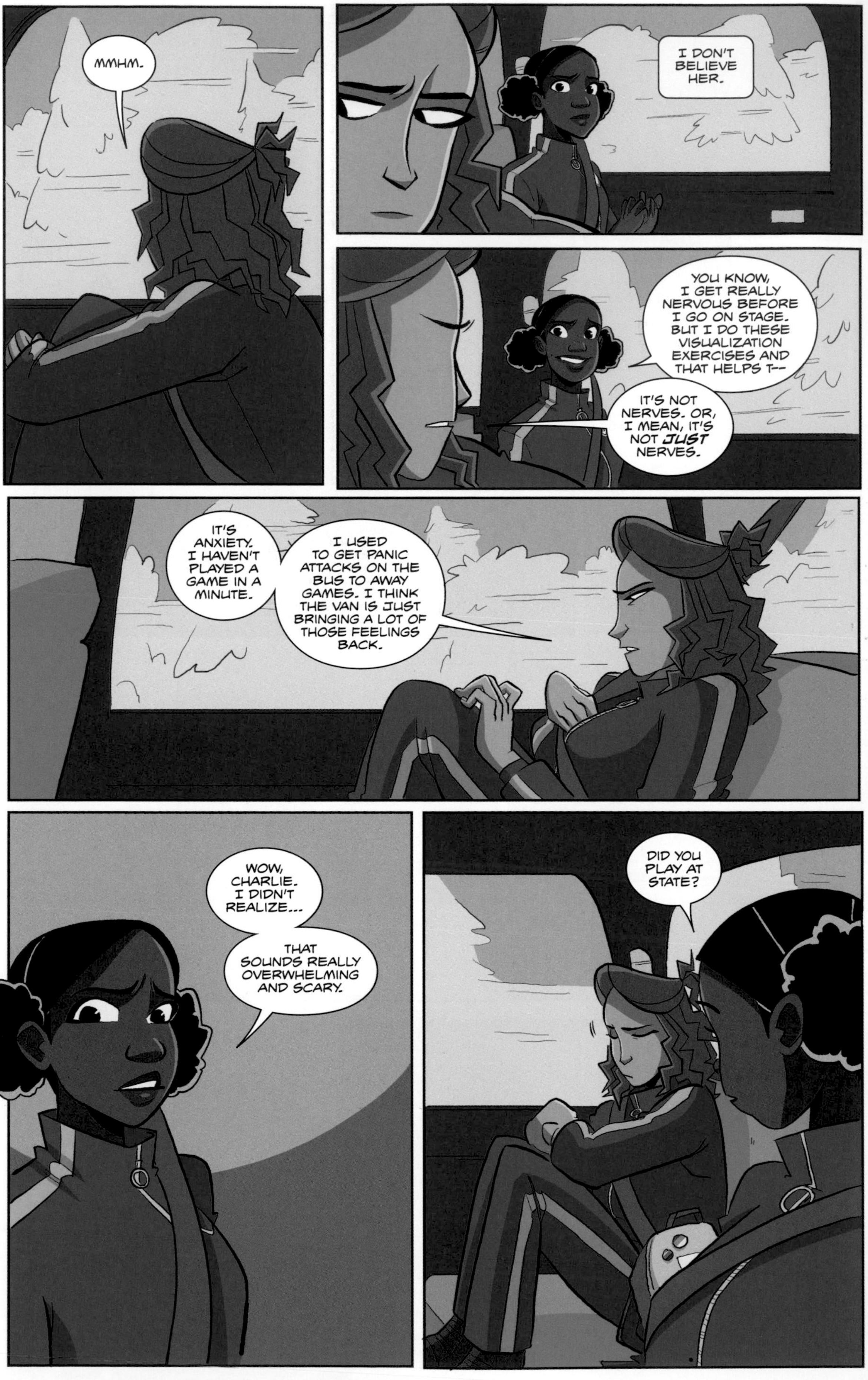
MMHM.
I DON'T BELIEVE HER.
YOU KNOW, I GET REALLY NERVOUS BEFORE I GO ON STAGE. BUT I DO THESE VISUALIZATION EXERCISES AND THAT HELPS T--
IT'S NOT NERVES. OR, I MEAN, IT'S NOT JUST NERVES.
IT'S ANXIETY. I HAVEN'T PLAYED A GAME IN A MINUTE.
I USED TO GET PANIC ATTACKS ON THE BUS TO AWAY GAMES. I THINK THE VAN IS JUST BRINGING A LOT OF THOSE FEELINGS BACK.
WOW, CHARLIE. I DIDN'T REALIZE...
THAT SOUNDS REALLY OVERWHELMING AND SCARY.
DID YOU PLAY AT STATE?

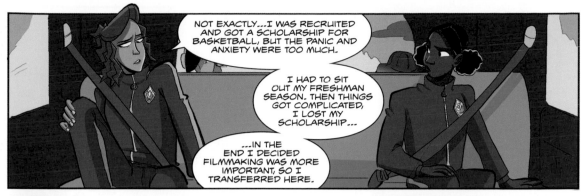

NOT EXACTLY...I WAS RECRUITED AND GOT A SCHOLARSHIP FOR BASKETBALL, BUT THE PANIC AND ANXIETY WERE TOO MUCH.

I HAD TO SIT OUT MY FRESHMAN SEASON. THEN THINGS GOT COMPLICATED, I LOST MY SCHOLARSHIP...

...IN THE END I DECIDED FILMMAKING WAS MORE IMPORTANT, SO I TRANSFERRED HERE.

AND NOW IT FEELS LIKE I'M RIGHT BACK WHERE I STARTED.

CHARLIE... I'M SO SORRY.

IF I HAD KNOWN--

LIV...YOU'RE PERSUASIVE, BUT YOU'RE NOT *THAT* PERSUASIVE...

HA HA.

I DUNNO. MAYBE YOU WERE RIGHT. I MEAN, THE TEAM SEEMS REALLY GREAT. IT'S PROBABLY GOOD FOR ME TO GET OUT OF MY COMFORT ZONE.

WHAT?

I WAS TRYING TO MAKE A GREAT "ZONE DEFENSE" JOKE THERE, BUT...

I GOT NOTHIN'.

JUST... STOP.

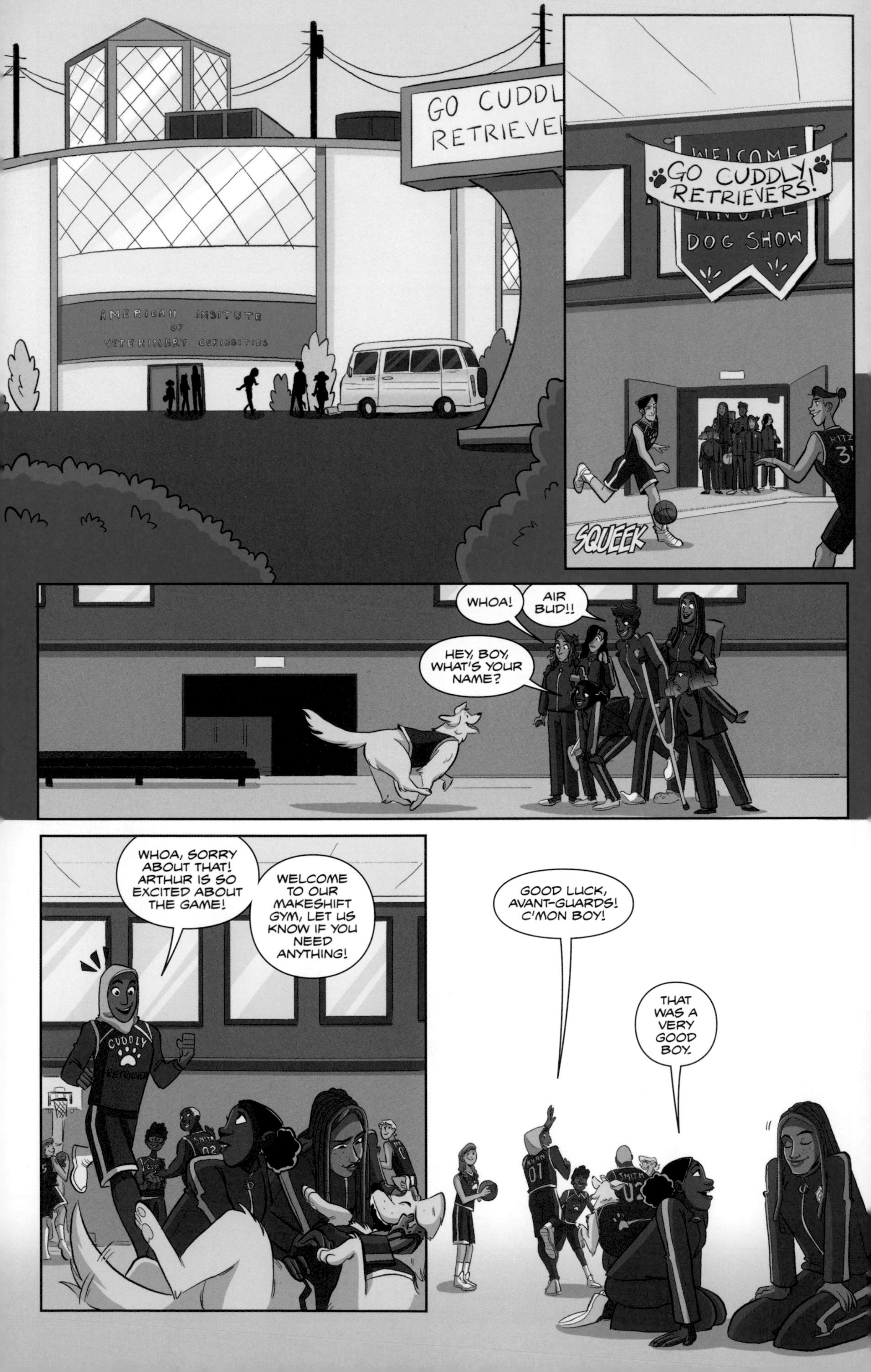
GO CUDDL
RETRIEVE
AMERICAN INSITUTE OF VETERINARY CURIOSITIES
GO CUDDLY RETRIEVERS!
DOG SHOW
SQUEEK
WHOA!
AIR BUD!!
HEY, BOY, WHAT'S YOUR NAME?
WHOA, SORRY ABOUT THAT! ARTHUR IS SO EXCITED ABOUT THE GAME!
WELCOME TO OUR MAKESHIFT GYM, LET US KNOW IF YOU NEED ANYTHING!
CUDDLY RETRIEVER
GOOD LUCK, AVANT-GUARDS! C'MON BOY!
THAT WAS A VERY GOOD BOY.

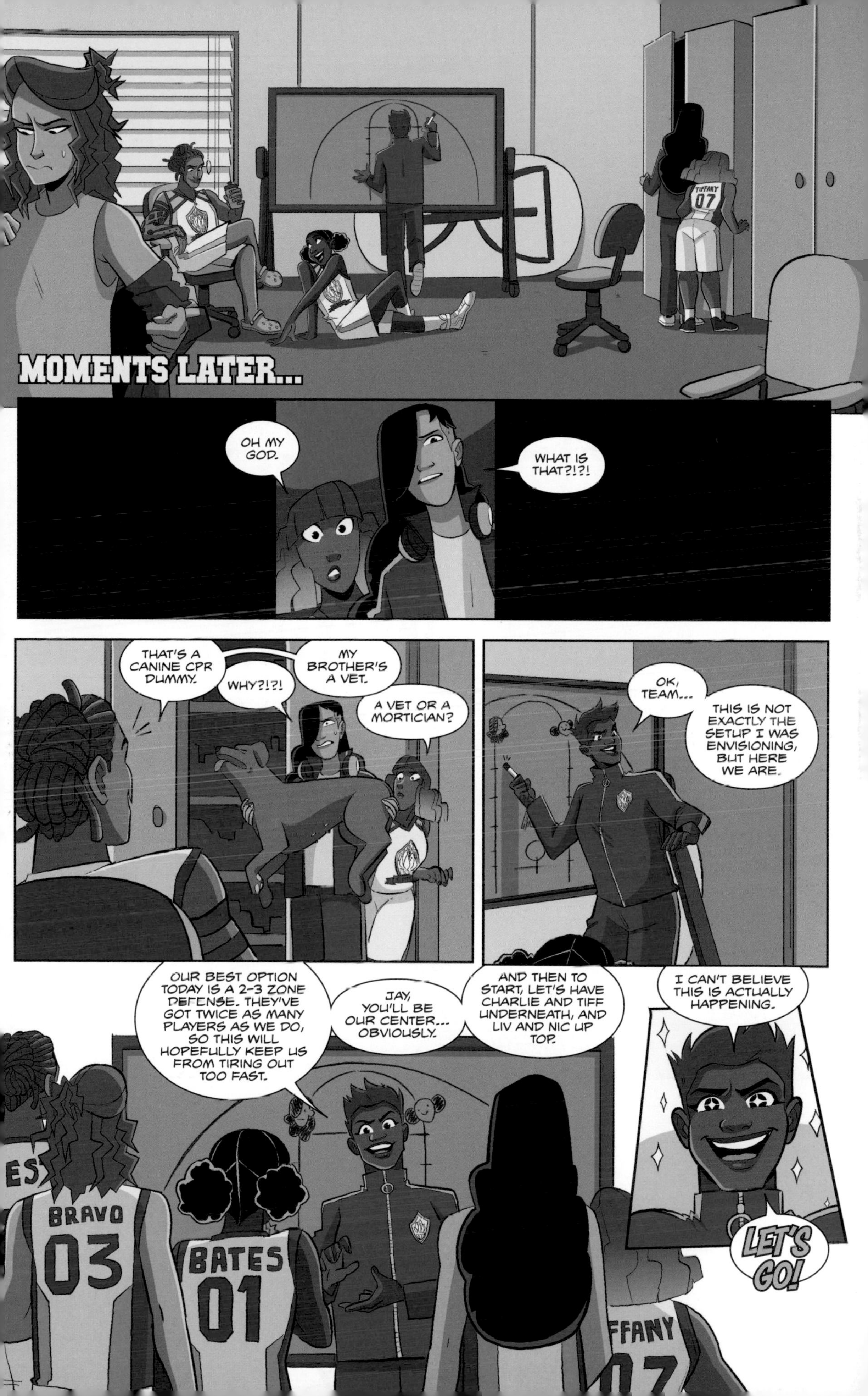
MOMENTS LATER...
OH MY GOD.
WHAT IS THAT?!?!
THAT'S A CANINE CPR DUMMY.
WHY?!?!
MY BROTHER'S A VET.
A VET OR A MORTICIAN?
OK, TEAM...
THIS IS NOT EXACTLY THE SETUP I WAS ENVISIONING, BUT HERE WE ARE.
OUR BEST OPTION TODAY IS A 2-3 ZONE DEFENSE. THEY'VE GOT TWICE AS MANY PLAYERS AS WE DO, SO THIS WILL HOPEFULLY KEEP US FROM TIRING OUT TOO FAST.
JAY, YOU'LL BE OUR CENTER... OBVIOUSLY.
AND THEN TO START, LET'S HAVE CHARLIE AND TIFF UNDERNEATH, AND LIV AND NIC UP TOP.
I CAN'T BELIEVE THIS IS ACTUALLY HAPPENING.
LET'S GO!
BRAVO 03
BATES 01

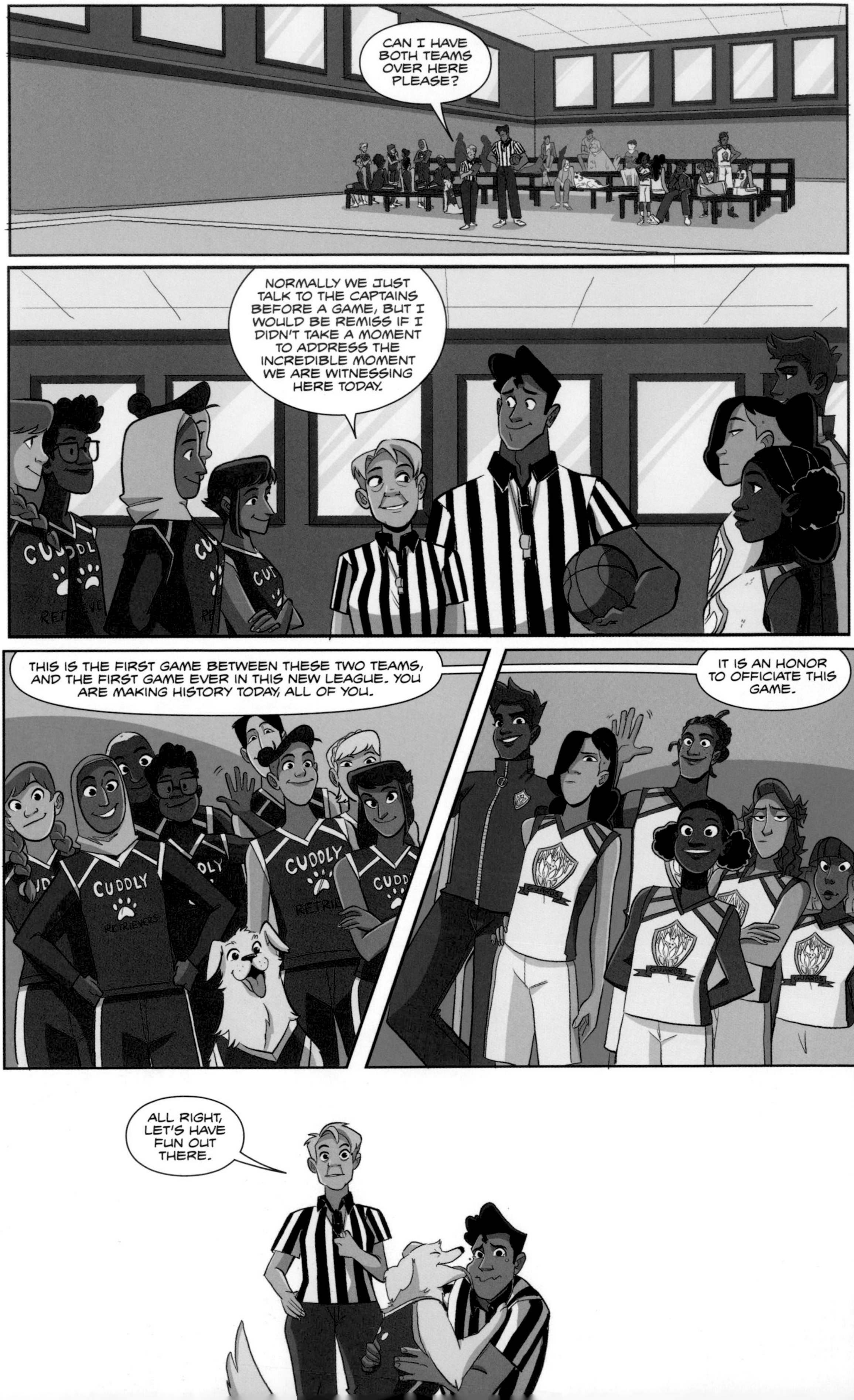
CAN I HAVE BOTH TEAMS OVER HERE PLEASE?
NORMALLY WE JUST TALK TO THE CAPTAINS BEFORE A GAME, BUT I WOULD BE REMISS IF I DIDN'T TAKE A MOMENT TO ADDRESS THE INCREDIBLE MOMENT WE ARE WITNESSING HERE TODAY.
CUDDLY
THIS IS THE FIRST GAME BETWEEN THESE TWO TEAMS, AND THE FIRST GAME EVER IN THIS NEW LEAGUE. YOU ARE MAKING HISTORY TODAY, ALL OF YOU.
IT IS AN HONOR TO OFFICIATE THIS GAME.
CUDDLY
RETRIEVERS
ALL RIGHT, LET'S HAVE FUN OUT THERE.

BUZZZZZZZZ
OK, BRING IT IN.
I GUESS IT'S TIME TO PLAY SPORTS NOW?
THAT WAS VERY REAL.
I'M REALLY PROUD OF ALL OF US. LET'S DO THIS.
AVANT-GUARDS ON 3...
1, 2, 3...
AVANT-GUARDS!!!

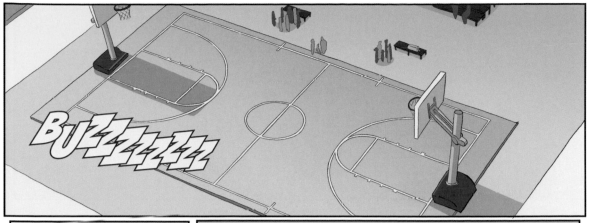

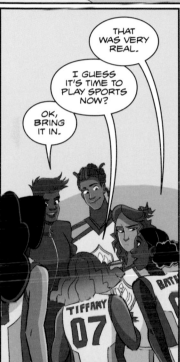

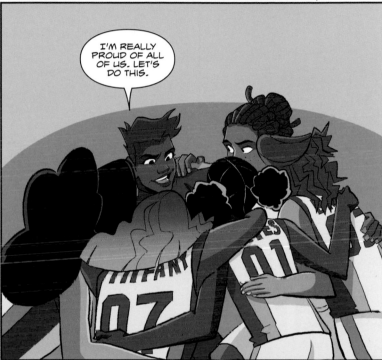

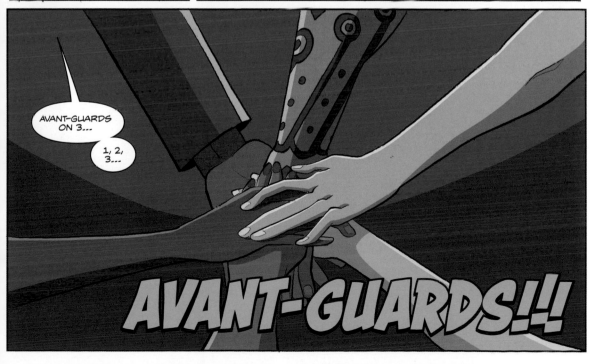

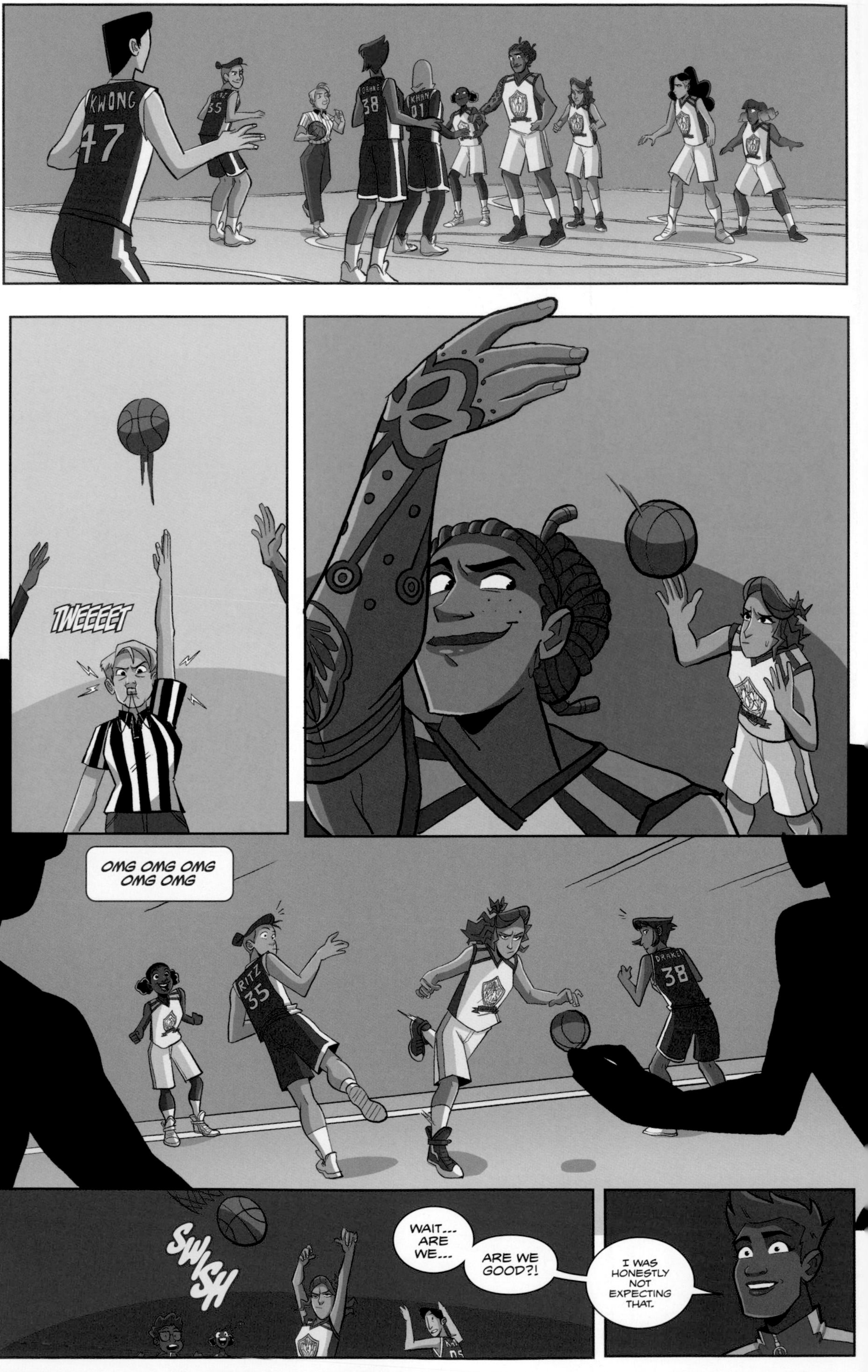
KWONG 47
35
DRAKE 38
KHAN 01
TWEEEET
OMG OMG OMG OMG OMG
RITZ 35
DRAKE 38
SWISH
WAIT... ARE WE...
ARE WE GOOD?!
I WAS HONESTLY NOT EXPECTING THAT.

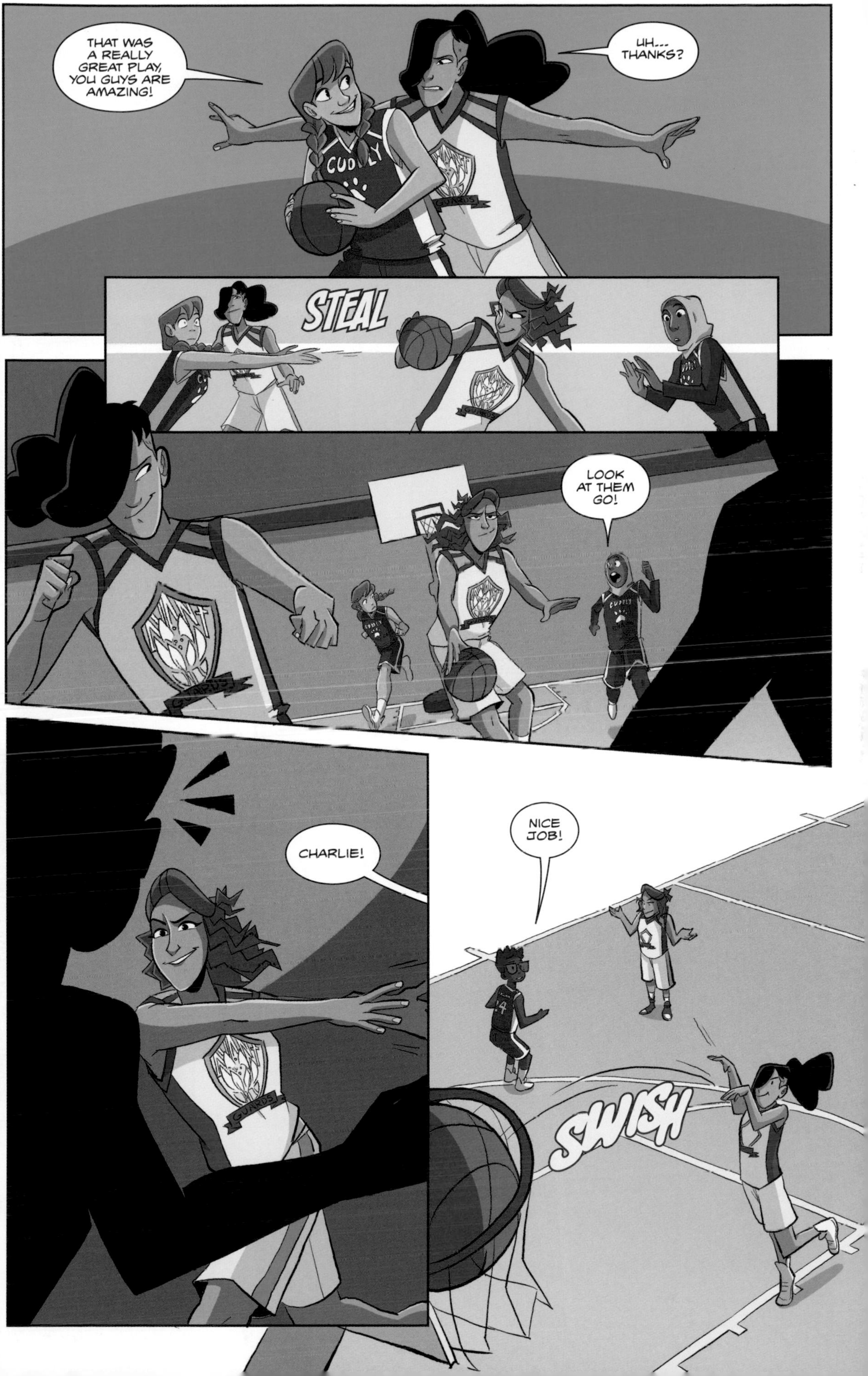
THAT WAS A REALLY GREAT PLAY, YOU GUYS ARE AMAZING!
UH... THANKS?
STEAL
LOOK AT THEM GO!
CHARLIE!
NICE JOB!
SWISH

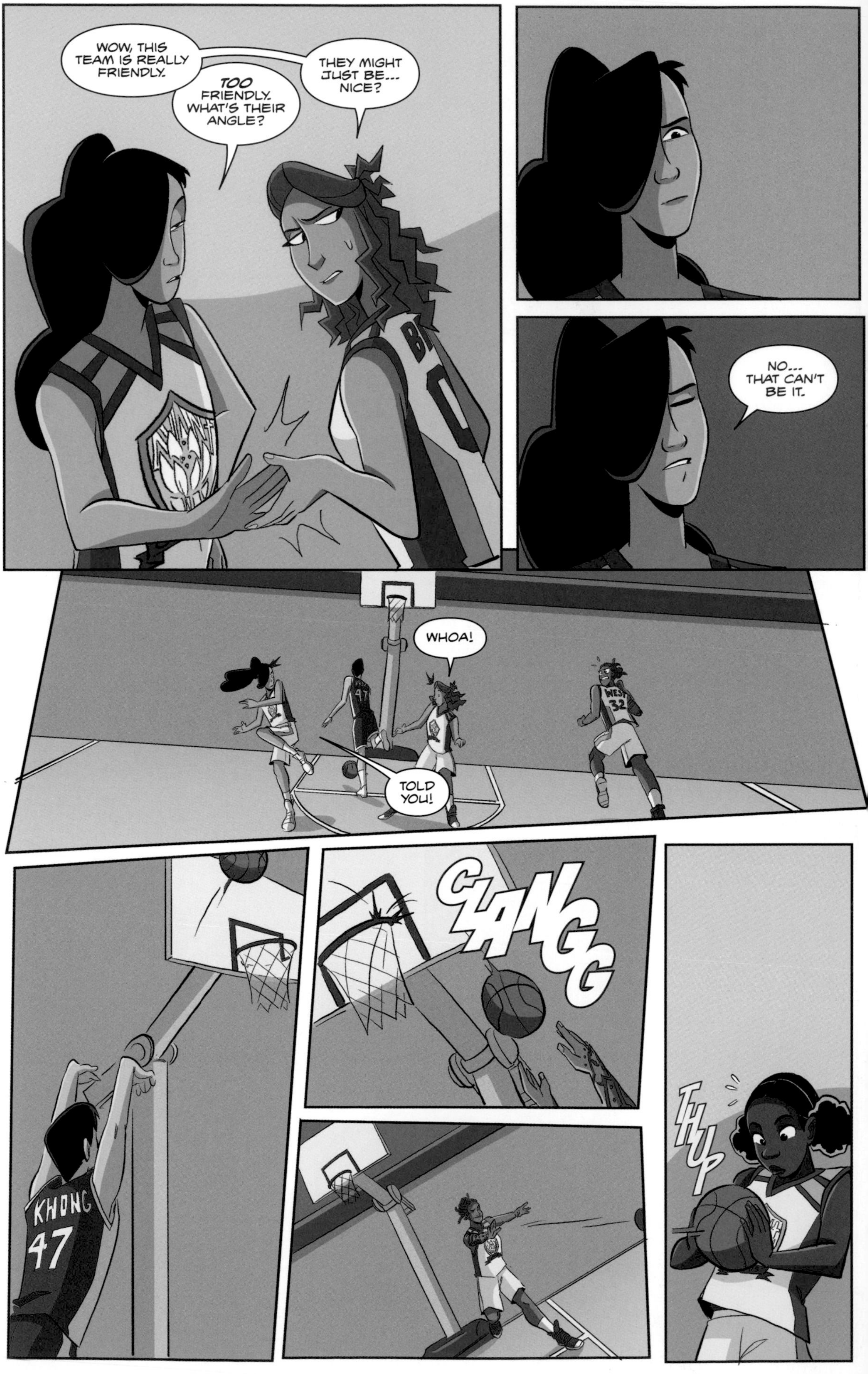
WOW, THIS TEAM IS REALLY FRIENDLY.
THEY MIGHT JUST BE... NICE?
TOO FRIENDLY. WHAT'S THEIR ANGLE?
NO... THAT CAN'T BE IT.
WHOA!
TOLD YOU!
KHONG 47
CLANGG
THUP

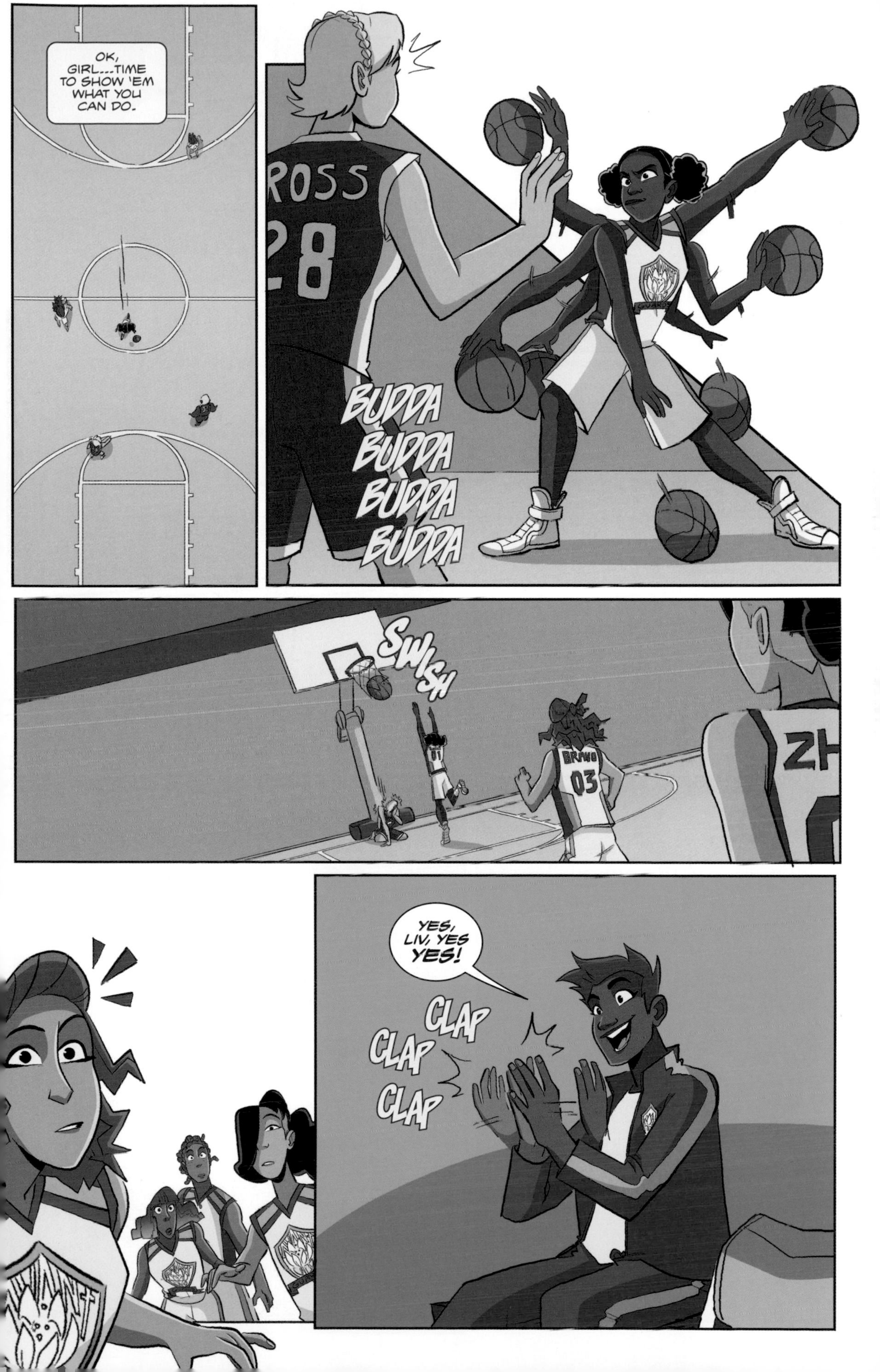
OK, GIRL...TIME TO SHOW 'EM WHAT YOU CAN DO.
ROSS
28
BUDDA
BUDDA
BUDDA
BUDDA
SWISH
BRAVO
03
ZH
YES, LIV, YES YES!
CLAP
CLAP
CLAP

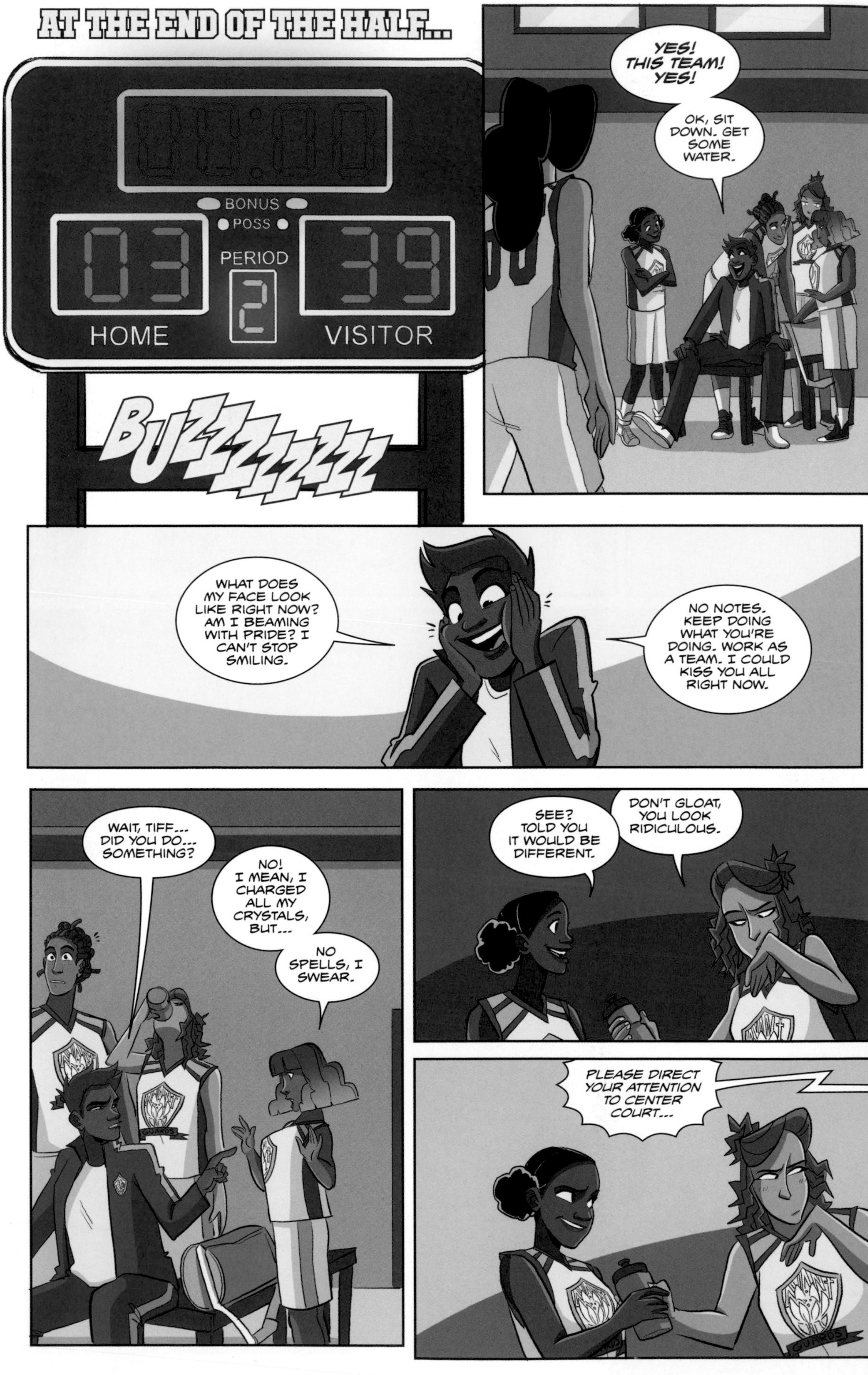
AT THE END OF THE HALF...
00:00
BONUS
POSS
03
PERIOD
2
39
HOME
VISITOR
BUZZZZZZZ
YES! THIS TEAM! YES!
OK, SIT DOWN. GET SOME WATER.
WHAT DOES MY FACE LOOK LIKE RIGHT NOW? AM I BEAMING WITH PRIDE? I CAN'T STOP SMILING.
NO NOTES. KEEP DOING WHAT YOU'RE DOING. WORK AS A TEAM. I COULD KISS YOU ALL RIGHT NOW.
WAIT, TIFF... DID YOU DO... SOMETHING?
NO! I MEAN, I CHARGED ALL MY CRYSTALS, BUT...
NO SPELLS, I SWEAR.
SEE? TOLD YOU IT WOULD BE DIFFERENT.
DON'T GLOAT, YOU LOOK RIDICULOUS.
PLEASE DIRECT YOUR ATTENTION TO CENTER COURT...

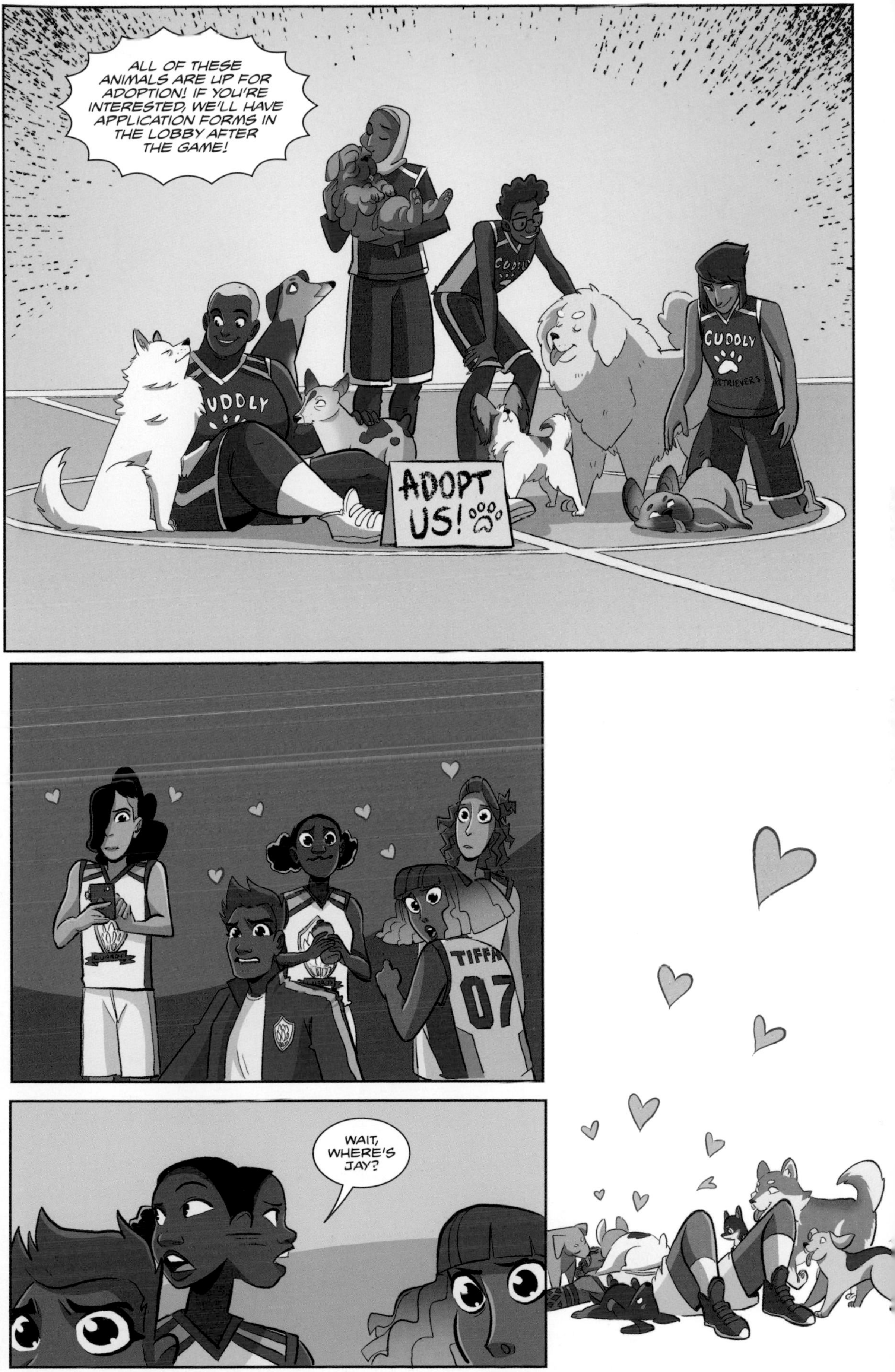
ALL OF THESE ANIMALS ARE UP FOR ADOPTION! IF YOU'RE INTERESTED, WE'LL HAVE APPLICATION FORMS IN THE LOBBY AFTER THE GAME!
CUDDLY
ADOPT US!
TIFFA
07
WAIT, WHERE'S JAY?

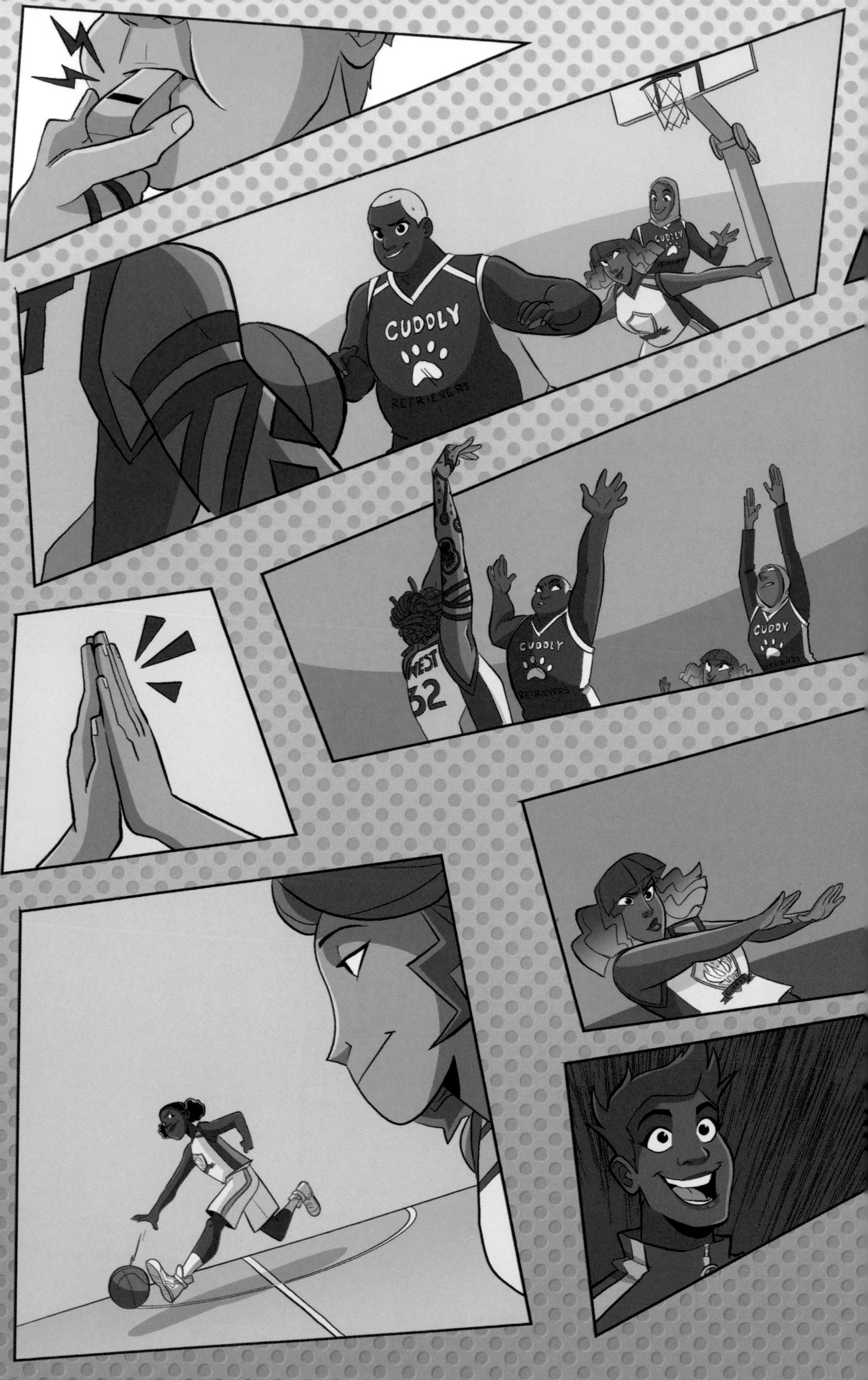
CUDDLY
RETRIEVERS
CUDDLY
RETRIEVERS
WEST
32
CUDDLY
RETRIEVERS

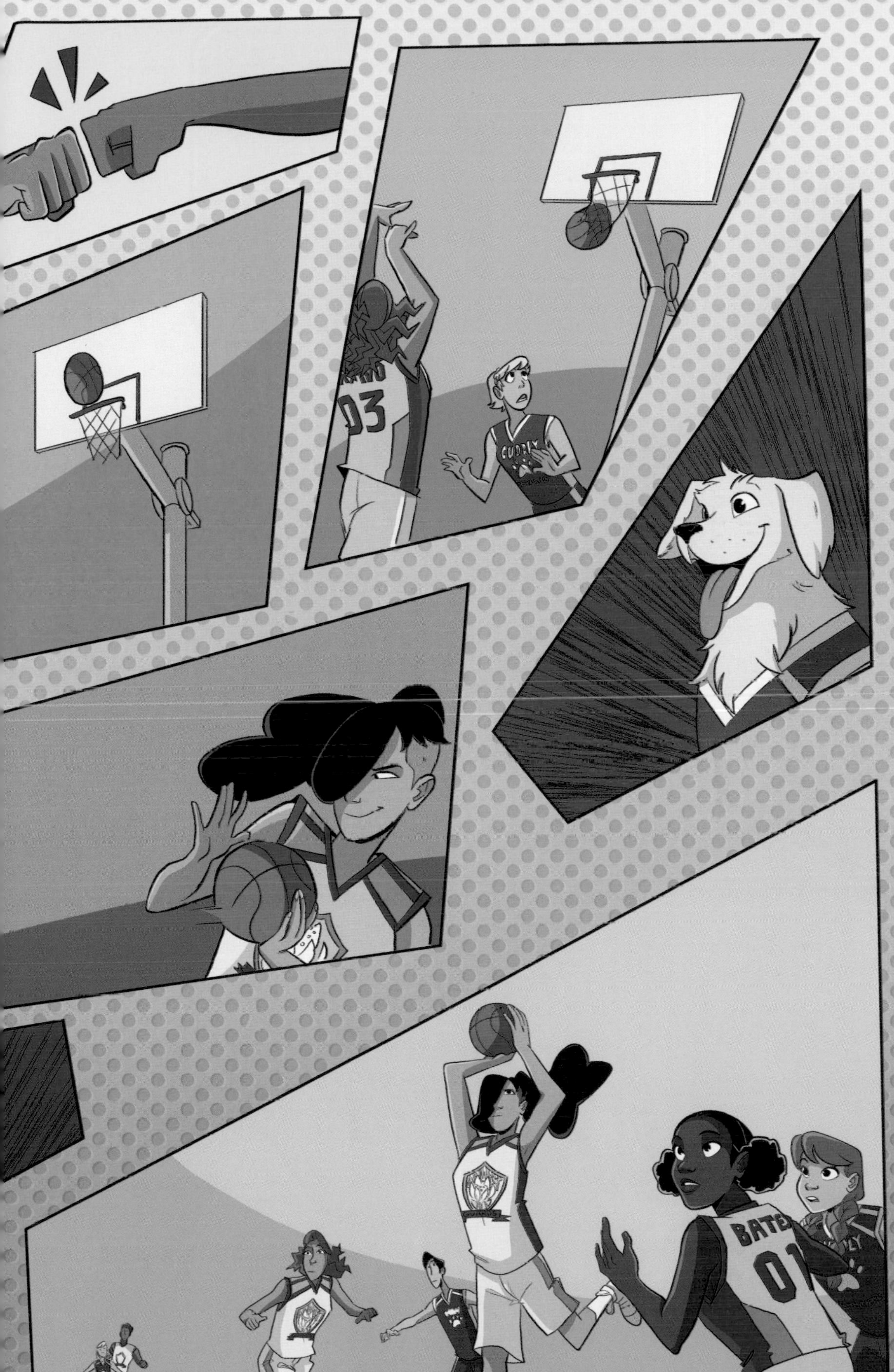

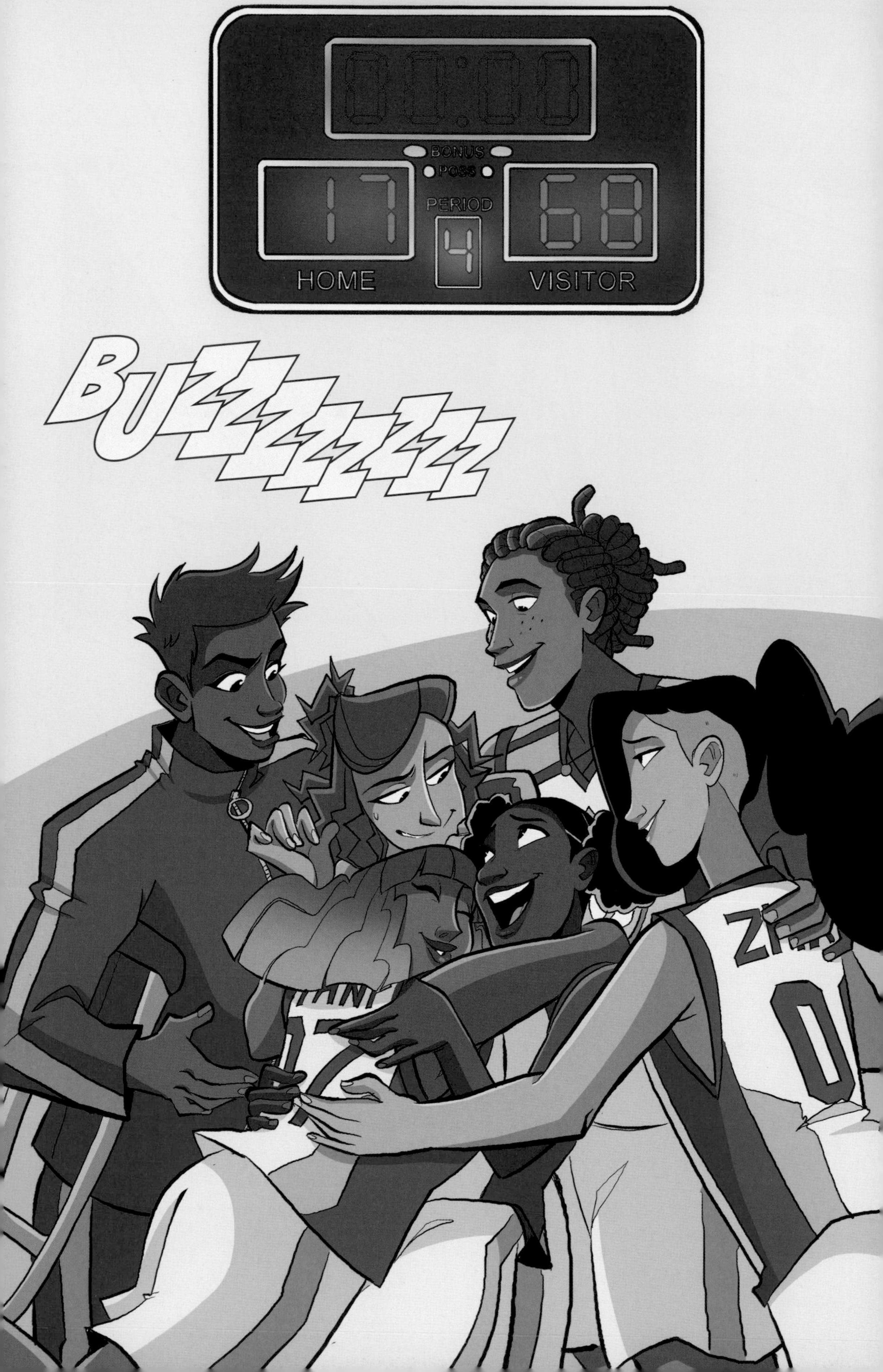
00:00
BONUS
POSS
17
PERIOD
4
68
HOME
VISITOR
BUZZZZZZZ

CHAPTER FOUR

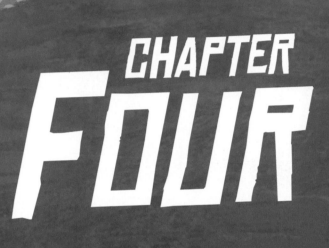

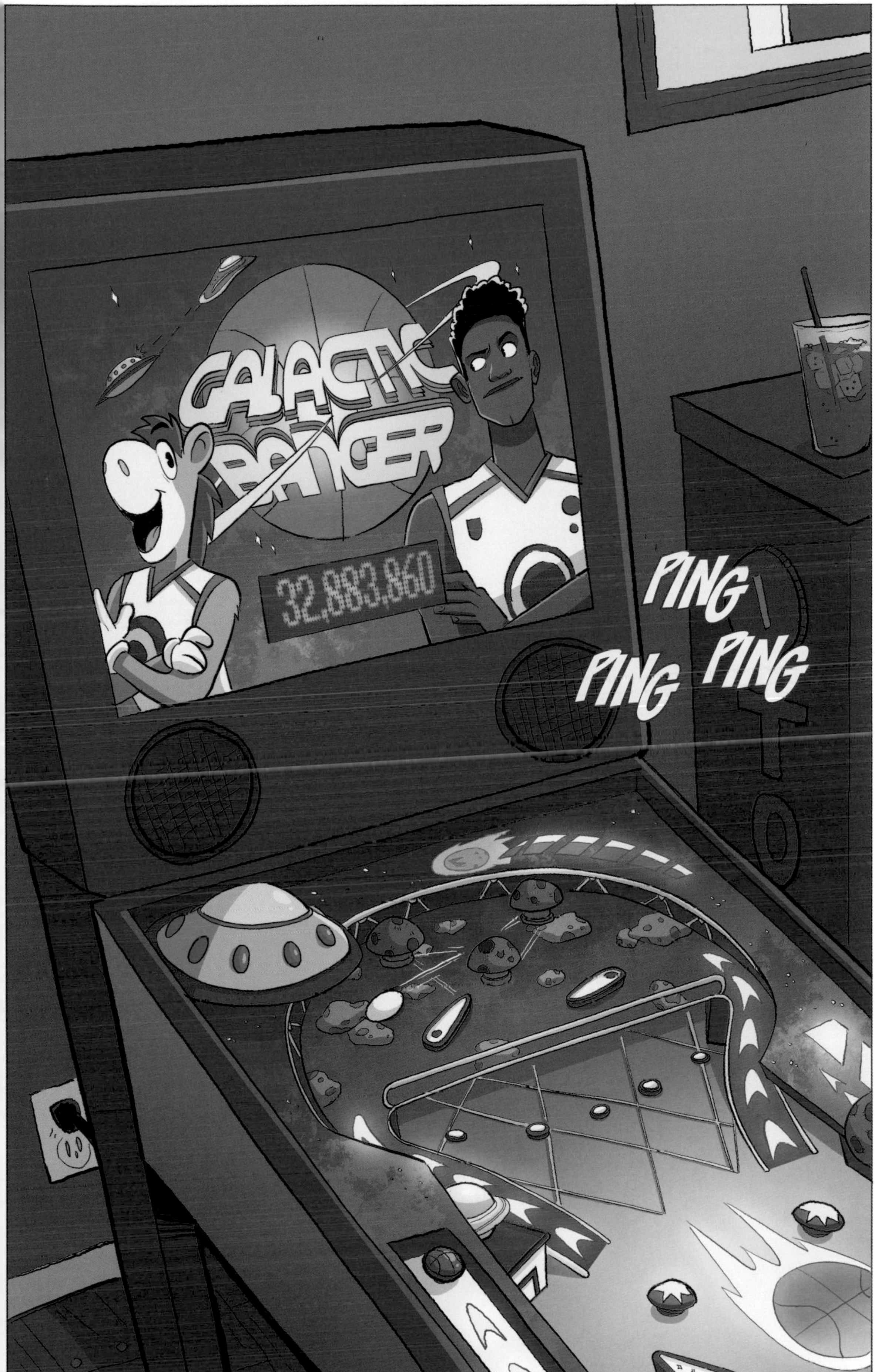
GALACTIC RANGER
32,883,860
PING
PING PING

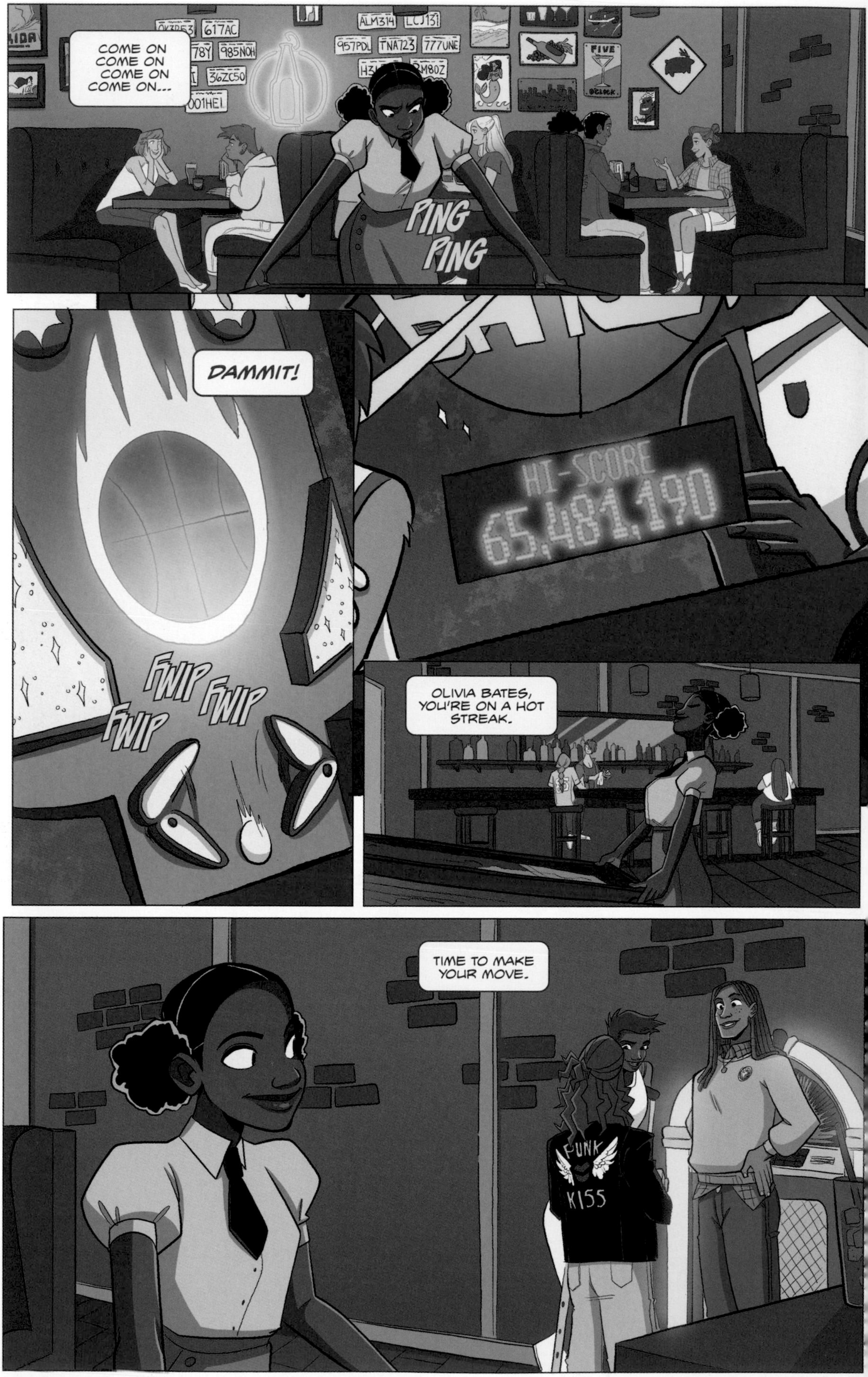

COME ON COME ON COME ON COME ON...
PING PING
DAMMIT!
FWIP FWIP FWIP
HI-SCORE
65,481,190
OLIVIA BATES, YOU'RE ON A HOT STREAK.
TIME TO MAKE YOUR MOVE.
PUNK KISS

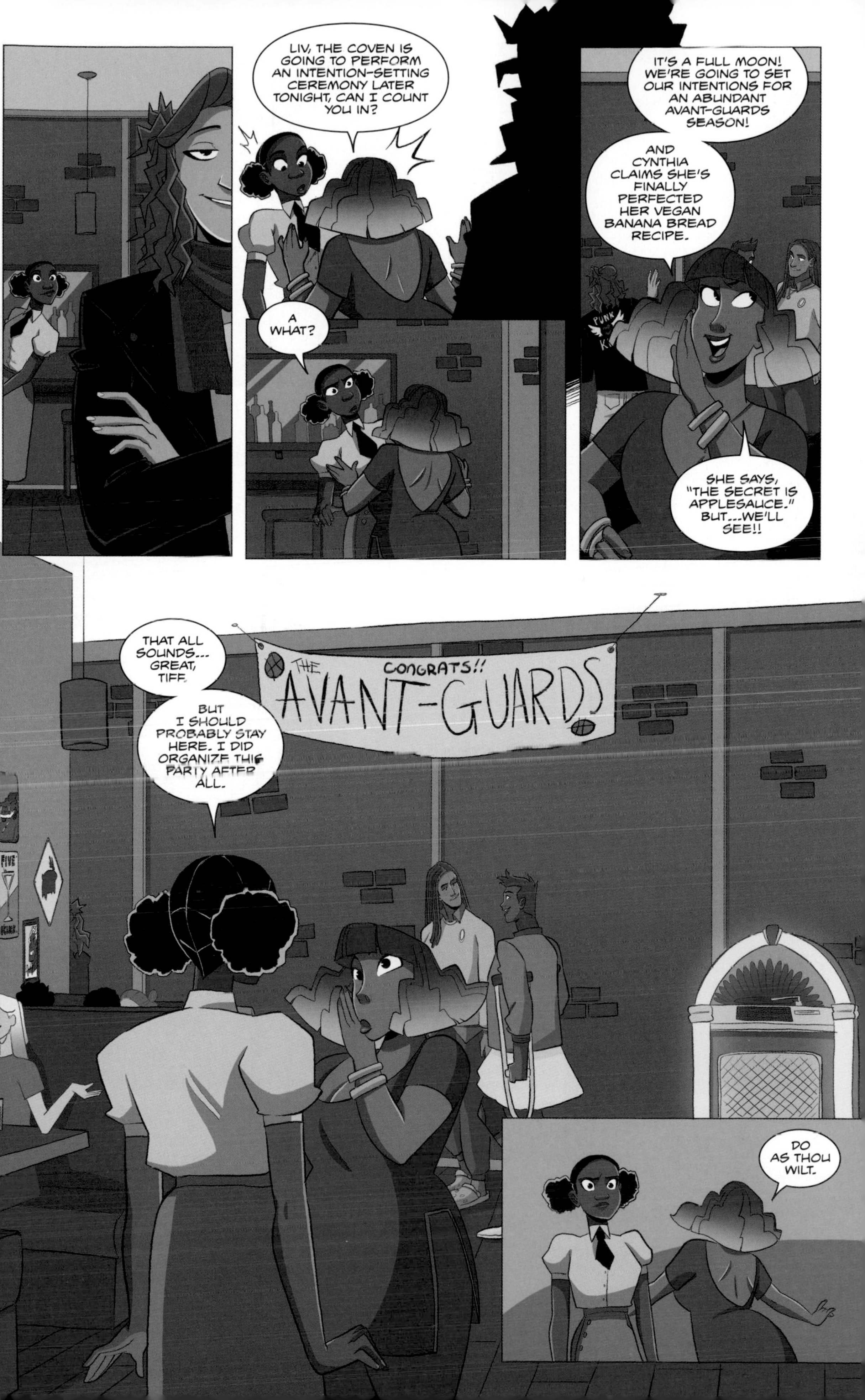
LIV, THE COVEN IS GOING TO PERFORM AN INTENTION-SETTING CEREMONY LATER TONIGHT, CAN I COUNT YOU IN?
A WHAT?
IT'S A FULL MOON! WE'RE GOING TO SET OUR INTENTIONS FOR AN ABUNDANT AVANT-GUARDS SEASON!
AND CYNTHIA CLAIMS SHE'S FINALLY PERFECTED HER VEGAN BANANA BREAD RECIPE.
SHE SAYS, "THE SECRET IS APPLESAUCE." BUT...WE'LL SEE!!
THAT ALL SOUNDS... GREAT, TIFF.
BUT I SHOULD PROBABLY STAY HERE. I DID ORGANIZE THIS PARTY AFTER ALL.
THE CONGRATS!! AVANT-GUARDS
DO AS THOU WILT.

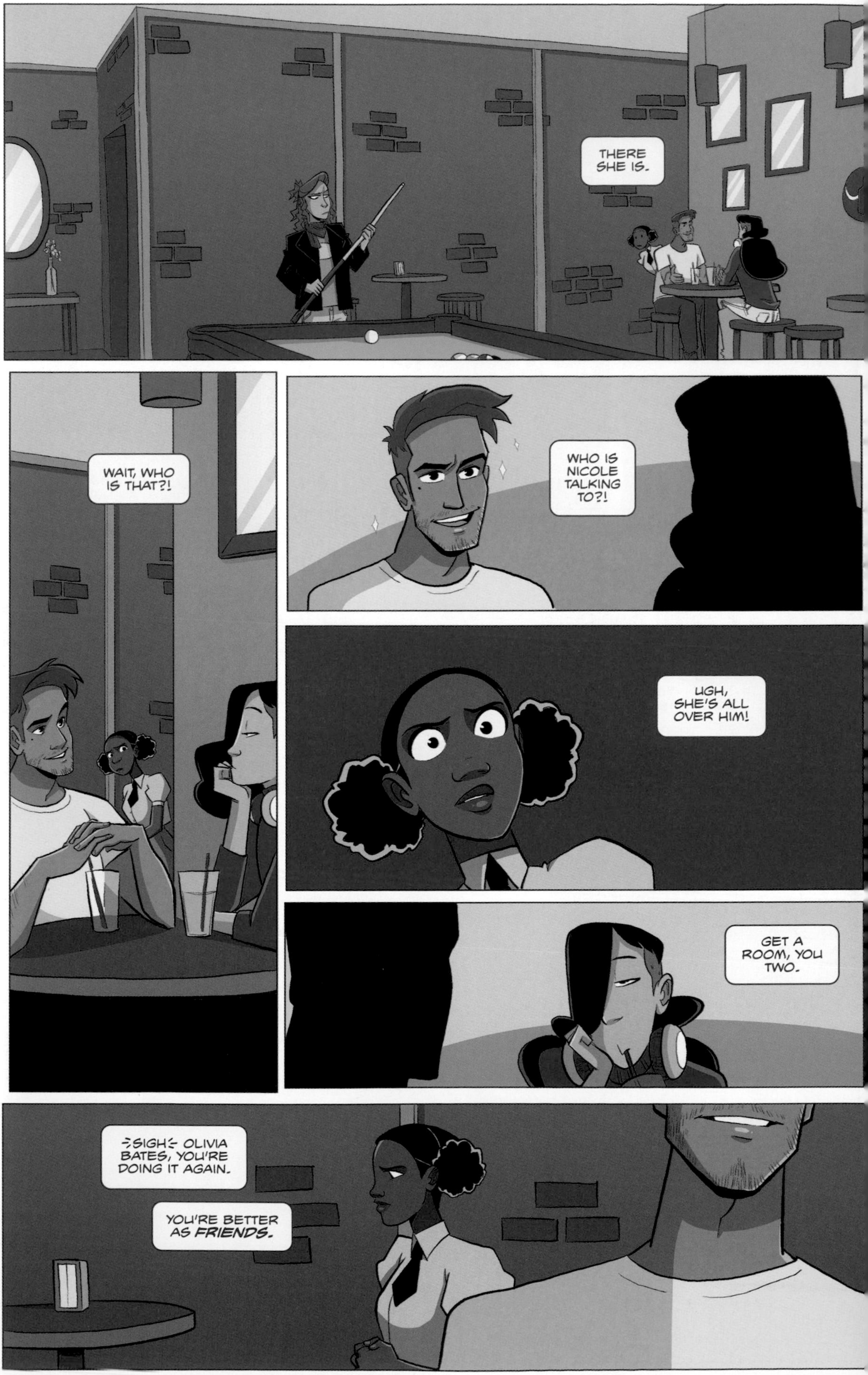
THERE SHE IS.
WAIT, WHO IS THAT?!
WHO IS NICOLE TALKING TO?!
UGH, SHE'S ALL OVER HIM!
GET A ROOM, YOU TWO.
=SIGH= OLIVIA BATES, YOU'RE DOING IT AGAIN.
YOU'RE BETTER AS *FRIENDS*.

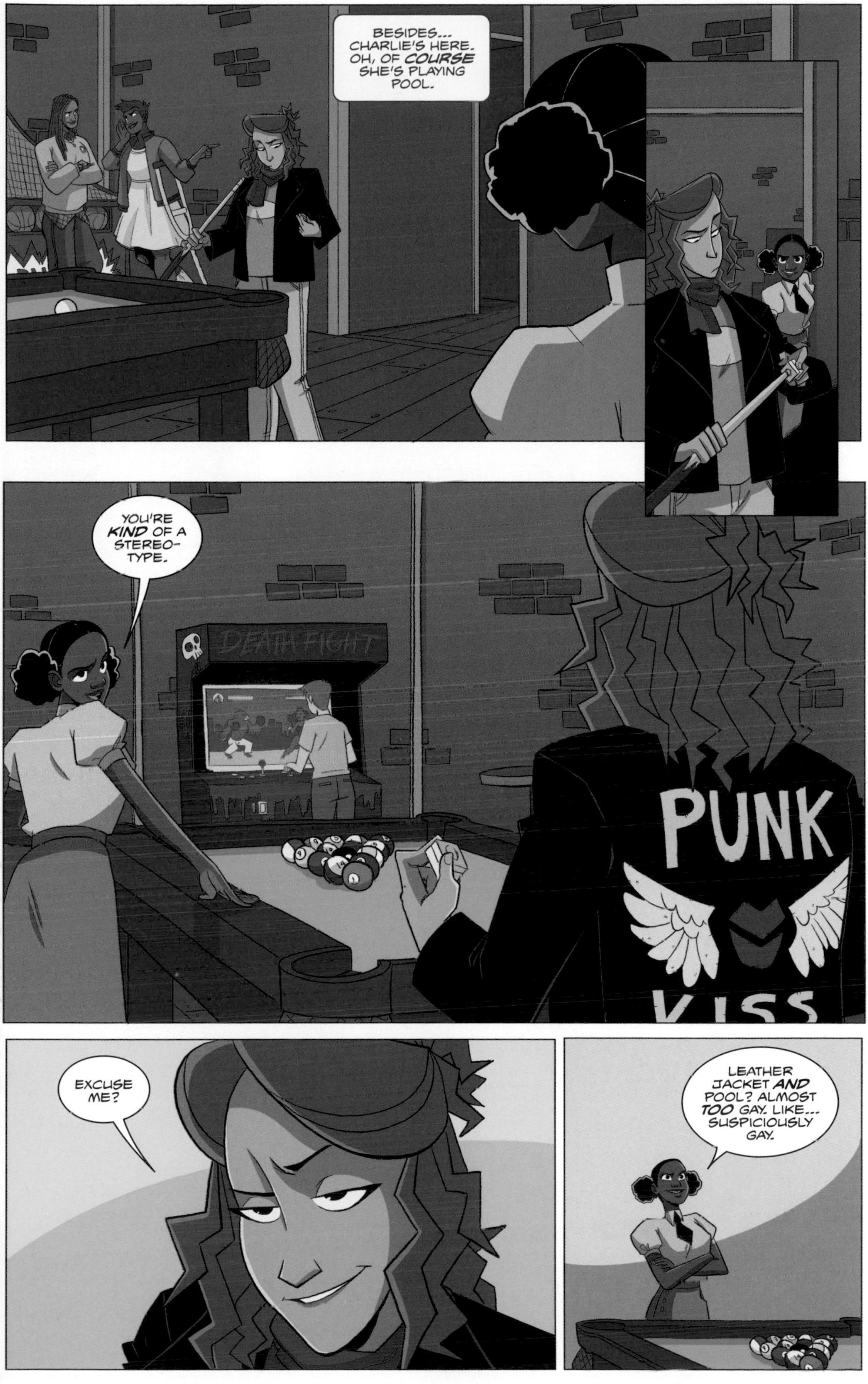
BESIDES... CHARLIE'S HERE. OH, OF COURSE SHE'S PLAYING POOL.
YOU'RE KIND OF A STEREO-TYPE.
DEATH FIGHT
PUNK
KISS
EXCUSE ME?
LEATHER JACKET AND POOL? ALMOST TOO GAY. LIKE... SUSPICIOUSLY GAY.

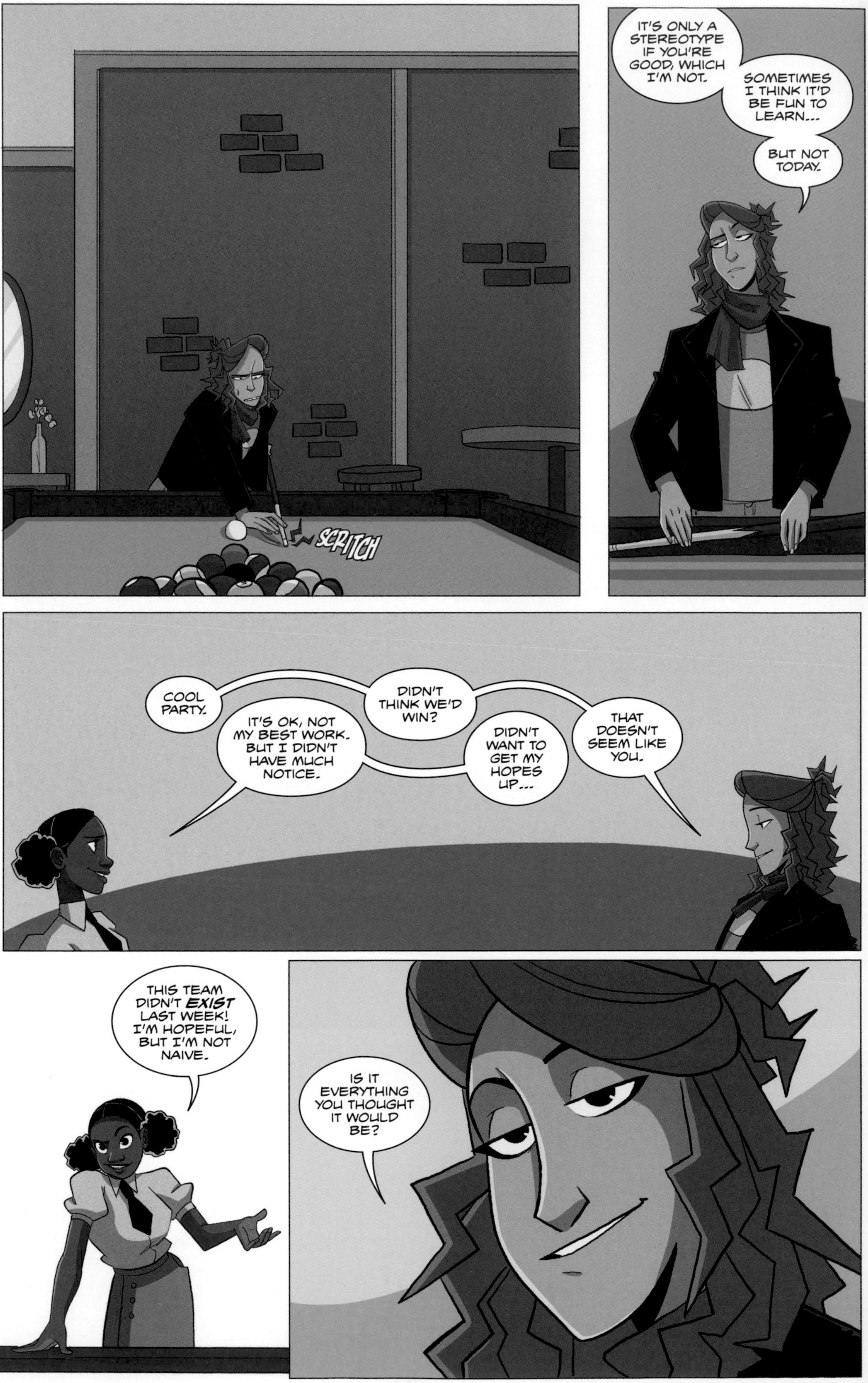
SCRITCH
IT'S ONLY A STEREOTYPE IF YOU'RE GOOD, WHICH I'M NOT.
SOMETIMES I THINK IT'D BE FUN TO LEARN...
BUT NOT TODAY.
COOL PARTY.
IT'S OK, NOT MY BEST WORK. BUT I DIDN'T HAVE MUCH NOTICE.
DIDN'T THINK WE'D WIN?
DIDN'T WANT TO GET MY HOPES UP...
THAT DOESN'T SEEM LIKE YOU.
THIS TEAM DIDN'T EXIST LAST WEEK! I'M HOPEFUL, BUT I'M NOT NAIVE.
IS IT EVERYTHING YOU THOUGHT IT WOULD BE?

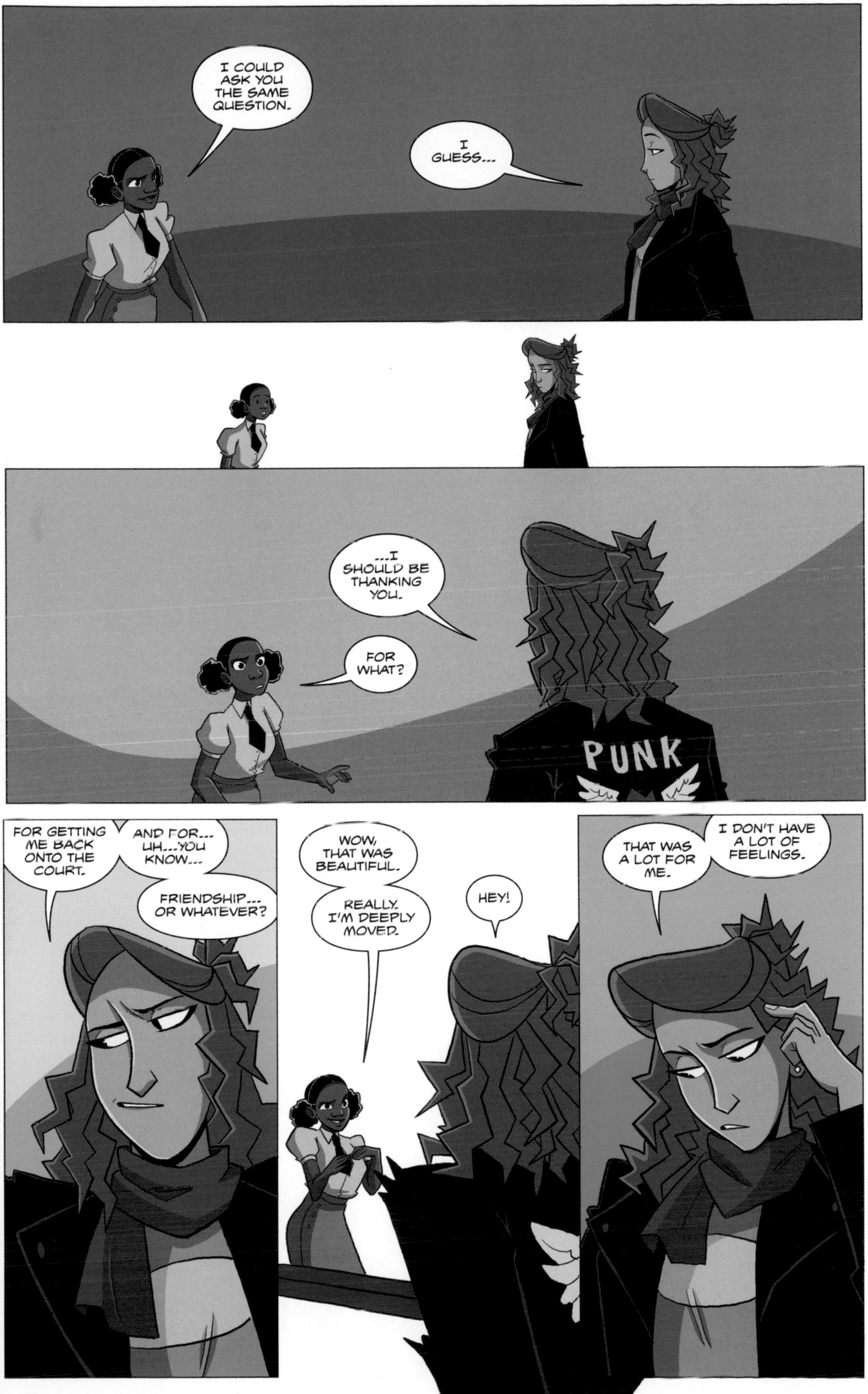
I COULD ASK YOU THE SAME QUESTION.
I GUESS...
...I SHOULD BE THANKING YOU.
FOR WHAT?
PUNK
FOR GETTING ME BACK ONTO THE COURT.
AND FOR... UH... YOU KNOW...
FRIENDSHIP... OR WHATEVER?
WOW, THAT WAS BEAUTIFUL.
REALLY. I'M DEEPLY MOVED.
HEY!
THAT WAS A LOT FOR ME.
I DON'T HAVE A LOT OF FEELINGS.

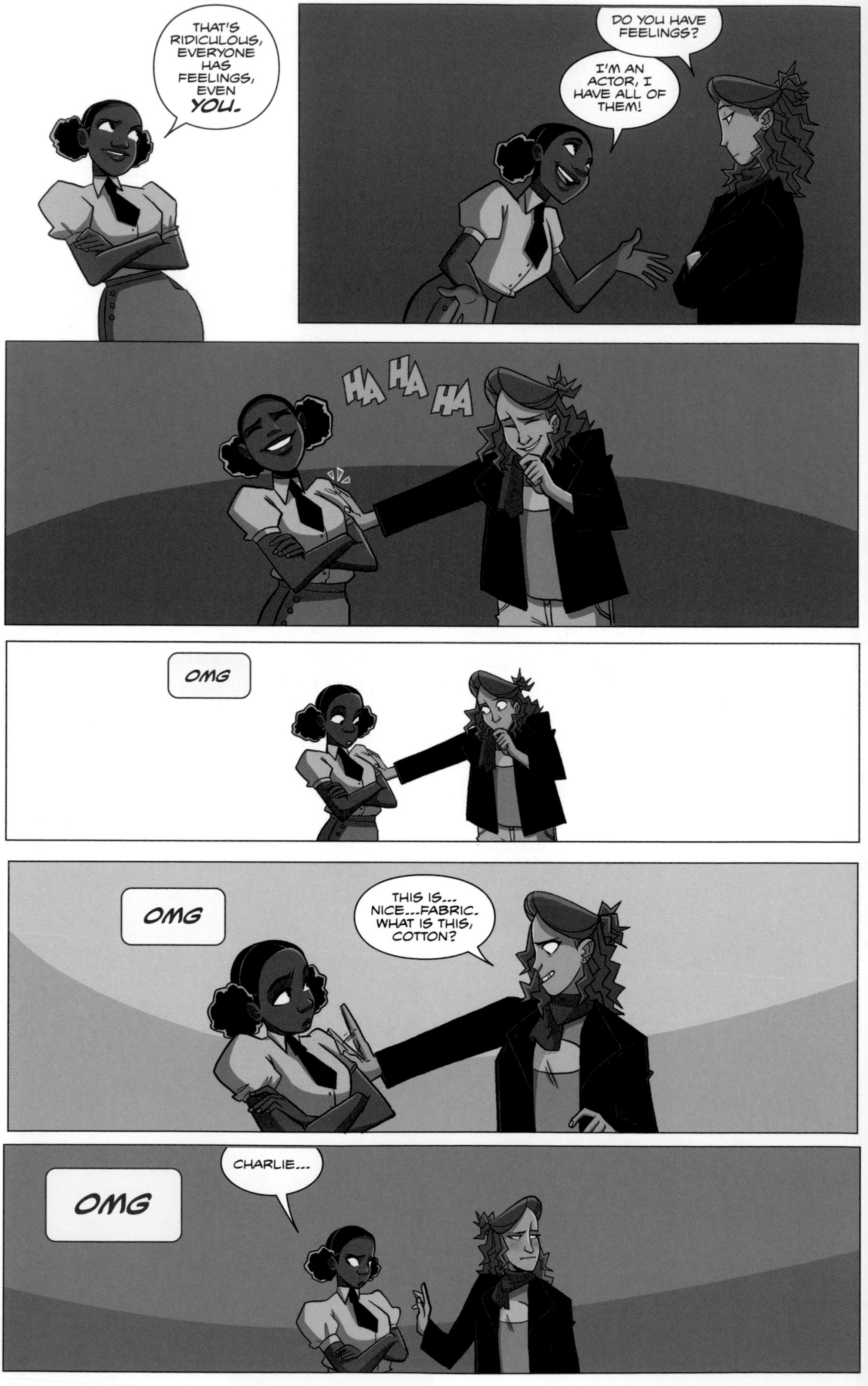

THAT'S RIDICULOUS, EVERYONE HAS FEELINGS, EVEN YOU.
DO YOU HAVE FEELINGS?
I'M AN ACTOR, I HAVE ALL OF THEM!
HA HA HA
OMG
OMG
THIS IS... NICE...FABRIC. WHAT IS THIS, COTTON?
OMG
CHARLIE...

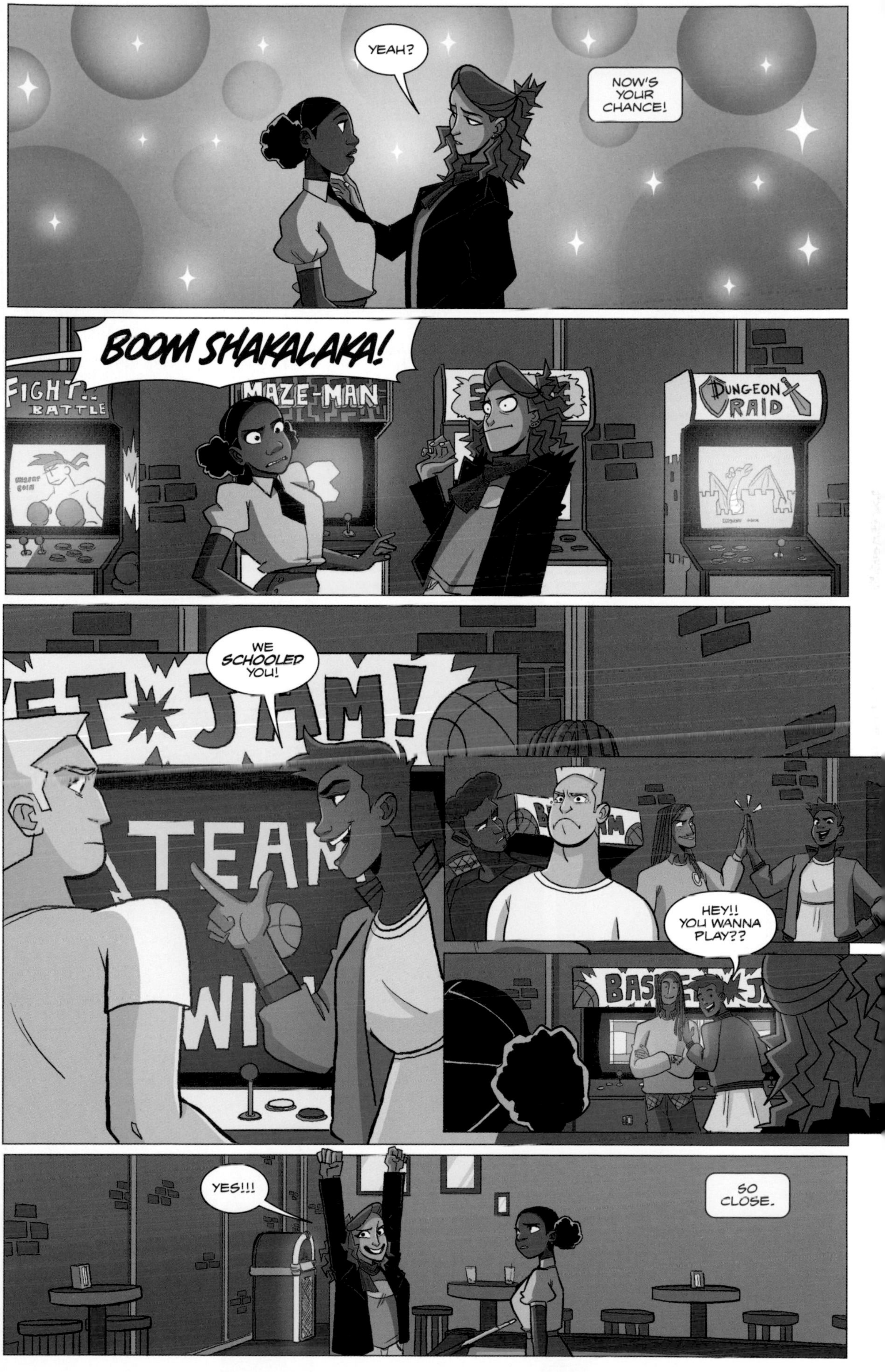
YEAH?
NOW'S YOUR CHANCE!
BOOM SHAKALAKA!
FIGHT.. BATTLE
MAZE-MAN
DUNGEON RAID
WE SCHOOLED YOU!
TEAM
HEY!! YOU WANNA PLAY??
YES!!!
SO CLOSE.

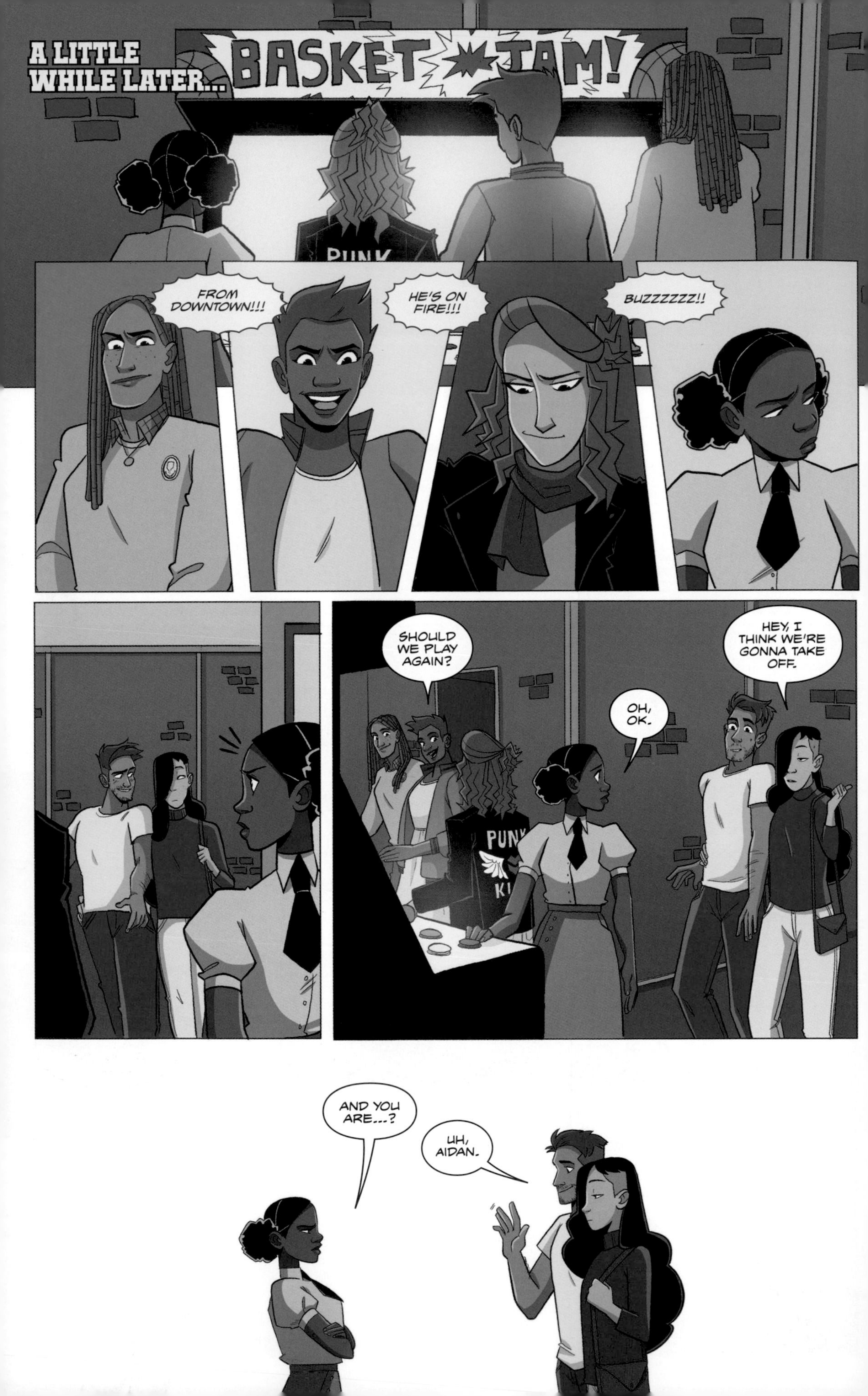
A LITTLE WHILE LATER...
BASKET JAM!
PUNK
FROM DOWNTOWN!!!
HE'S ON FIRE!!!
BUZZZZZZ!!
SHOULD WE PLAY AGAIN?
HEY, I THINK WE'RE GONNA TAKE OFF.
OH, OK.
PUNK
AND YOU ARE...?
UH, AIDAN.

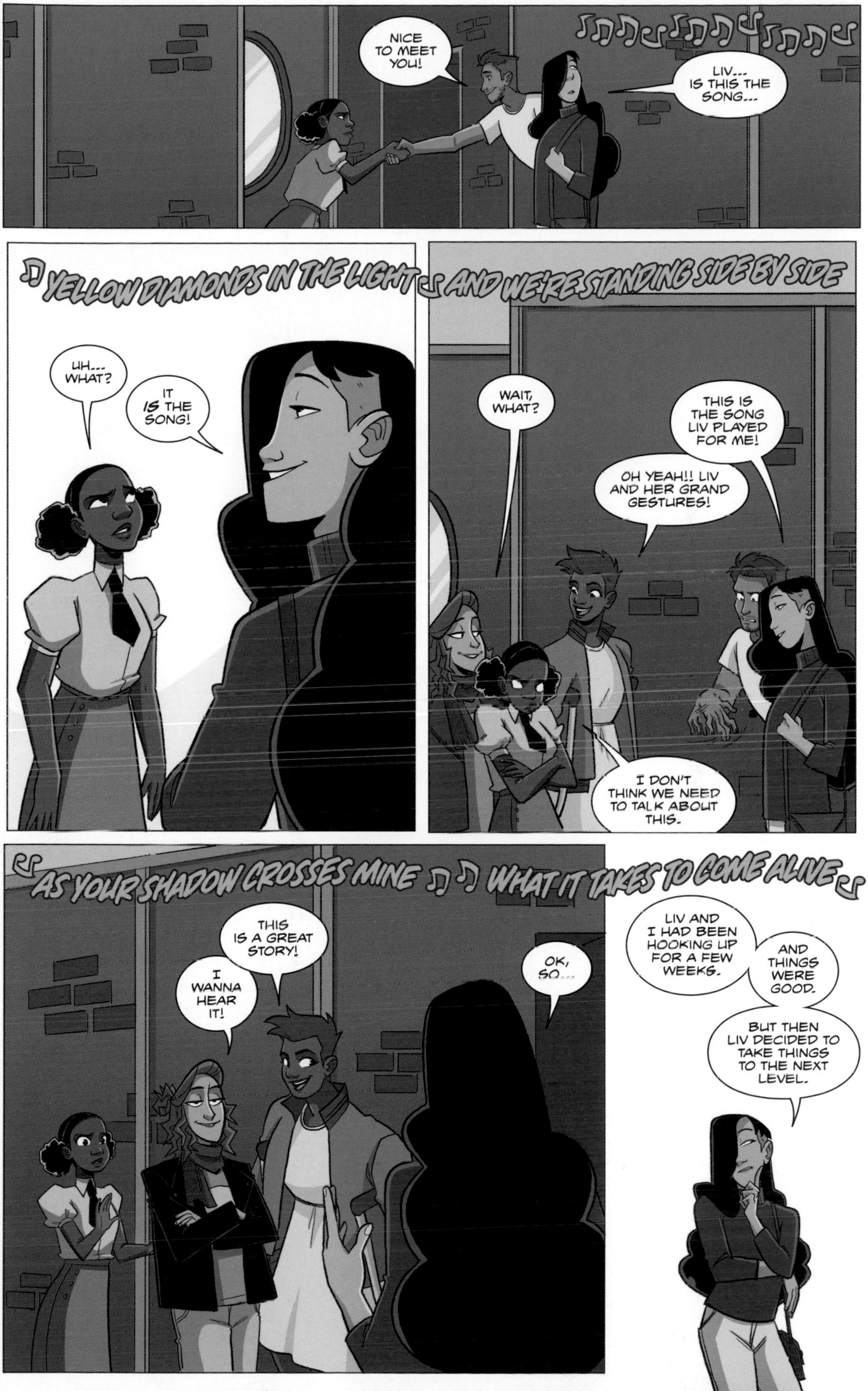
NICE TO MEET YOU!
LIV... IS THIS THE SONG...
YELLOW DIAMONDS IN THE LIGHT
UH... WHAT?
IT IS THE SONG!
AND WE'RE STANDING SIDE BY SIDE
WAIT, WHAT?
THIS IS THE SONG LIV PLAYED FOR ME!
OH YEAH!! LIV AND HER GRAND GESTURES!
I DON'T THINK WE NEED TO TALK ABOUT THIS.
AS YOUR SHADOW CROSSES MINE
THIS IS A GREAT STORY!
I WANNA HEAR IT!
OK, SO...
WHAT IT TAKES TO COME ALIVE
LIV AND I HAD BEEN HOOKING UP FOR A FEW WEEKS.
AND THINGS WERE GOOD.
BUT THEN LIV DECIDED TO TAKE THINGS TO THE NEXT LEVEL.

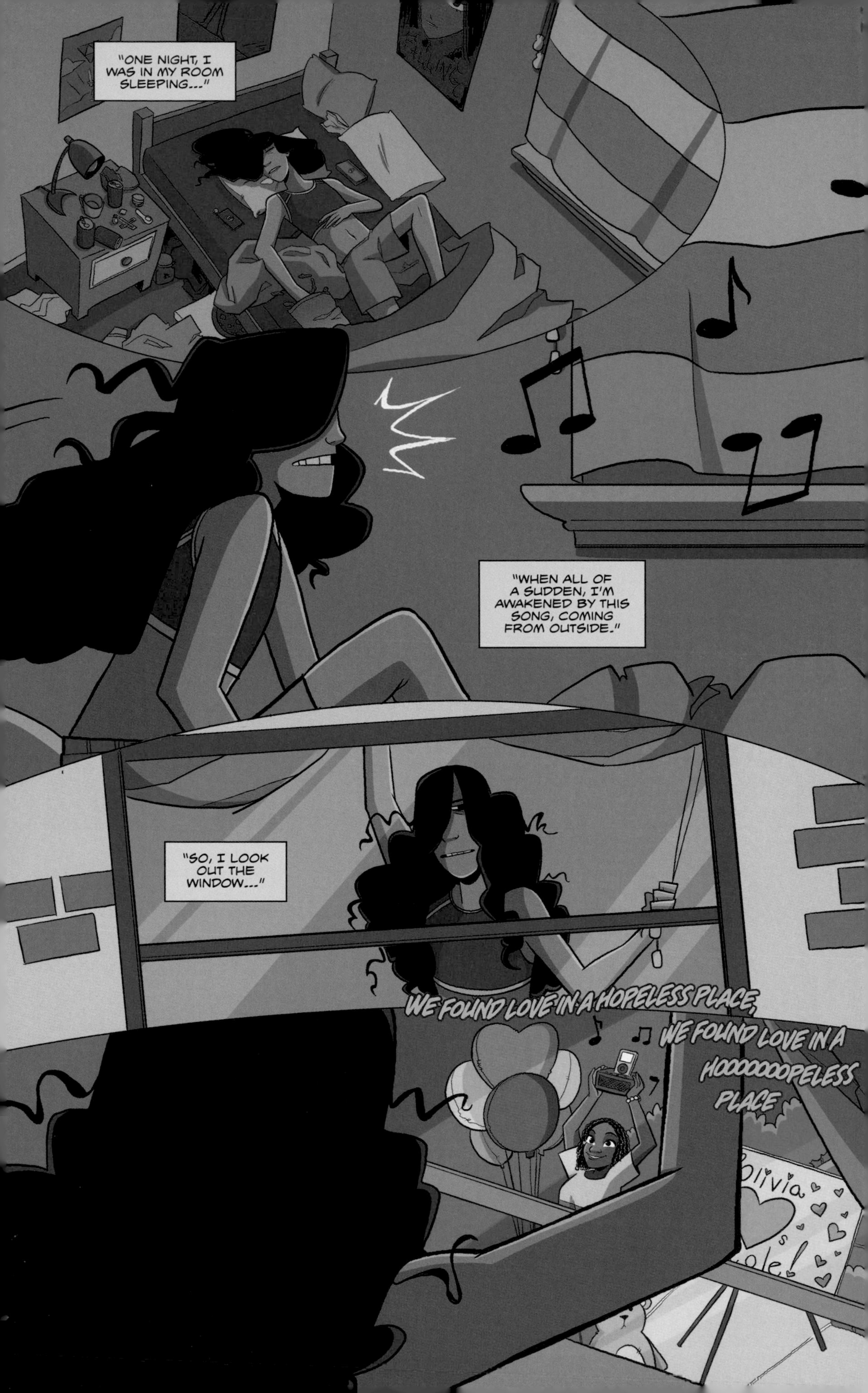
"ONE NIGHT, I WAS IN MY ROOM SLEEPING..."
"WHEN ALL OF A SUDDEN, I'M AWAKENED BY THIS SONG, COMING FROM OUTSIDE."
"SO, I LOOK OUT THE WINDOW..."
WE FOUND LOVE IN A HOPELESS PLACE,
WE FOUND LOVE IN A HOOOOOOOPELESS PLACE
Olivia

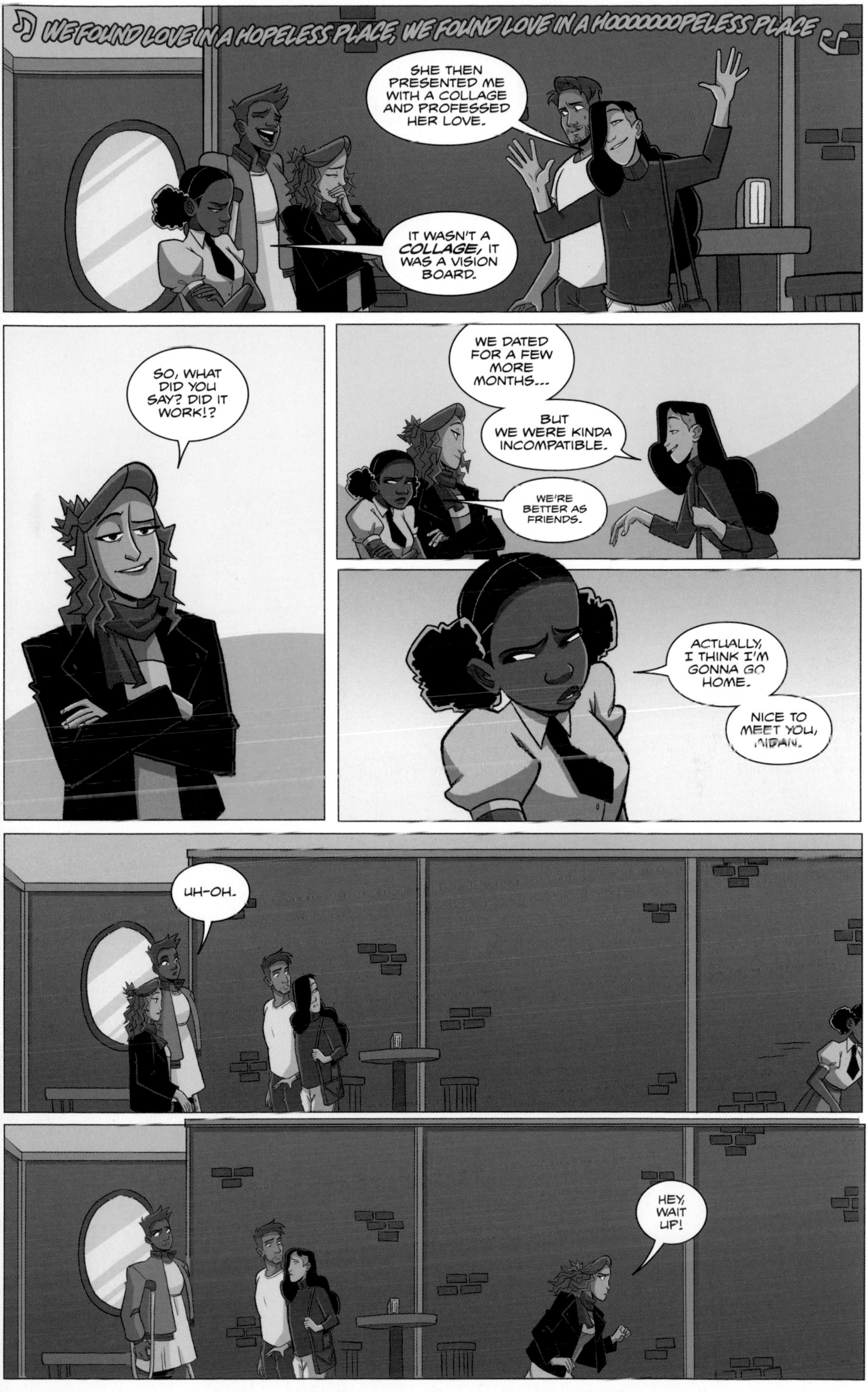
WE FOUND LOVE IN A HOPELESS PLACE, WE FOUND LOVE IN A HOOOOOOOPELESS PLACE
SHE THEN PRESENTED ME WITH A COLLAGE AND PROFESSED HER LOVE.
IT WASN'T A *COLLAGE,* IT WAS A VISION BOARD.
SO, WHAT DID YOU SAY? DID IT WORK!?
WE DATED FOR A FEW MORE MONTHS...
BUT WE WERE KINDA INCOMPATIBLE.
WE'RE BETTER AS FRIENDS.
ACTUALLY, I THINK I'M GONNA GO HOME.
NICE TO MEET YOU, AIDAN.
UH-OH.
HEY, WAIT UP!

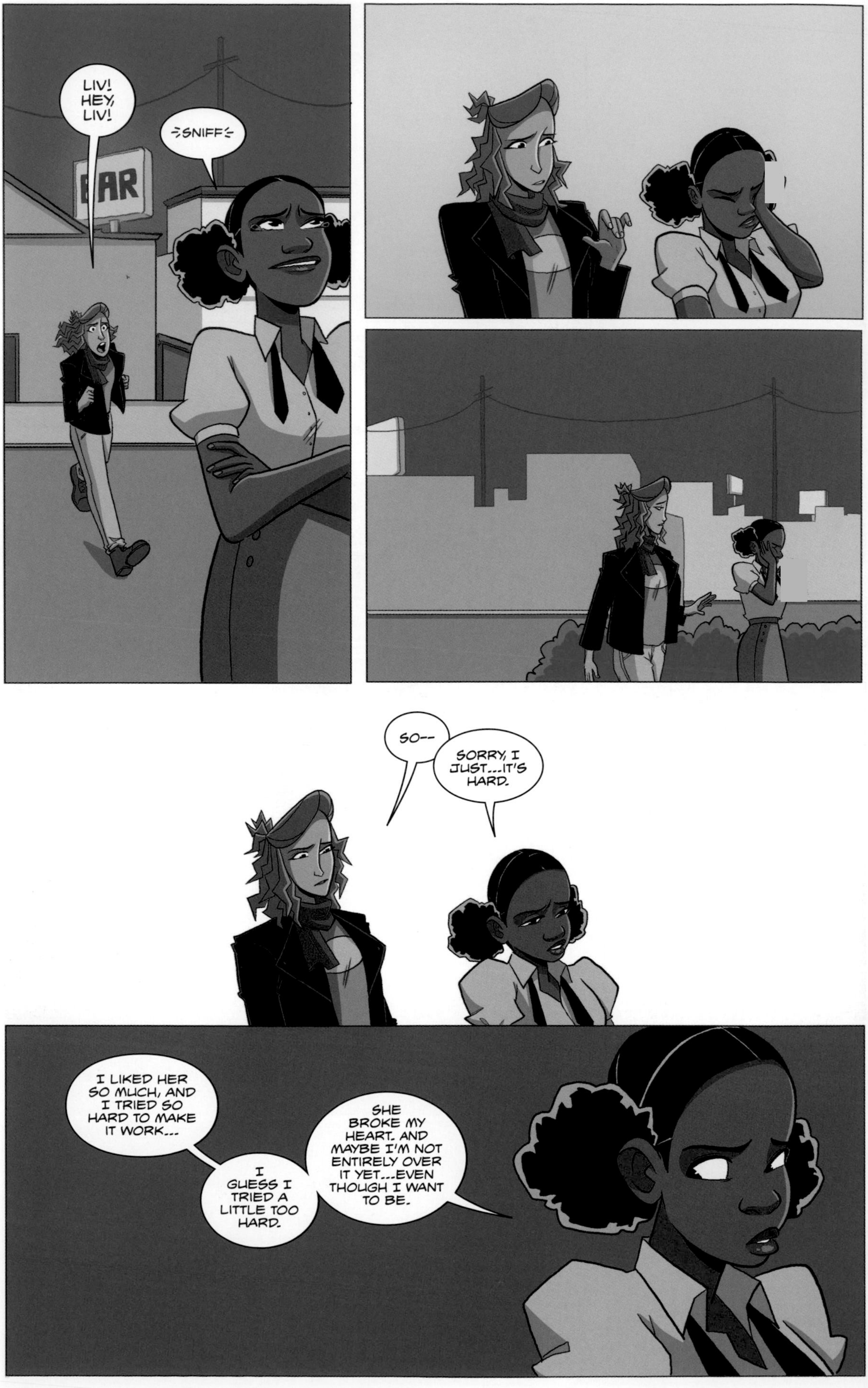
LIV! HEY, LIV!
SNIFF
SO--
SORRY, I JUST...IT'S HARD.
I LIKED HER SO MUCH, AND I TRIED SO HARD TO MAKE IT WORK...
I GUESS I TRIED A LITTLE TOO HARD.
SHE BROKE MY HEART. AND MAYBE I'M NOT ENTIRELY OVER IT YET...EVEN THOUGH I WANT TO BE.

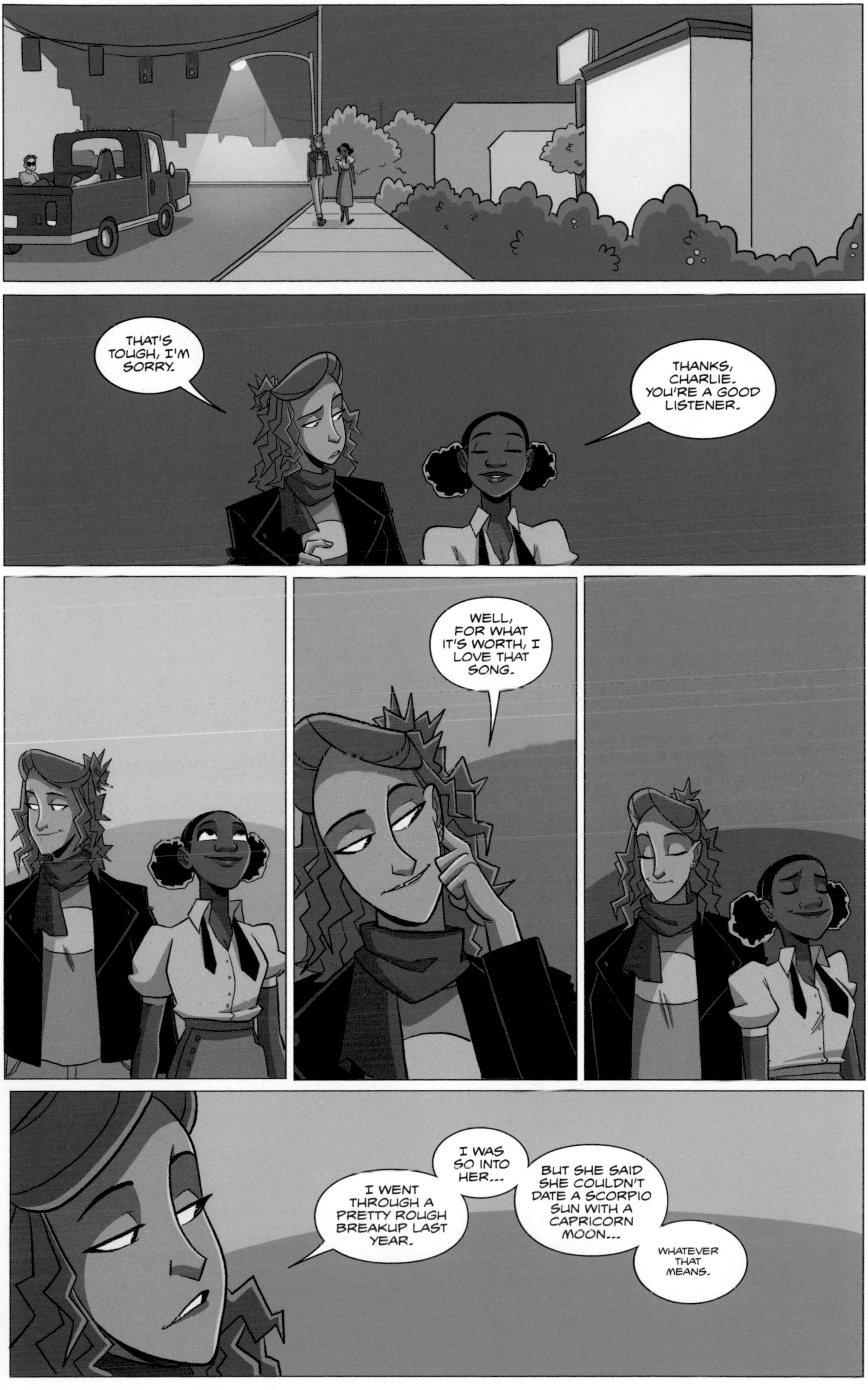
THAT'S TOUGH, I'M SORRY.
THANKS, CHARLIE. YOU'RE A GOOD LISTENER.
WELL, FOR WHAT IT'S WORTH, I LOVE THAT SONG.
I WENT THROUGH A PRETTY ROUGH BREAKUP LAST YEAR.
I WAS SO INTO HER...
BUT SHE SAID SHE COULDN'T DATE A SCORPIO SUN WITH A CAPRICORN MOON...
WHATEVER THAT MEANS.

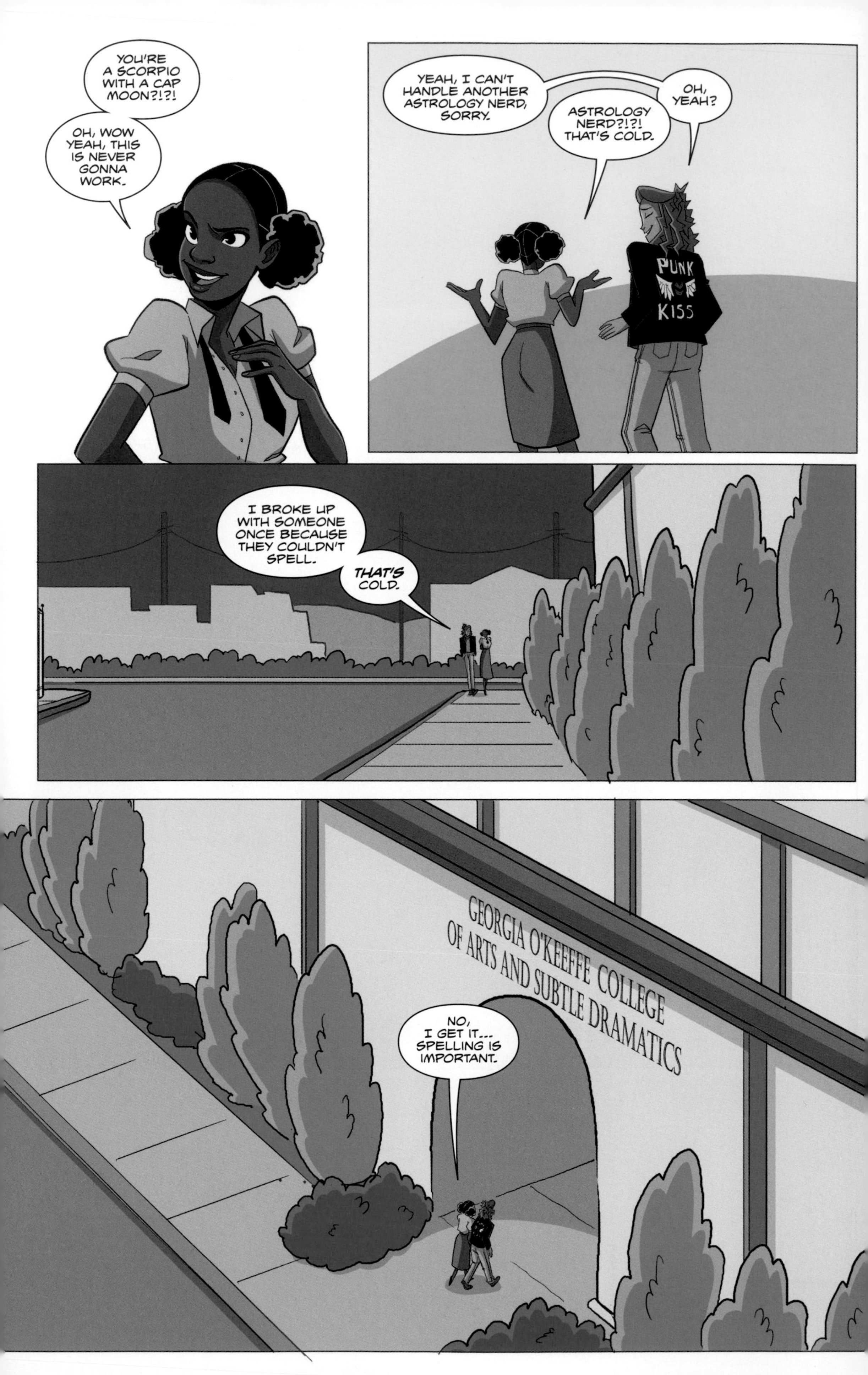
YOU'RE A SCORPIO WITH A CAP MOON?!?!
OH, WOW YEAH, THIS IS NEVER GONNA WORK.
YEAH, I CAN'T HANDLE ANOTHER ASTROLOGY NERD, SORRY.
OH, YEAH?
ASTROLOGY NERD?!?! THAT'S COLD.
PUNK KISS
I BROKE UP WITH SOMEONE ONCE BECAUSE THEY COULDN'T SPELL.
THAT'S COLD.
GEORGIA O'KEEFFE COLLEGE OF ARTS AND SUBTLE DRAMATICS
NO, I GET IT... SPELLING IS IMPORTANT.

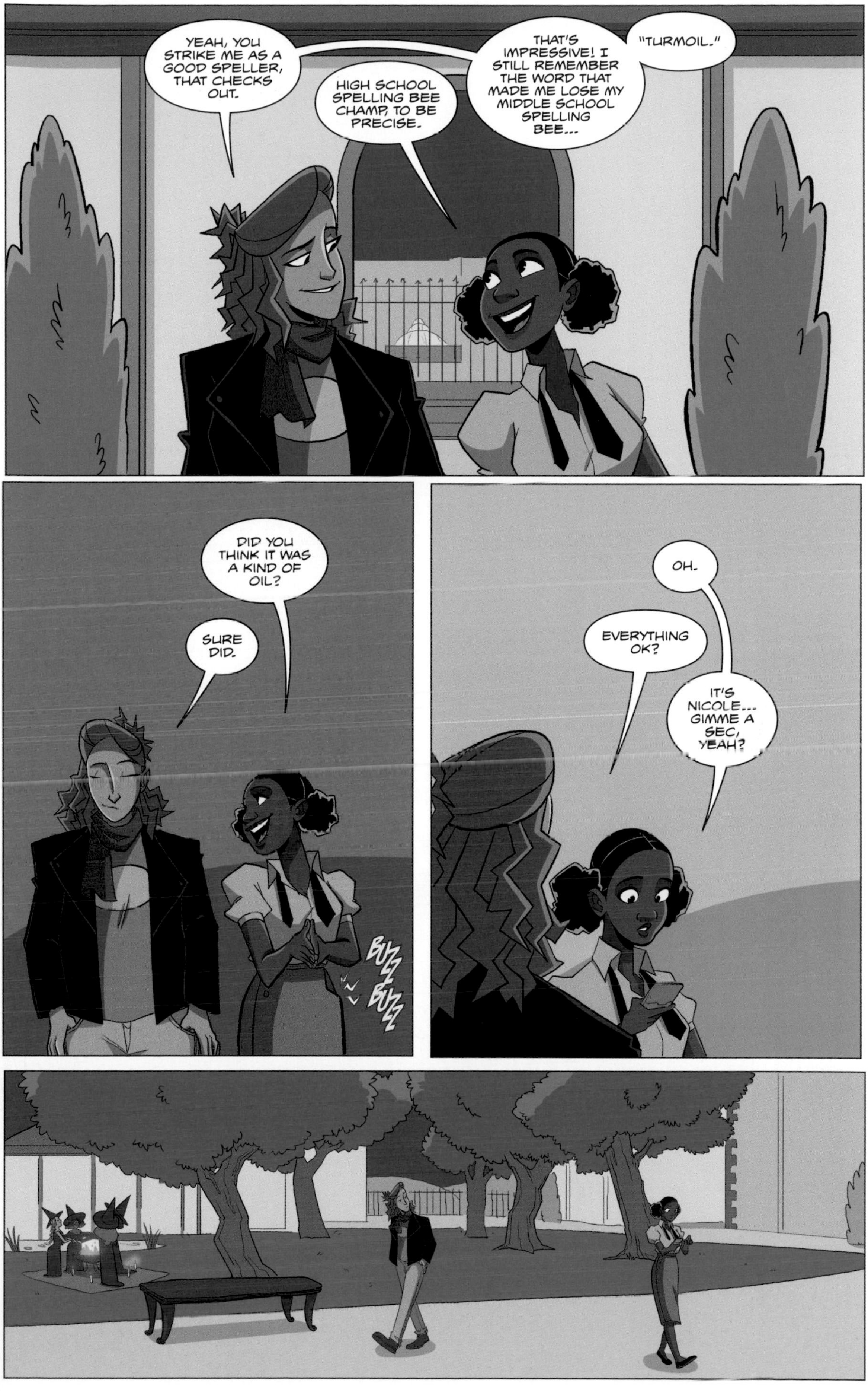
YEAH, YOU STRIKE ME AS A GOOD SPELLER, THAT CHECKS OUT.
HIGH SCHOOL SPELLING BEE CHAMP, TO BE PRECISE.
THAT'S IMPRESSIVE! I STILL REMEMBER THE WORD THAT MADE ME LOSE MY MIDDLE SCHOOL SPELLING BEE...
"TURMOIL."
DID YOU THINK IT WAS A KIND OF OIL?
SURE DID.
BUZZ BUZZ
OH.
EVERYTHING OK?
IT'S NICOLE... GIMME A SEC, YEAH?

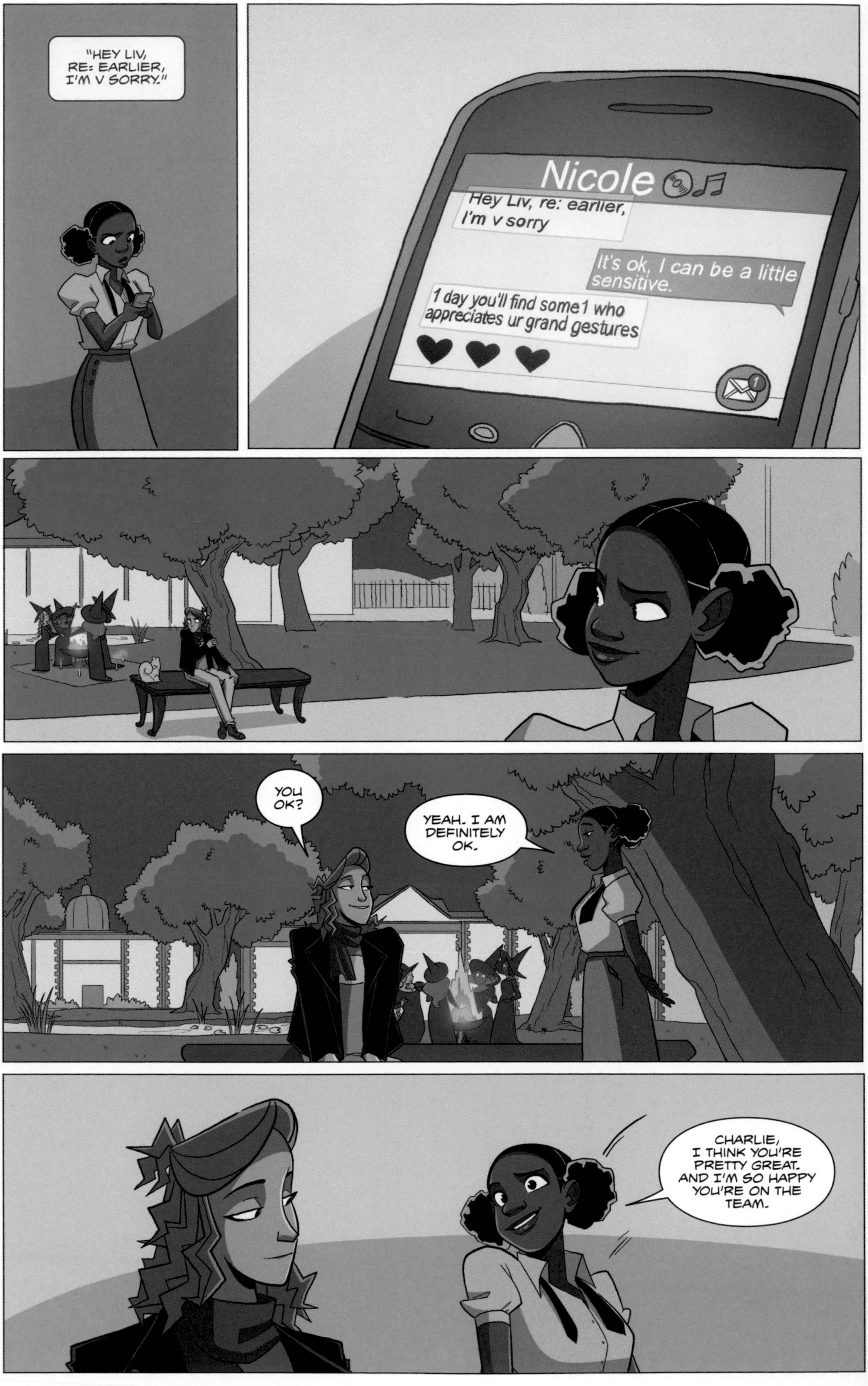
"HEY LIV, RE: EARLIER, I'M V SORRY."
Nicole
Hey Liv, re: earlier, I'm v sorry
It's ok, I can be a little sensitive.
1 day you'll find some1 who appreciates ur grand gestures
YOU OK?
YEAH. I AM DEFINITELY OK.
CHARLIE, I THINK YOU'RE PRETTY GREAT. AND I'M SO HAPPY YOU'RE ON THE TEAM.

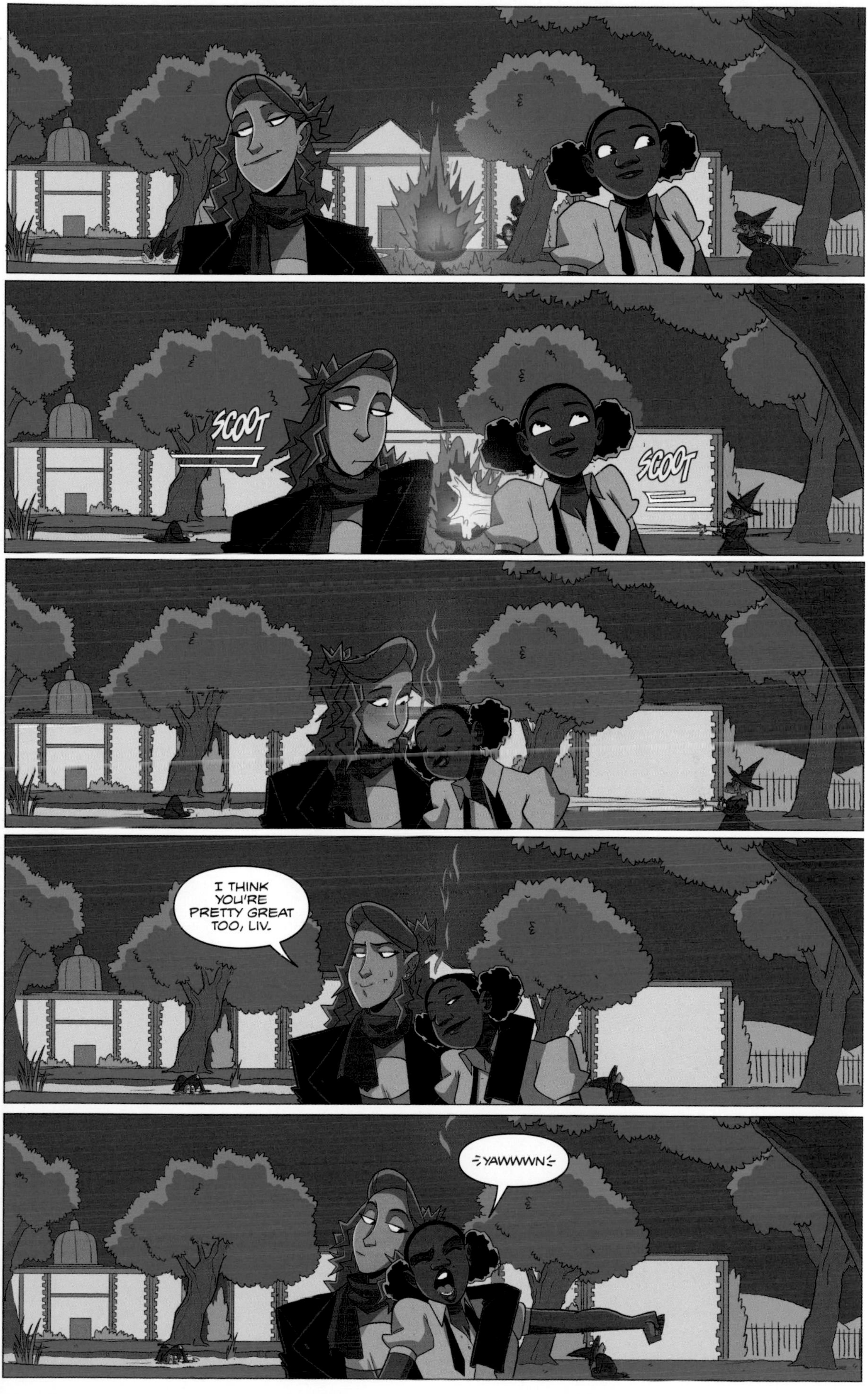
SCOOT
SCOOT
I THINK YOU'RE PRETTY GREAT TOO, LIV.
YAWWWN

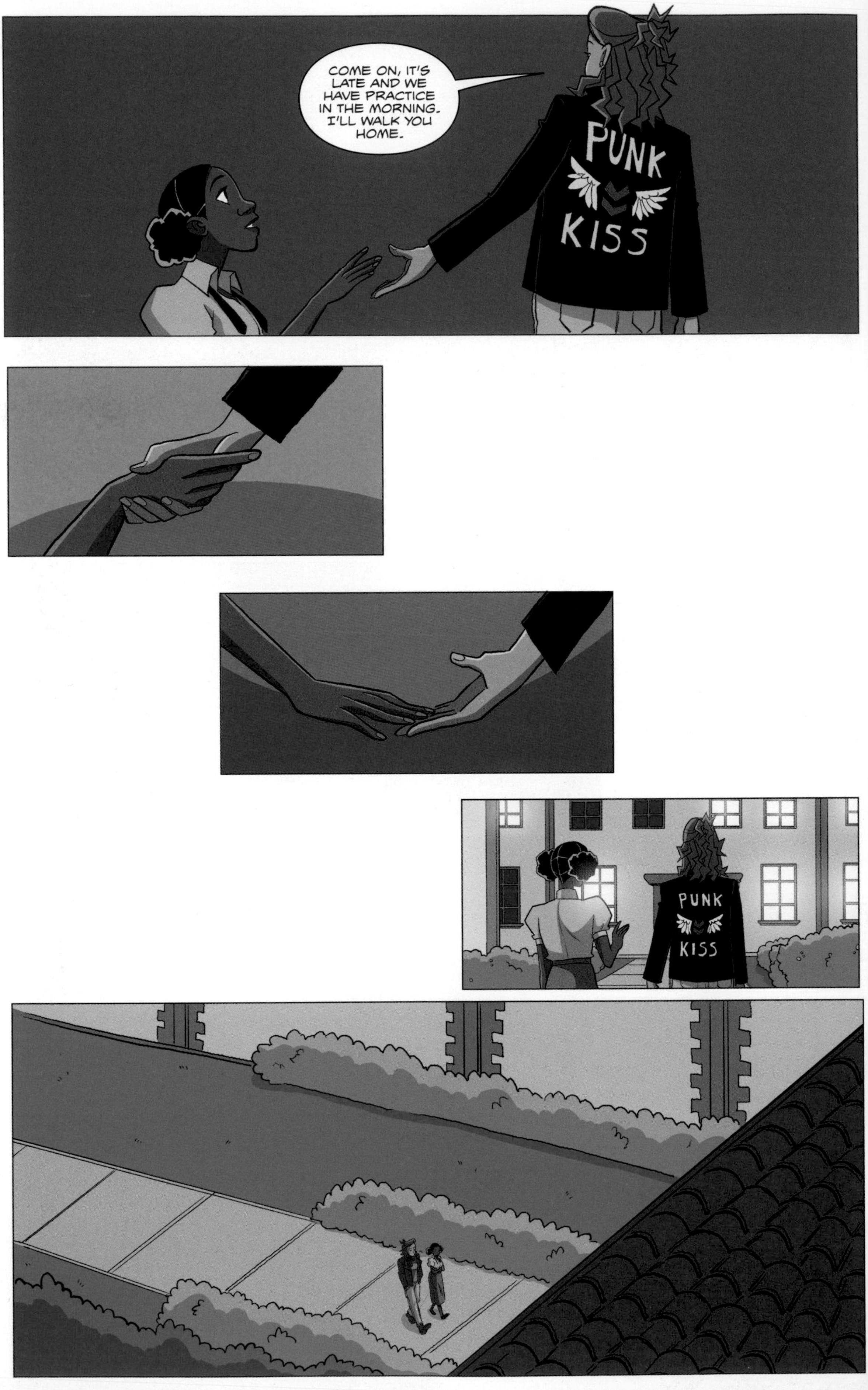
COME ON, IT'S LATE AND WE HAVE PRACTICE IN THE MORNING. I'LL WALK YOU HOME.
PUNK KISS
PUNK KISS

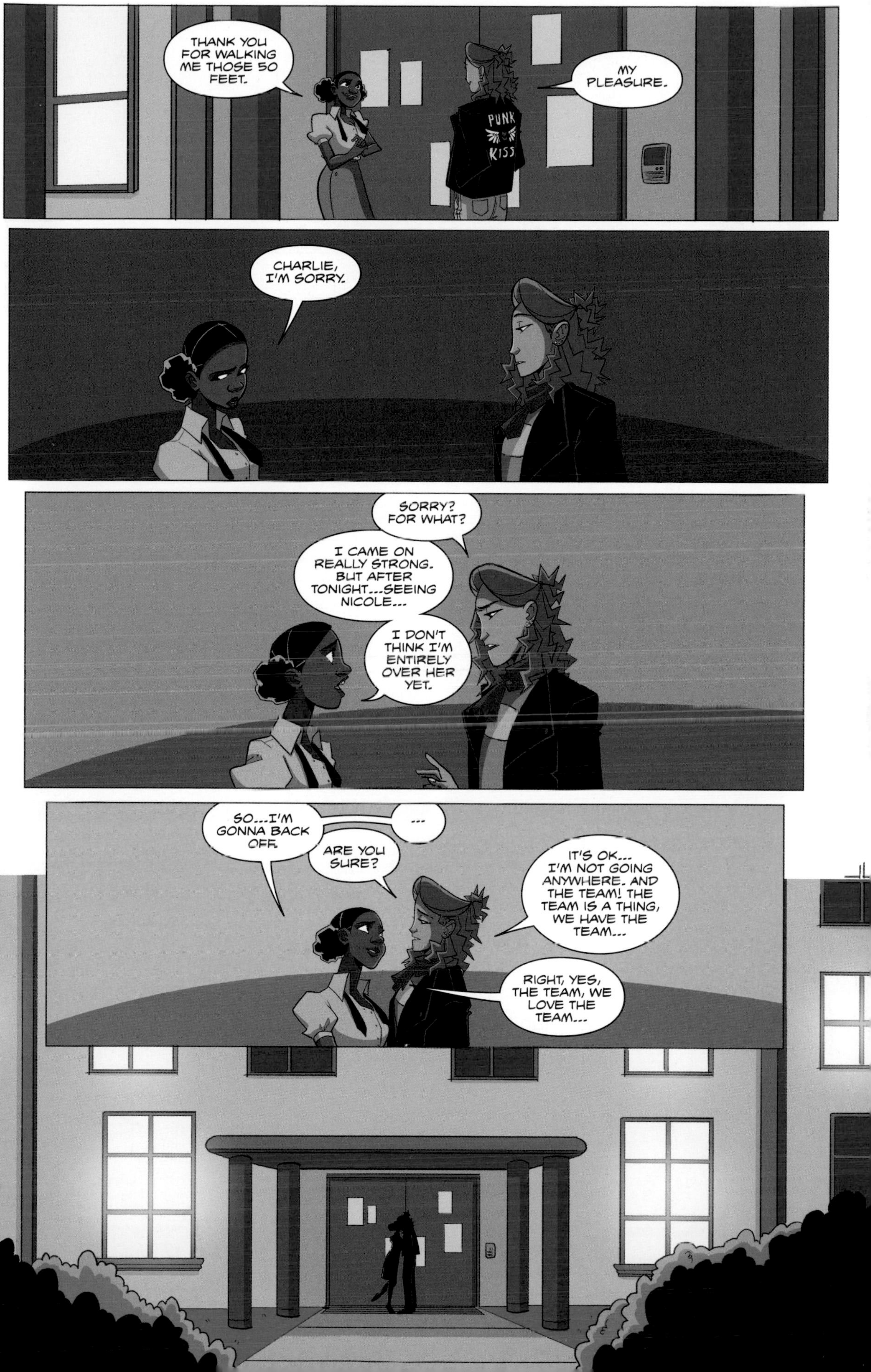
THANK YOU FOR WALKING ME THOSE 50 FEET.
MY PLEASURE.
PUNK KISS
CHARLIE, I'M SORRY.
SORRY? FOR WHAT?
I CAME ON REALLY STRONG. BUT AFTER TONIGHT...SEEING NICOLE...
I DON'T THINK I'M ENTIRELY OVER HER YET.
SO...I'M GONNA BACK OFF.
...
ARE YOU SURE?
IT'S OK... I'M NOT GOING ANYWHERE. AND THE TEAM! THE TEAM IS A THING, WE HAVE THE TEAM...
RIGHT, YES, THE TEAM, WE LOVE THE TEAM...

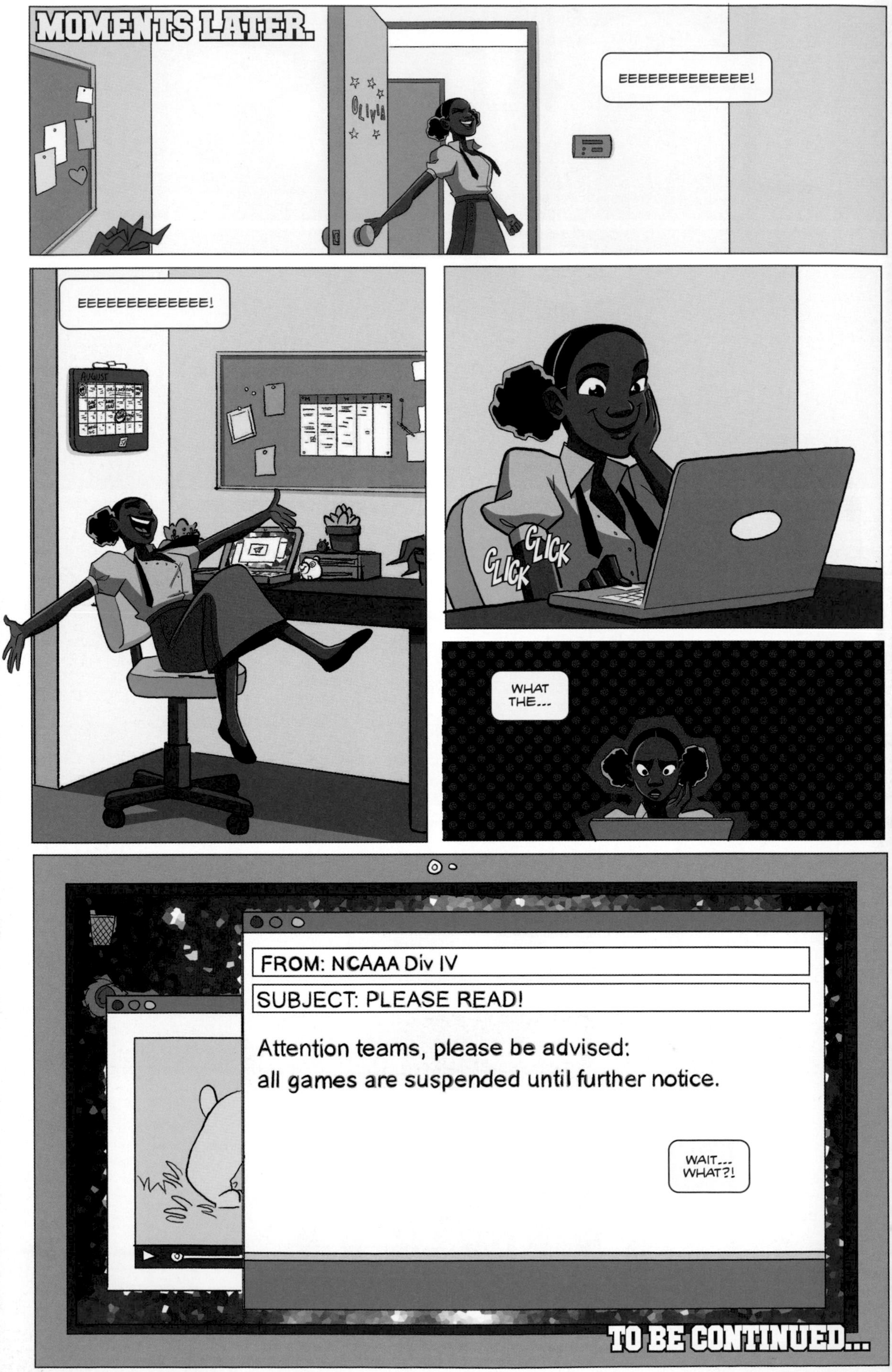
MOMENTS LATER.
OLIVIA
EEEEEEEEEEEEE!
EEEEEEEEEEEEE!
AUGUST
CLICK
CLICK
WHAT THE...
FROM: NCAAA Div IV
SUBJECT: PLEASE READ!
Attention teams, please be advised:
all games are suspended until further notice.
WAIT... WHAT?!
TO BE CONTINUED...

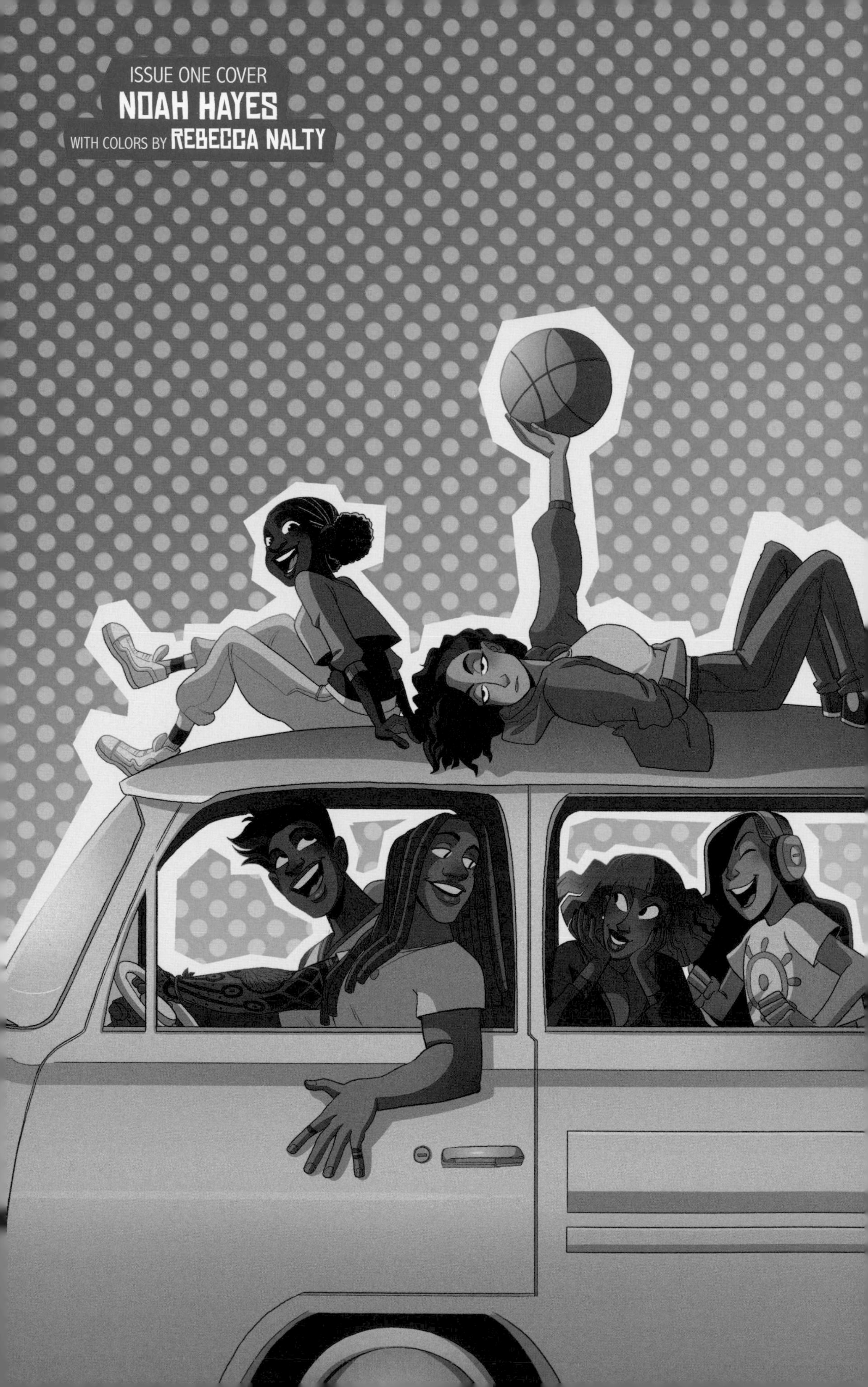

ISSUE ONE COVER
NOAH HAYES
WITH COLORS BY **REBECCA NALTY**

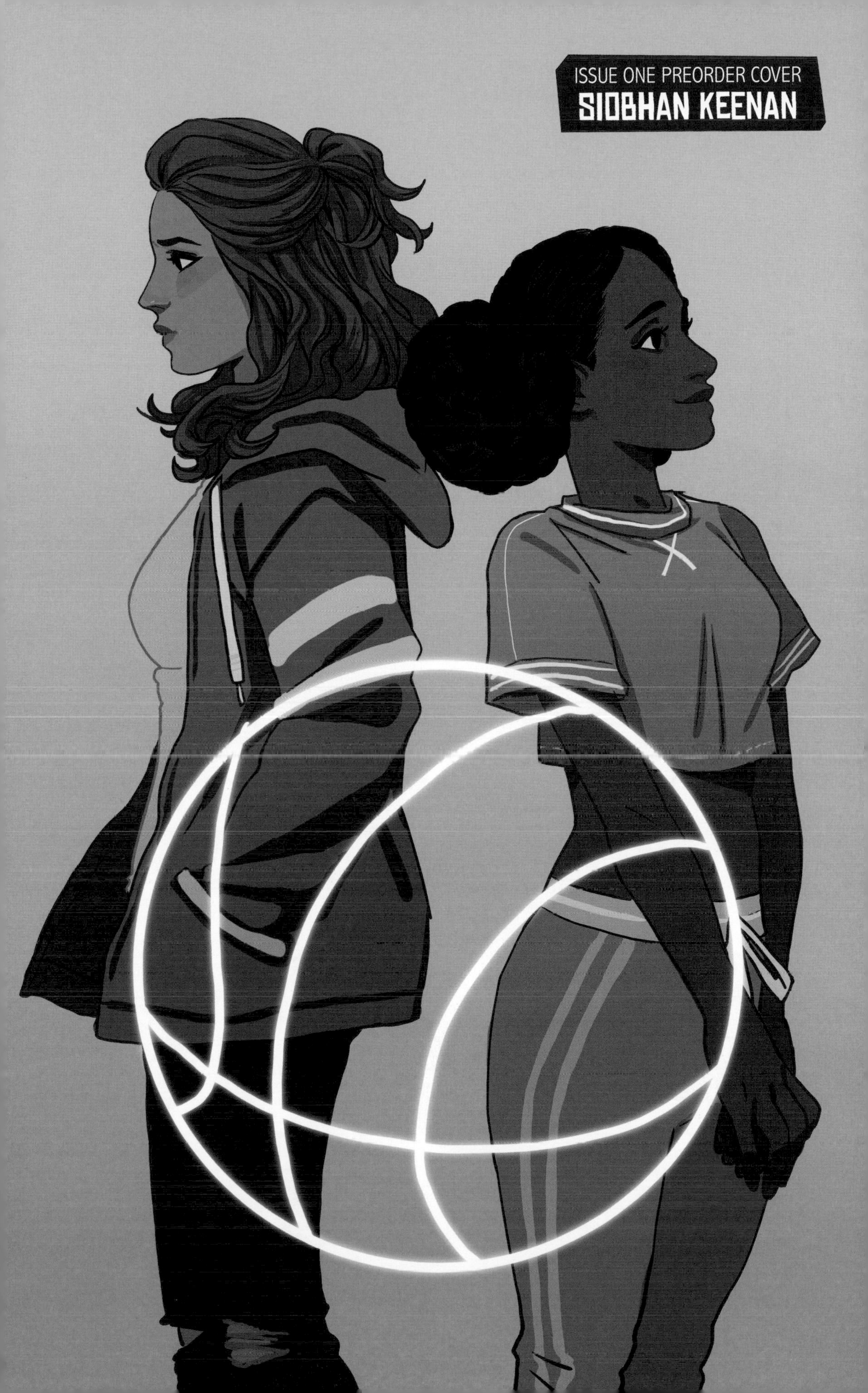

ISSUE ONE PREORDER COVER
SIOBHAN KEENAN

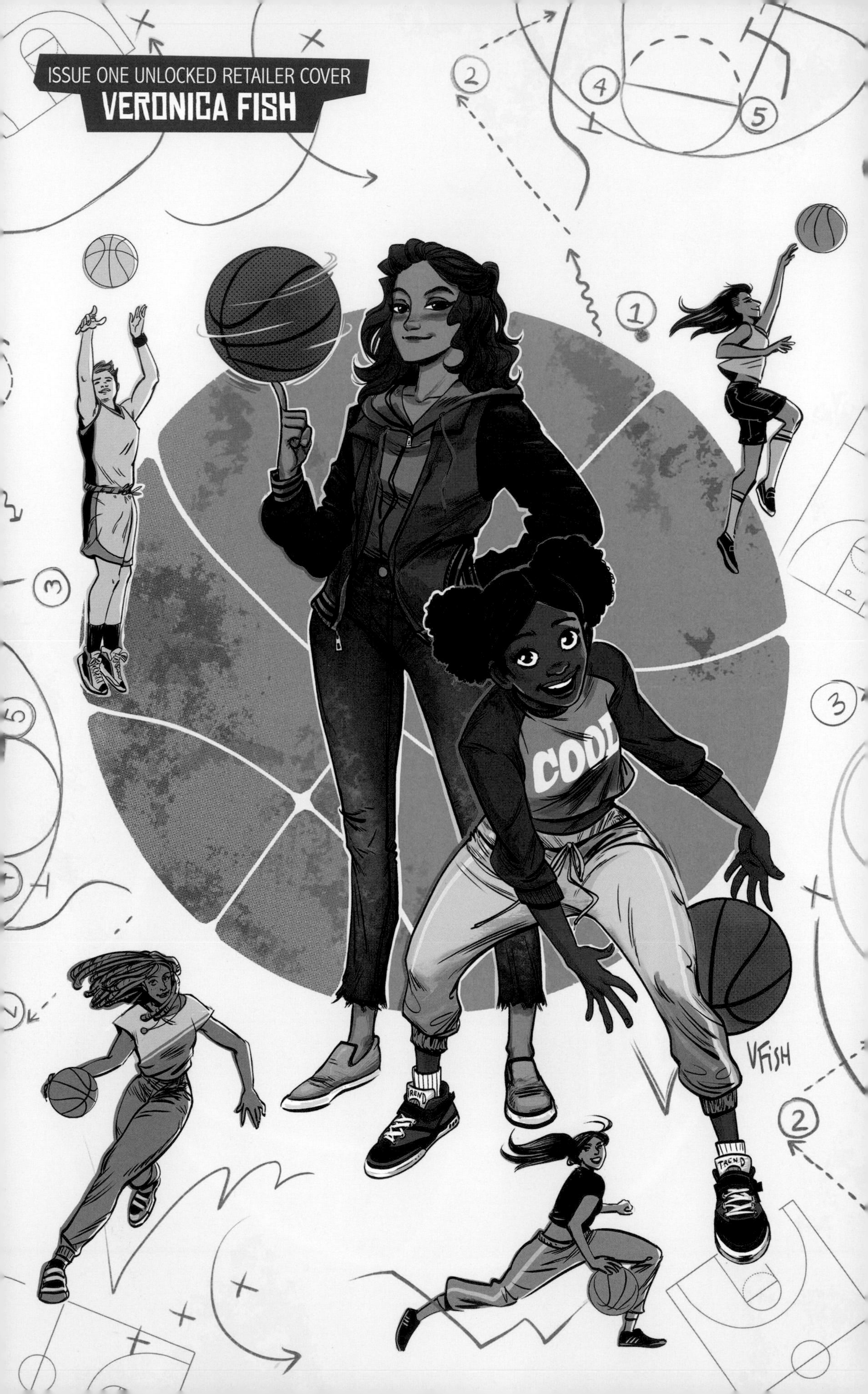
COO
VFISH

ISSUE ONE UNLOCKED RETAILER COVER
VERONICA FISH

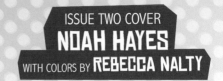

ISSUE TWO COVER
NOAH HAYES
WITH COLORS BY **REBECCA NALTY**

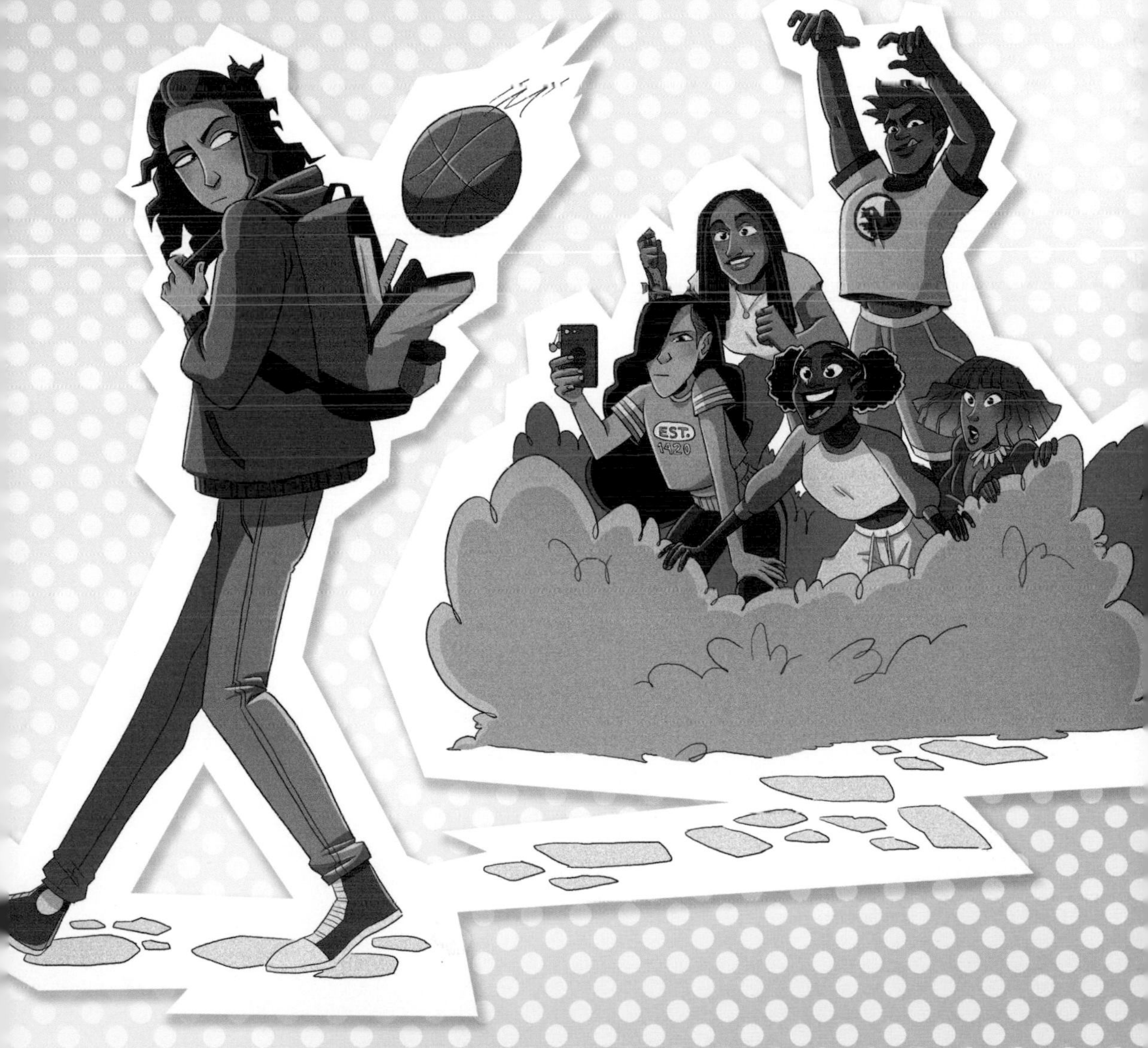
EST.
1420

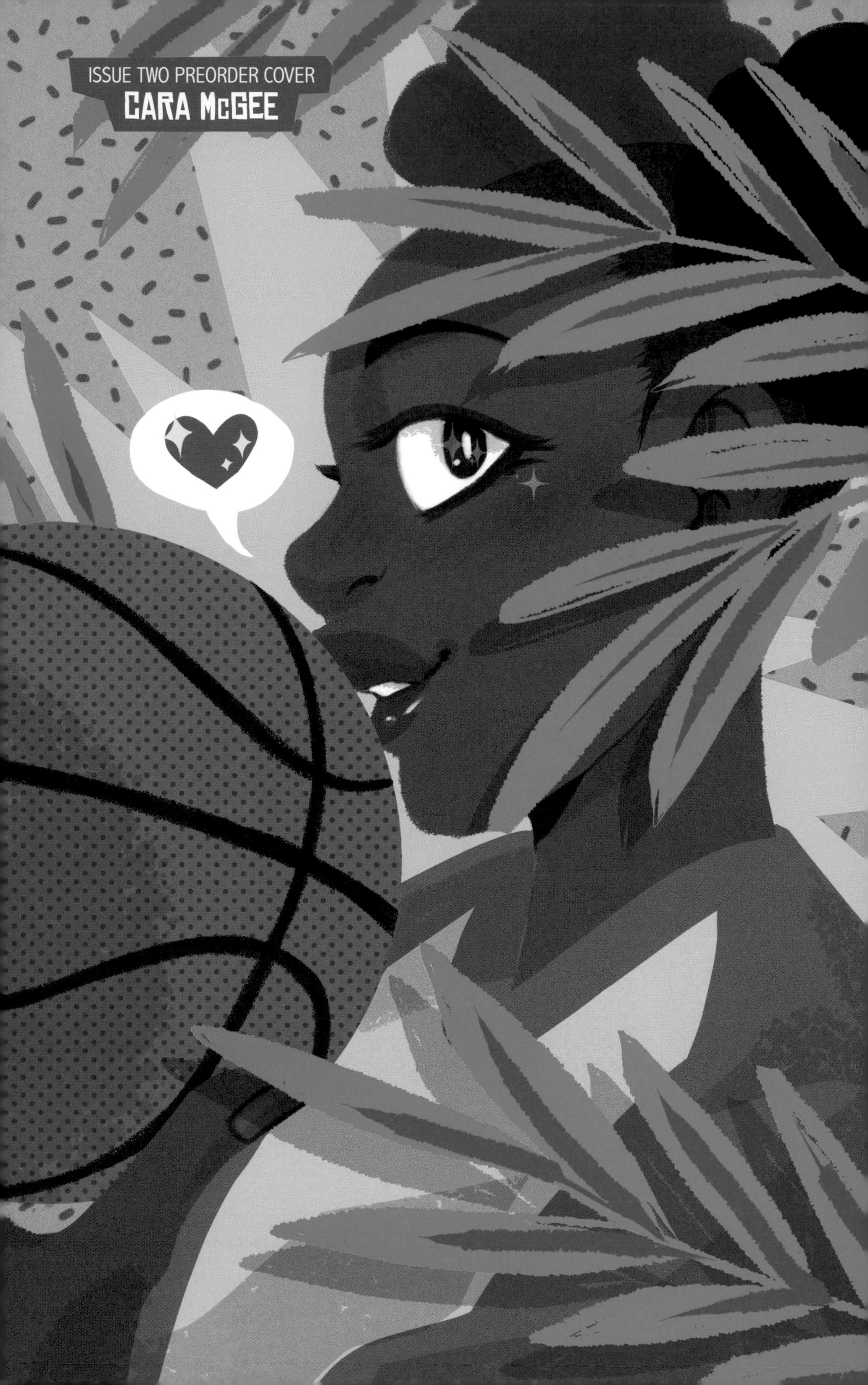
ISSUE TWO PREORDER COVER
CARA McGEE

ISSUE THREE COVER
NOAH HAYES
WITH COLORS BY **REBECCA NALTY**

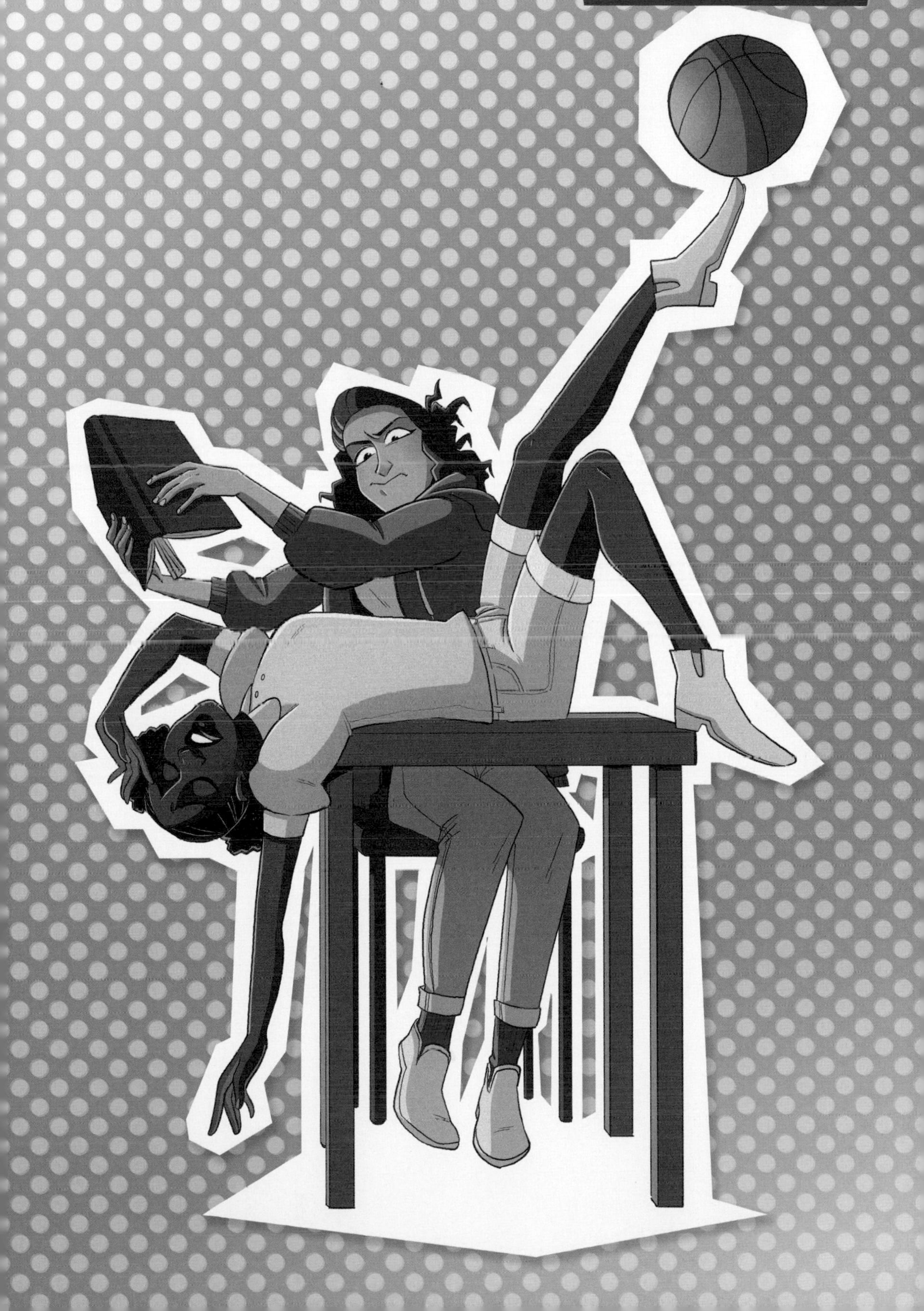

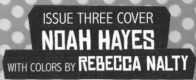

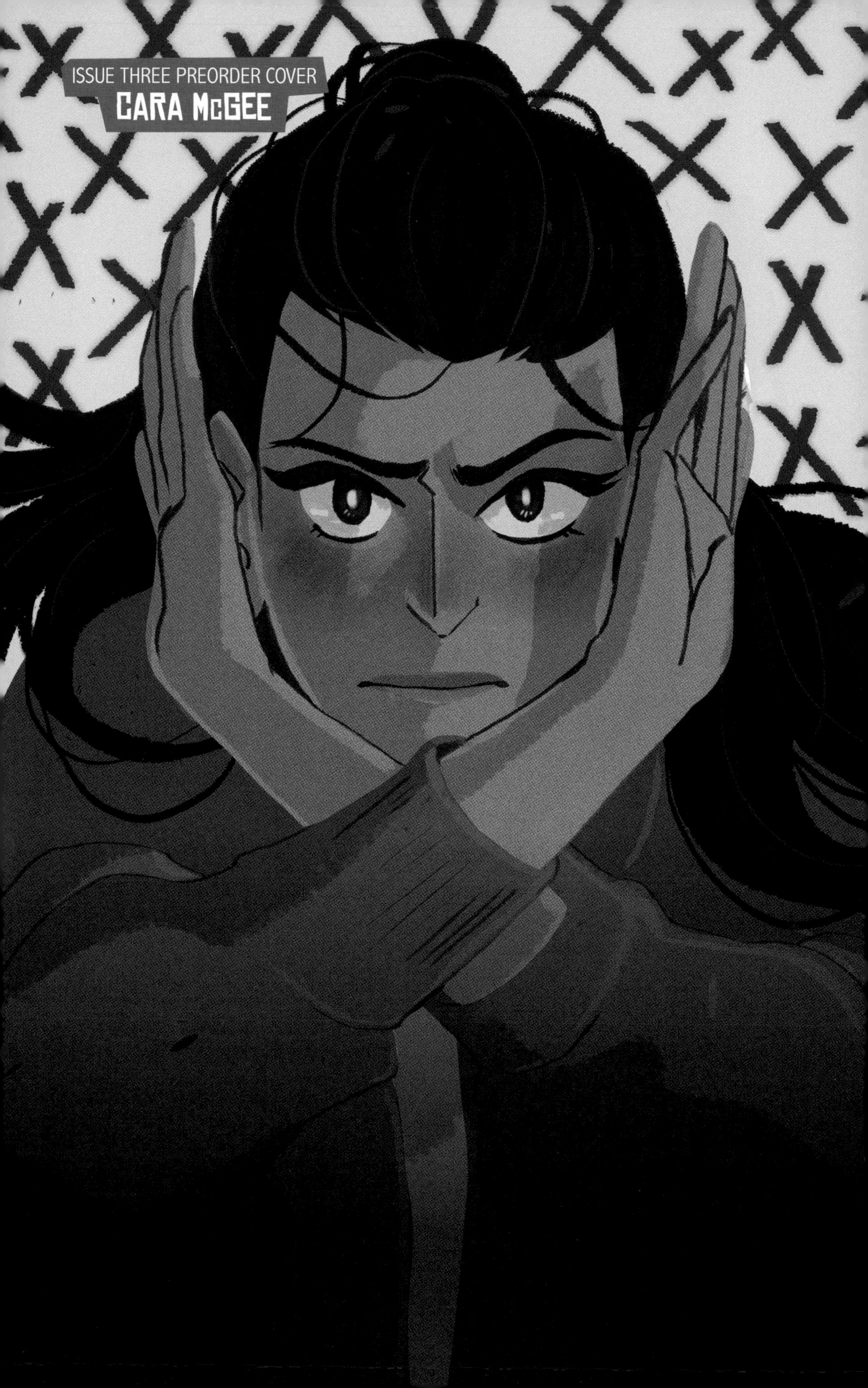

ISSUE THREE PREORDER COVER
CARA McGEE

ISSUE FOUR COVER
NOAH HAYES
WITH COLORS BY **REBECCA NALTY**

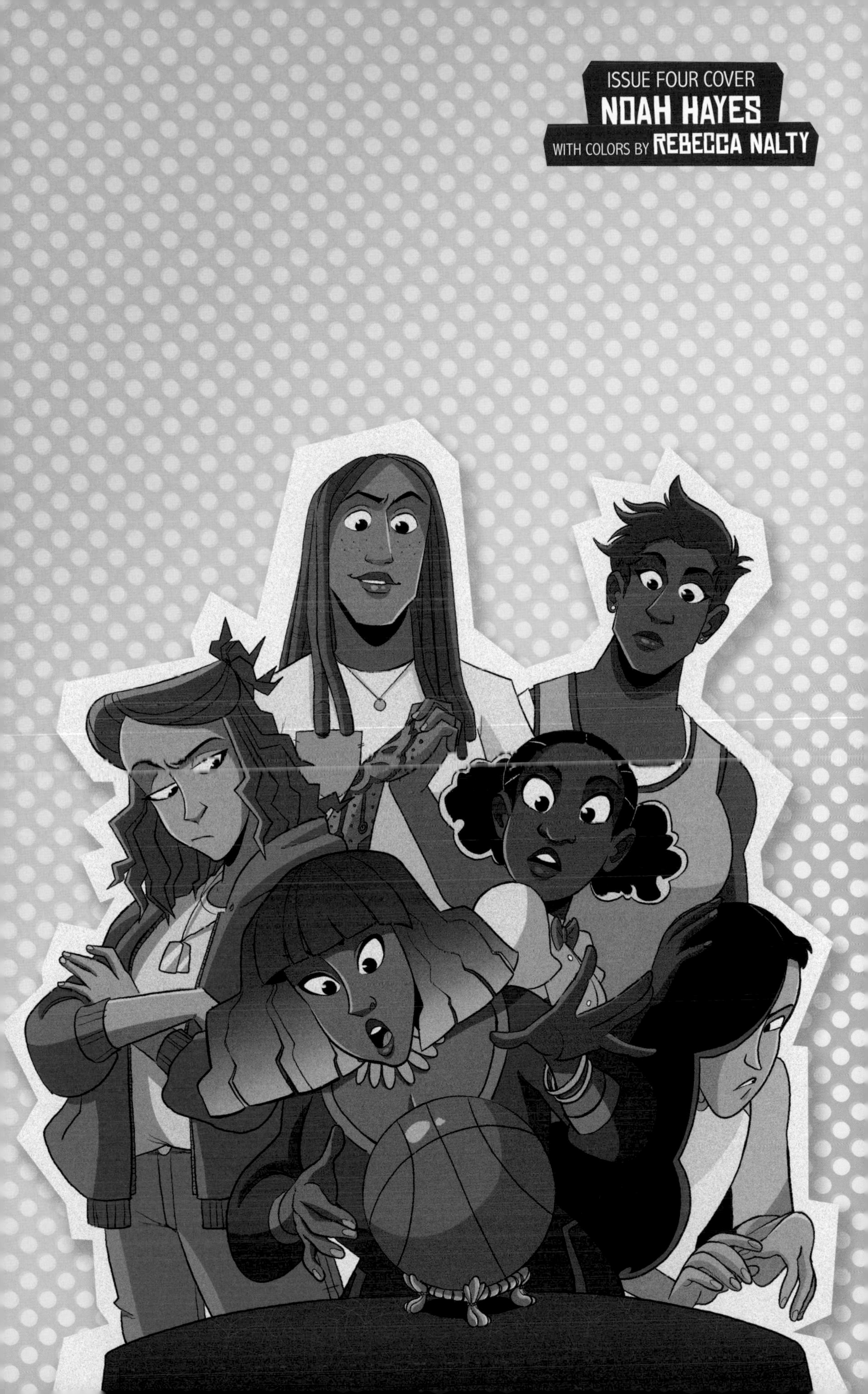

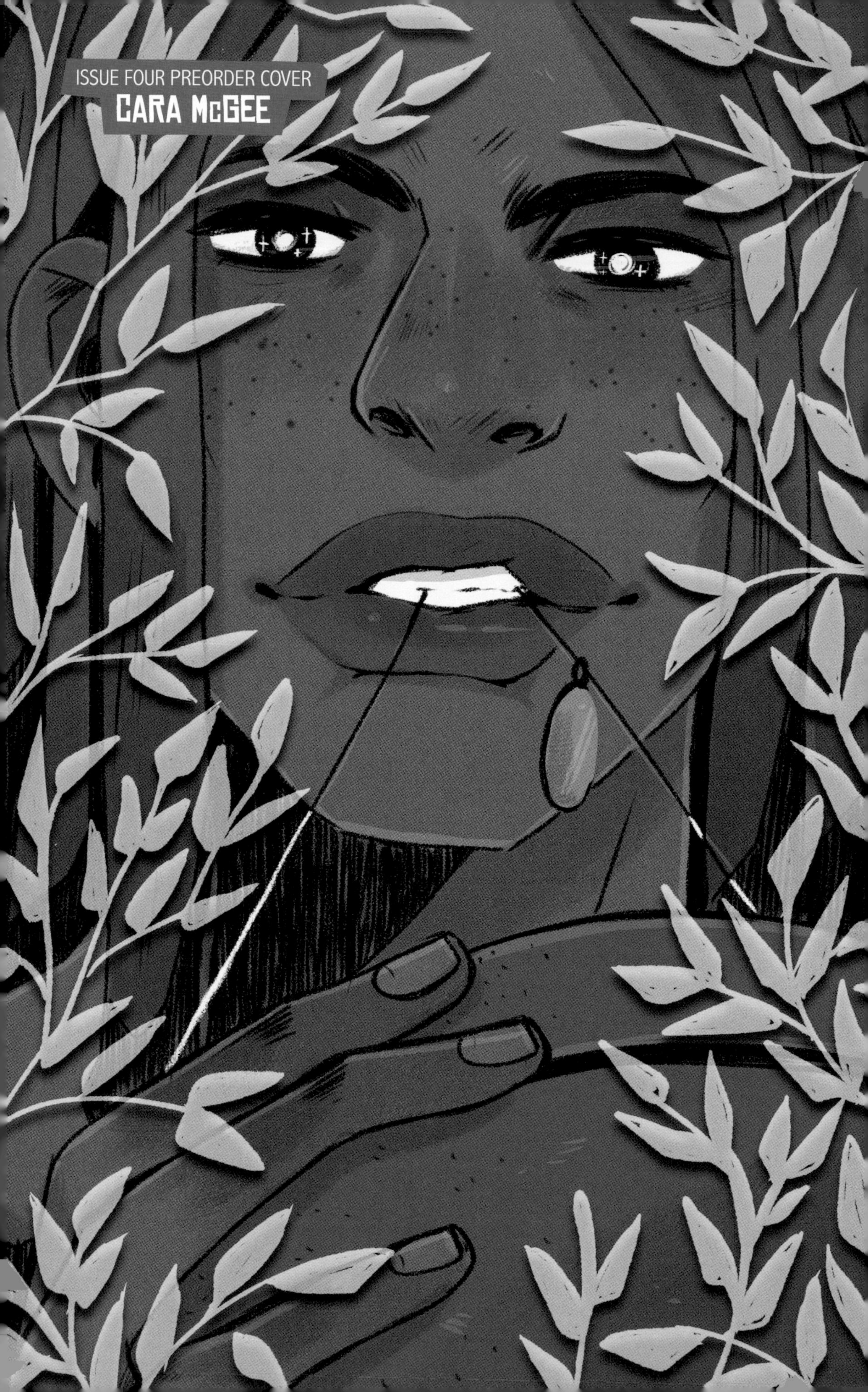
ISSUE FOUR PREORDER COVER
CARA McGEE